DIAMONDS IN THE DUST

DIAMONDS IN THE DUST

Beryl Matthews

This first world edition published in Great Britain 2008 by
SEVERN HOUSE PUBLISHERS LTD of
9–15 High Street, Sutton, Surrey SM1 1DF.
This first world edition published in the USA 2008 by
SEVERN HOUSE PUBLISHERS INC of
595 Madison Avenue, New York, N.Y. 10022.

British Library Cataloguing in Publication Data

Matthews, Beryl
  Diamonds in the dust
  1. Brothers and sisters - Fiction 2. Widows - Fiction
  3. Missing persons - Investigation - Fiction 4. Police -
  Fiction 5. London (England) - Social conditions - 20th
  century - Fiction 6. Domestic fiction
  I. Title
  823.9'2[F]

  ISBN-13: 978-0-7278-6612-7   (cased)
  ISBN-13: 978-1-84751-046-4   (trade paper)

All Severn House titles are printed on acid-free paper.

Typeset by Palimpsest Book Production Ltd.,
Grangemouth, Stirlingshire, Scotland.
Printed and bound in Great Britain by
MPG Books Ltd., Bodmin, Cornwall.

One

'Where's Mum?'

'I expect she's had to stay late at the factory.' Dora resisted the temptation to glance at the clock on the shelf. The last thing she must do is show she was worried; Lily was only six and very sensitive. She smiled at her little sister. 'Eat your bread and jam.'

Lily's green eyes fixed on Dora anxiously. 'Mum's always home for breakfast and to take me to school.'

'Don't worry, I'll take you today.'

'What about after?' Lily nibbled on a piece of bread.

'Mum'll be home by then, but if she's too tired and can't come for you, I'll get off work early and collect you.'

'You'd better let me do that.' Tom didn't look worried – he was very annoyed. 'You'll lose your job if you're not careful. Mum knows she's got to be back by breakfast to take care of Lily!'

Dora gave her brother a grateful look. At twelve years old he was turning into a strapping lad, and a sensible one. She disliked her job as a daily housemaid, but she didn't want to get the sack. Jobs weren't easy to come by. 'Thanks Tom. I'll go to the factory first and see what's keeping Mum.'

'It isn't like her. She's never missed breakfast with us before.' Tom groaned when he saw Lily. She'd finished the bread and now had jam all over her face and hands. He got a damp cloth and began cleaning her up, making her laugh as he teased. 'You're supposed to spread the jam on the bread, not all over yourself.'

Dora watched her brother and sister fooling around. They all had fair hair like their mother, and green eyes like their father. But there the similarity ended. Tom was a strong character and so was she, but Lily was delicate, very sensitive, and they all felt protective towards her. Their mum would sometimes be a few minutes late, but she never missed being home in time to have breakfast with them. Although they didn't see much of her because she worked all night and slept most of the day, she loved them and was working the night shift because the pay was better. Their dad had been killed in the war and things had been tough for a while. Mum had been determined that her children would have a decent life, and things had improved since she'd got this night job two years ago. They'd moved out of the slums and now rented a nice house, and they never went short of food. They were much better off than a lot of people, and that was all because their mum worked so hard for them. But where was she this morning? She had *never* been late before. Joining them for breakfast was one thing she had always said was important.

'That's better.' Tom studied Lily carefully. 'You'll have to be careful the flies don't stick to you.'

Lily giggled and grabbed her brother's hand. 'I might stick to you.'

He made a pretence of trying to free himself from her hand, making her dance around in delight. 'It's no good, Dora, I'm stuck to her. I'll have to take her to school now.'

'I guess you will, but you'll have to get free by the time you get there, because you'll look out of place in the little class.' She joined in the teasing. Tom had successfully taken Lily's mind off her worry about her mum, but she wasn't fooled. Tom wouldn't hesitate to tell their mother what he thought about her not being here this morning. It was the only time they saw her really. By six o'clock every evening she was gone again. Since their father had been killed, he considered himself to be the man of the house, and was not afraid to speak out if he thought something wasn't right.

Still holding his sister's hand, he leant towards Dora. 'I'll be outside the Barringtons' at lunchtime to see what you've found out. This isn't right. She must have been taken bad, or something.'

'If that's the case then someone should have let us know, not left us to worry like this. I'll go to Grant's factory now.'

Tom nodded, then turned his attention to Lily. 'Come on you sticky thing, or we'll be late.'

Lily turned and waved to Dora, showing no sign of her earlier distress as she gazed up at her adored big brother. As they saw very little of their mother it was left to Dora and Tom to look after Lily. Not that they minded – they both loved the little girl.

As soon as they'd left the house, Dora checked that she had enough in her purse for the bus ride, and ran up the road. She caught a bus straight away, and in fifteen minutes was standing outside the gates of Grant's. Dora had never been inside the clothes factory, but knew it had a reputation for being a sweatshop. Whenever she'd mentioned to her mum that she ought to try and find a better job, she had just laughed and said it wasn't too bad.

'We ain't got no jobs going,' a man on the gate told her briskly.

'I'm not after work. I've come about my mum. She works here on the night shift and hasn't come home this morning.'

He narrowed his eyes. 'We ain't got no night shift.'

'Of course you have.' If Dora hadn't been so worried she would have laughed. Was the man daft? 'She's worked here for two years. Her name's Harriet Bentley. Go and ask someone for me . . . please,' she added.

He shrugged and ambled off, muttering, 'Waste of time. We ain't got no night shift.'

It seemed an age before he returned, and Dora was relieved to see another man with him – a man in a proper suit. Perhaps she'd get some sense out of him?

'Now then, what's this all about?' he asked when he reached her.

'I'm looking for my mum, Harriet Bentley. She works here on the night shift and hasn't come home this morning.'

'I told her we ain't got no night shift, Mr Rogers, but she don't believe me.' The gatekeeper cast Dora an aggrieved glance.

Mr Rogers opened the large book he was carrying, scanning down the list of names. Then he closed it and shook his head. 'No one by the name of Bentley works here, and Dave's right, we don't have a night shift.'

Dora was stunned, unable to take in what she was hearing. 'But . . . but . . . Mum said she works here. I'm not simple, I know what I was told. She leaves home at six every evening and comes home in time for breakfast, except Sunday when she has the day off.'

'I'm sorry, but she doesn't work here, and never has done, according to our books.'

It felt as if the ground had been pulled out from under her. What was going on? Dora was confused – and she never got confused. Her mum always said she had a good clear head on her. She curled her fingers around the wrought iron gate to steady herself. There had been a mistake, that was all. Taking a deep breath, she asked, 'Is there another factory near here that does have a night shift?'

'Not that I know of.' Mr Rogers tucked the book securely under his arm and said kindly, 'Why don't you go home? I expect your mum's there by now.'

Bewildered as she was, Dora didn't forget her manners. 'Thank you for seeing me, sir.'

'Sorry I couldn't help.'

Dora stood there for a moment as he walked away, questions racing through her head. Why had her mum told her she worked here when she didn't? And she was positive she had the right place. What should she do now? Go home like the man said? No, there was no point. Tom and Lily were at school. If Mum came home she would send word to the Barrington house, knowing Dora would be worried.

That thought galvanized her into motion, making her spin round and run for the bus stop, forcing her legs to move. She was late! Whatever was going on today, she mustn't lose her job.

Dora burst into the kitchen and nearly sent the housekeeper flying. 'I'm so . . . sorry . . .' she gasped, bending over in an effort to draw air into her lungs.

'You're twenty minutes late.' Mrs Marsden studied the clock for a moment and then glared sternly at Dora. 'I hope you have a good reason for this tardiness?'

'The bus didn't come.' It was the only excuse she could think of. Whatever had happened to their mum was their business, and no one else's. She made a great show of still gasping for air. 'I ran all the way.'

The housekeeper's expression relaxed a little. 'I can see you've made a great effort to be here on time, and you're usually reliable, so I'll overlook it this time. But make sure it doesn't happen again.'

'I will, Mrs Marsden. And thank you, Mrs Marsden.'

Dora was handed a list of her duties for the day and, breathing a quiet sigh of relief that she'd got away with being late, she wasted no time in getting down to her allotted tasks. It was a relief to be busy because she still couldn't believe what the man at the factory had told her. Now she'd had time to think she was quite frightened. Their mum would never abandon them – she cared about them. But where was she?

Dora scrubbed and dusted with total concentration in an effort to push away the worry – but it was impossible. All the time she silently prayed that there was a simple explanation for all of this, and they would be laughing about it tonight. Yes, that was right, she assured herself, they would be finding it all a great joke tonight.

When it was time for her lunch break, she slipped out the back and found her brother waiting for her. He was pacing, a deep frown on his face.

'I nipped home first, Dora, but she still isn't there. What did you find out?'

She explained and watched her brother's mouth drop open in disbelief.

'You mean she's been telling us lies all this time? Bloody hell, Dora, what's going on? And where is she?'

'Watch your language, Tom,' Dora reprimanded sharply. 'Swearing won't help to solve this mystery.'

By way of an apology he grimaced and held up his hands. 'You're right. But what are we going to do? I thought it would be simple. All you had to do was go to the factory and they'd tell you where she was. We've got to find her. But where do we start?'

'We'll have to decide that tonight, and Lily will have to be told.'

Tom nodded agreement. 'This is going to upset her, but she's a bright kid, and it'll be better if she knows what's going on. I'll collect her from school.' Tom ran a hand through his hair. 'Er . . . I'd better get something for our supper. You got any money, Dora?'

Keeping enough for her bus fare, Dora gave him the two shillings she had left in her purse. 'I've got to get back to work now, Tom. I'll see you tonight, and if Mum still isn't home, we'll decide what we're going to do.'

He pocketed the coins. 'I hope she's all right?'

'Me too.' Dora lifted her head, a determined look in her eyes. 'We'll find her, Tom.'

'Course we will. It's all some daft mistake, I expect.'

The afternoon seemed never ending, but eventually the day was over and Dora could head for home. She felt sick with worry. Every time a visitor came to the house she waited anxiously, hoping it was word from her mum. But it never was, and as the day dragged on, the knot in her stomach got tighter and tighter.

As she stepped through the door she was greeted with a scene so normal that it stopped her in her tracks. Tom was busy cooking the supper, and Lily was reading a book, following every word with her finger. She loved books, and Dora was sure she hadn't been able to read as well when she'd been Lily's age. She showed all the signs of being very bright.

Lily glanced up. 'Mum hasn't come home. Has she left us? Doesn't she love us any more?'

When her sister's bottom lip trembled, Dora was immediately by her side. 'Of course she still loves us, sweetie.'

'Then where is she?'

'We don't know, but we'll find out, and we'll need your help as well.'

Tom put the plates of sausages and mash on the table. 'Eat up before it gets cold, then we'll put our heads together and decide what we're going to do.' He smiled at Lily. 'Don't you worry. People don't just disappear. We'll soon have her back with us.'

Dora knew her brother was only saying this to comfort the little girl. They knew all too well that people did disappear for no apparent reason. And they'd already run up against a dead end with the discovery that their mum had never worked at Grant's.

Lily stopped with a forkful of sausage halfway to her mouth, fear in her eyes. 'You won't leave me, will you?'

'Not a chance!' Tom pinched the piece of sausage off her fork and popped it into his mouth. 'The three of us are in this together, and we're going to look after each other.'

Happy with this reply, Lily cut another piece of sausage and ate it quickly before her brother could take it again. Then she smiled at both of them and began to eat with obvious enjoyment. She trusted her brother and sister, and if they said it was going to be all right, then it was going to be.

As soon as the meal was finished, Dora washed, Tom dried and Lily put the crocks away. Then they settled around the table again. There was silence as each one tried to come up with a way to find their mum.

After a while Dora shook her head. 'I don't know what to do. I was sure it would just be a case of checking with the factory, but they say she's never worked there. Where on earth do we start looking?'

'We could try the hospitals,' Tom suggested.

Dora nodded. 'Tomorrow's my half day off so I'll visit the local ones.'

Lily was kneeling on the chair and leaning across the table, her little face serious. 'We ought to tell the police. They're good at finding people.'

'Not yet.' Tom shook his head. 'Suppose Mum turns up soon and finds out we've made a fuss. She'll be furious. You know how strict she is about people knowing our business, Lily, so we'd better keep this to ourselves for the time being. We don't know what's happened, but she might turn up at any minute.'

The little girl looked worried.

'Tom's right, sweetie, and someone might try to split us up if they know we're on our own. I'm eighteen in a couple of weeks, and the local authorities will probably consider I'm old enough to take care of you and Tom. I don't know much about it, of course, but let's not risk it just yet.'

'But you take care of us now.' Lily was puzzled. 'Mum isn't here very much.'

'I know, but the authorities might not like the idea of us living on our own.'

Lily huffed. 'You take good care of us, and I'll tell them.'

'I'm sure that will help.' Dora reached across and patted her sister's hand. 'But I think we'll keep it quiet for the moment. There's something very strange about Mum's disappearance, and I'd like to find out for myself why she lied to us.'

Lily nodded.

'I agree with you, Dora,' Tom said. 'But I don't think we can do this on our own. We do need help, but who is there we can we ask? We haven't got any other family that we know of.'

'Mr Crawford used to be a copper.'

'What, the man who lives two doors down?' Tom frowned. 'How do you know that? We've never spoken to him.'

Lily wriggled until she was nearly on the table. 'June at school told me. He's her uncle. He was a policeman before the war, but he got hurt in the fighting and they won't take him back. He'd know what to do. June said he's very nice, so I 'spect he'd keep quiet if we asked him to.'

'Even so, Lily, I can't imagine he'd want to help us . . .'

'There's no harm in going to see him, Dora. We haven't got anyone else to turn to. He can only tell us to clear off. And we don't have to tell him who we're looking for until we know he will help us.'

'You're right, of course . . .'

Lily scrambled off her chair. 'It's still light so we can go now.'

'He might not be in,' Dora protested. She had grave doubts about this. They'd seen Mr Crawford around, but he'd never spoken to them. He seemed badly injured, and she didn't believe he could be much help. But Lily was insistent.

'He don't go out much.' Lily was already on her way.

Dora and Tom followed their determined little sister. She was the only one who had come up with an idea. Dora didn't think it was a very good idea, but it was all they had at the moment.

Two

Stanley Crawford gazed out of the window, frustration gnawing away at him. He was twenty-eight, in the prime of life, and he felt as if he'd been thrown on the rubbish heap. A generation of young men had been slaughtered, and some of the maimed and mentally damaged were begging in the streets in a desperate effort to support themselves and their families. What had their sacrifices been for? What had that bloody war been for? Thank the Lord he didn't have to resort to begging, though the police force wouldn't have him back. That was what he really wanted to do, but he was desperate enough to take any job. The trouble was that as soon as he walked in on crutches, there suddenly weren't any jobs. He'd dumped the damned things in the shed and was struggling to make do with a stick. It was hard going, but he was determined to get around like that.

He leant heavily on the stick and sighed. It was a beautiful May evening and he should go to the local pub for a pint, but it all seemed so aimless. What he needed was something to make him feel useful and occupy his mind. The doctors didn't hold out much hope that he would ever gain full use of his leg again, but he wasn't listening to them. He *was* going to walk properly, and then the police force would have to consider him. He knew he was going to have to fight as fiercely as he had in the trenches, but he had to succeed, or there would be only empty years ahead of him. In the meantime he mustn't allow self-pity to overwhelm him. He was a lot better off than many of the men who'd fought in that terrible war. This house was his, left to him by his grandfather along with a small inheritance. It wasn't much, but if he was careful he could manage quite well. The money wouldn't last much more than another year or two, though, so he'd have to find employment soon.

He watched three youngsters walking along hand in hand and recognized them as the Bentley children. From the little he'd seen of them they were well behaved and always clean and tidy. A rare smile touched his mouth as he studied the youngest. She was going to be a real beauty when she grew up. The eldest girl wasn't bad, either. She was quite pretty in a serious kind of way, with a strong sense of responsibility, he guessed. They did have a mother, he knew, because he had seen her a few times, but she never spoke, and didn't appear to be around much.

The smile disappeared as they hesitated at his gate, had a hurried discussion, and then came up the path. What the . . . ? He swore as he turned too quickly and nearly lost his balance. He was tempted not to answer the knock on his door, but curiosity got the better of him.

When he opened the door he glanced at the youngest and found himself mesmerized by a pair of bright green eyes.

'I'm at school with June.' Lily didn't give anyone else a chance to speak. 'She said you used to be a policeman. We need help.'

'That was a long time ago.'

'You're clever. June said so.'

'I can't imagine how I could be of any help to you.' He tapped the stick, wanting to get rid of them now. 'As you can see, I can't get around very well.'

Lily looked at the stick, and then up at his face. 'You can tell us what to do. You don't have to be able to walk to do that.'

'Lily!' The older girl scolded. 'I'm sorry, Mr Crawford, we shouldn't have bothered you.'

He could feel the concern coming from them as they turned away, and their crestfallen expressions at his response tugged at him. He must be mad, but what else did he have to do? 'Wait! Why don't you come in and tell me all about it?'

Lily rushed in without hesitation, pulling her brother and sister behind her, declaring, 'There, I told you he was nice.'

He ushered them into the front room and waited as they all sat close together on the settee, clearly nervous. Then he eased himself into a chair. 'First of all tell me your names.'

'I'm Dora, this is Tom and Lily, my brother and sister.'

He nodded. 'What's the problem, and how do you think I can help you?'

'We need to find someone and we don't know how to do it.'

He leant forward, intrigued. Dora had said someone, not something. 'Do you know where they live?'

Tom nodded. 'They're not there.'

'If they've got a job you could check with their employers.'

'We've done that, sir,' Tom said. 'We was told they worked at Grant's on the night shift, but they haven't got a night shift, and they told Dora that sh . . . this person's never worked there.'

He sat bolt upright as a picture came into his head of their mother leaving the house every evening around six o'clock. 'Are you talking about your mother?'

'Blimey, sir, you soon worked that one out.' Tom was impressed.

Lily's face had drained of all colour at the mention of her mother. 'You mustn't tell anyone, Mr Crawford. Dora said that people might not like us being on our own, but she takes good care of us, always has.'

For a moment he was speechless. Then it began to dawn on him the predicament these youngsters now found themselves in. He didn't know how old Dora was, but her suitability for caring for her siblings might well be questioned.

'Please!' Lily had scrambled off the settee and was now standing in front of him, her eyes pleading. 'I don't want no one to take me away. Dora's eighteen soon. We'll be all right then.'

'I promise not to mention it. Whatever you tell me is between us only.' He smiled reassuringly at Lily, noting that Dora was older than he had first thought. 'Don't you worry. We'll sort this out.'

A little colour seeped back into Lily's face, and she returned to her seat.

Stan could feel his mind beginning to work, just like the old days. It was odd that the children believed their mother worked nights when she clearly didn't. He was intrigued – no, more than that, he was excited by the mystery. 'Let's deal with the practical things first. Are you renting the house you live in?'

'Yes.'

'Right, then don't tell the landlord your mother isn't there. Dora, can you afford to pay the rent, and who usually gives him the money?'

'I have a little put by. It'll last for a couple of weeks, and I've got a job. I usually pay the rent collector when he calls.'

'Good, then he won't be suspicious if he doesn't see your mother. Now you'd better tell me the whole story. Don't leave anything out even if it seems trivial to you. I need every detail.'

As he listened to Dora explain about their missing mother, Stan felt the back of his neck begin to tingle. He didn't like what he was hearing. This woman obviously thought a lot of her children, and they of her. She would not have walked out on them without a word. The lie about the kind of work she was doing was worrying. He rubbed his hand over the back of his neck. He hoped he was wrong, but his instinct was telling him that something bad had happened here.

By the end of the story he knew that he was going to help them. To get involved in an investigation like this was just what he needed to put the life back in him. But more than that, he wanted to do what he could for these children. They were showing great courage, and he admired them for that. However, before he began the search he felt honour bound to suggest the obvious, although he already knew they didn't want to do this. 'You should report your mother's disappearance to the police.'

'We know that.' Tom was immediately on his feet, agitated. 'But it's only been one day and we don't want anyone sticking their noses in our business just yet. If that's the only suggestion you've got then we'll find someone else to help us!'

Ah, the boy had a quick temper, Stan noted, but it was also clear that all three of them were intelligent. They must be frightened and confused, but they hadn't panicked.

Tom held out his hand to Lily. 'Come on, we're wasting our time here.'

Stan pulled himself out of the chair, and even leaning on the stick, he towered over Tom. 'No you're not. I'll do what I can for you. I've still got friends at the local station. They know I'm desperate to get back so they won't think it odd if I drop in to see them from time to time, eager to hear about cases they're working on. Whatever's happening in this area goes through them. But if she doesn't turn up in two or three days, the police will have to be told.'

'You won't say anything about our mum for the moment,

will you?' Dora looked worried at his insistence that the disappearance be reported soon.

'I won't break my promise to you. I'll listen, and if anything seems odd, I'll investigate it on my own. They'll never know I'm only interested in one person.'

'We'll help,' Dora suggested, eyeing the stick he was leaning on. 'You don't find it easy getting around.'

'I'll manage.' He grimaced. 'The exercise will do me good, but I'll ask if I need you to do things for me now and again.'

'I was going to the hospitals tomorrow. It's my half day off.'

'You leave that to me. I want the three of you to act as normal, and don't do anything to draw attention to the fact that your mother isn't there.' He turned to Lily, who was examining the dog's head on his stick. 'Now, young lady, if your mother does come home, I want you to rush round here and let me know at once. Can you do that?'

'Yes, sir.' She rested the stick back against his chair again and gave a wan smile. 'That's pretty.'

'It was my father's.' He glanced at the boy and saw that he had now calmed down. 'Rest assured, I'll do everything I can for you. And I can be trusted, Tom.'

Tom nodded. 'Sorry I lost my temper, sir. We don't understand why Mum hasn't come home, or why she told us lies about where she worked. It doesn't make sense.'

'It's a mystery, I agree. Have you been through your mother's things?'

'Oh, no.' Dora was horrified. 'We *never* touch Mum's room.'

'You'll have to now, Dora.' Stan spoke gently. 'There might be papers, or something there to tell where she went every night. And I'll need a photograph of your mother, if you've got one.'

'Yes, of course, we'll let you have that in the morning, and anything else we find.' Dora got to her feet. 'It's your bedtime, Lily. Thank Mr Crawford for seeing us and listening to our troubles.'

'Thank you.' Lily held on to her sister's hand and gazed up at him. 'It was my idea to come to you. We haven't got anyone else, you see.'

'I'm glad you did.' Much to Stan's surprise he meant it. There was a bubble of excitement and anticipation running through him, and he hadn't felt anything like that for a long time. 'You sleep well, and you never know, she might be home in the morning. But if she isn't, we'll find out what's happened to her.'

At the door, Tom whispered, 'It doesn't look good, does it? No way would Mum leave us unless she was . . .'

Stan placed a comforting hand on the boy's shoulder to stop him finishing the sentence. 'Let's not jump to any conclusions. It's too early yet.'

'No, you're quite right, sir. Hope we can find her soon, though.'

'We'll do our best. And the name's Stan.'

Tom gave him a grateful smile, and then hurried to catch up with his sisters.

The first job was to get Lily to bed. It had been a long and worrying day for all of them, and the little girl was almost asleep before they'd tucked her in. She was even too tired to listen to a bit of the story Dora read to her every night at bedtime.

Tom and Dora hesitated outside their mother's bedroom.

'We've got to do it, Dora,' Tom urged. 'I know Mum always made her room off limits to us, but this is different. We have to see if there's anything here that will help Stan get the search going.'

'Stan?'

'He told me to call him that,' Tom told her proudly. 'Nice bloke. Shame he got messed up in the war.'

Dora silently agreed. Stan Crawford was an impressive man. He looked to be over six feet, even leaning on the stick for support, hair as dark as night and the clear blue eyes a startling contrast. A shiver rippled through her when she remembered how he had studied her – all of them – and she'd felt as if he could read every thought in her head. It was silly, of course, but the intensity of his bright eyes gave the impression that nothing was hidden from him. He would be handsome if his face wasn't grey and lined with pain. So many were still suffering because of the war, and it always upset her when she saw them. So many young lives had been ended or ruined with crippling injuries.

Tom opened their mother's bedroom door. 'Come on, Dora, let's see if we can find anything.'

The room was clean and tidy, as was the whole house. Their mother had always made them put everything away when they'd finished with it. That's what drawers and cupboards are for, she had told them. The room was sparsely furnished, containing only a bed, wardrobe and dressing table.

'This won't take long. You start with the wardrobe, Tom, and I'll go through the dressing table.'

Fifteen minutes later Dora closed the last drawer. 'There's nothing here. How are you doing?'

'Only clothes and shoes inside.' He dragged a chair up to the wardrobe and climbed on it, running his hands over the top. 'Nothing here either.'

Frowning in puzzlement Dora scanned the room. 'That's strange. I would have expected to find photos, letters and things like that. There's nothing personal here except makeup and clothes, and we know there's nothing in the front room. I always assumed she kept papers and things in here.'

Tom peered under the bed and then pulled himself up to sit on the edge. 'There isn't even any dust under there. If there's anything here, then she's hidden it well.'

Dora didn't like the idea of their mother hiding things from them, but after today that was something they would have to accept. 'We haven't looked behind the wardrobe. Help me pull it out, Tom.'

After struggling with the heavy piece of furniture they found nothing, and the same with the dressing table.

'That's it then.' Dora was despondent. 'There's nowhere else to look. What are you doing, Tom?'

He was tugging the covers off the bed and dropping them on the floor. 'If I wanted to hide something, this is where I'd put it.'

Dora was very uneasy about this, and reluctant to admit that there were things their mother had kept from them.

Tom saw the expression on her face. 'Come on, Dora, Mum's been lying to us about her job. What else has she kept from us? Give me a hand with this mattress.'

They pulled the huge feather mattress off the bed, and gazed at what they had uncovered. At the foot of the bed was a small parcel, neatly wrapped in brown paper and tied with string.

Dora felt tears of disappointment prick her eyes and murmured, 'What have you been hiding from us, Mum?'

They sat on the floor and opened it. It contained a small notebook, a batch of letters tied up with ribbon and a black velvet box.

Tom was turning the pages of the notebook and shaking his head. 'It doesn't make sense. It's all numbers.'

'Well, it's Mum's writing.' Dora examined it carefully, but Tom was right. Each page had a series of numbers grouped together. 'We'll give this to Mr Crawford in the morning. He might be able to make some sense of it.'

Dora ran her fingers through the bundle of letters, and then put them down.

'Shouldn't we read them?' Tom asked.

'They're personal letters, Tom. Probably from Dad over the years. I wouldn't feel easy about reading them.'

'Suppose not. Wow! Look at this.' Tom had opened the velvet box and held out a sparkly necklace. 'Cor, it looks like diamonds.'

Dora took it from him and held it up to the light. 'It's only glass, Tom. Where would Mum get diamonds? It's just a keepsake with happy memories, I expect.'

He pulled a face. 'You're right. The likes of us don't have diamonds. It must have meant a lot to her though, or else she wouldn't have hidden it. Perhaps it was a present from Dad when they were courting.'

'Must have been. Isn't there anything else?'

'Don't think so.' He shook the brown paper packet and something fell out. 'Hold on a minute, what's this?'

Dora knew as soon as she saw it. 'Money. How much is there, Tom?'

He counted it. 'Five pounds! What the bloody hell is she hiding that for?'

'I've told you about swearing, Tom. Now cut it out!'

'This business is enough to make a saint swear.'

She silently agreed with him, but wasn't going to admit it. 'Let's put everything back except the book. We might need the money later on, but I'll use my savings first.'

'Er . . . I still think we ought to read the letters.'

'Certainly not, Tom! They're private.'

It didn't take them long to put the room back as it had been, and after a cup of cocoa, they got ready for bed, exhausted and troubled.

'I'm really glad Mr Crawford has agreed to help us because I'm completely confused.'

'If Mum turns up tomorrow she'll have a lot of explaining to do.'

'I don't think she's coming back, Tom,' Dora said quietly.

'Nor me. She's gone, Dora, but where?'

'I haven't the faintest idea, but I'm sick with worry that something dreadful has happened. We'll have to hope Mr Crawford can find her.'

Three

He'd been awake most of the night, but that wasn't unusual. It was damned difficult to sleep with the pain. The doctors had wanted to amputate his leg, but he'd yelled at them until they'd agreed to patch it up. Pain was the price he was prepared to pay for keeping his leg. Though some nights when it was particularly bad he did wonder if he'd made the right decision.

After finishing his breakfast, Stan sat at the kitchen table, tucked the photograph of Mrs Bentley in his pocket, then opened the little book Tom had brought him before going to school. He turned the pages, frowning. Whatever information the book held, it had been put in such a way that only Mrs Bentley could understand it. It might just be a diary, but he doubted it. She had gone to a lot of trouble to keep whatever was in it a secret. But he couldn't understand why she would want to keep a collection of numbers a secret. Unless they were a code? He would have to give it some thought later. It was intriguing.

'Oh, you've had your breakfast.'

He started at the sound of his sister's voice. Irritated, he said, 'Don't you ever knock, Winnie?'

Ignoring his scowl, she sat down. 'Had a bad night, did you?'

'Just like all the others.'

She reached across the table and grasped his hand. 'I wish you'd come and live with Reg and me. You know June would love to have her favourite uncle living with us. We don't like you being here on your own. What if you fall down or something?'

'We've been over this a dozen times.' He softened his tone, knowing his sister's concern. 'I'm not going to be a burden to you. I've got to keep my independence. It's important to me.'

Winnie sighed. 'I know it is, but that doesn't stop me worrying about you. I'm sure it was the worry that took Mum and Dad so close to each other.'

Stan looked up sharply. 'They were both already sick when I came home. Are you trying to make me feel guilty?'

'No, of course not! I didn't mean it like that. It was the war that took them to an early grave. Losing their eldest son was terrible, and then seeing you return so badly injured was more than they could stand. They were heartbroken, Stan.'

'I know it. But what happened to me was beyond my control, Win. And I always did my best to stay cheerful around them. You've got to stop fretting over me. I won't give up my independence. I'm coping all right, and I've done away with the crutches at last. I only need a stick now.'

She nodded, knowing when to give in. Then she noticed the book. 'What's that?'

Slipping the book into his pocket, away from her prying eyes, he smiled. 'Some friends have asked me to see if I can work something out for them.'

'And you're not going to tell me?'

'No, I promised.' He sat back, his expression animated for a change. 'If I make a success of this I might be able to go into business solving people's problems.'

'A private detective you mean? You're joking!' When a deep rumbling chuckle came from him, the sound tugged at her heart. 'Oh Stan, I haven't heard you do that since you came back.'

'Told you I'm fine, didn't I? Now, off you go. I've got a lot to do today. I'll probably pop into the station and see Reg this morning.'

Winnie laughed. 'And give him some advice on his case load, I expect.'

'Why not? I was a good copper, Win, and I've still got all my mental faculties.'

She leant over and kissed his cheek. 'I'll get you some shopping today. Your larder's nearly bare.'

'Thanks.'

As soon as his sister had gone, Stan had another look at the book. He didn't know what kind of an education Mrs Bentley had had, but if she'd worked out a code, then it was bound to be something simple. All he had to do was put his mind to the

puzzle, but that would have to wait for tonight. The first thing
he had to decide was how he was going to get around. Buses
would mean a lot of walking to and from the stops, and getting
on and off was still difficult for him. But there was an answer,
if he could manage it.

He stood up and went out to the shed. His old bicycle was
filthy dirty after years of not being used. A quick check showed
it only needed a wipe down and a bit of oil on the chain. He
could tie his stick to the crossbar, and he would have trans-
port for the day. He was well aware that it wasn't going to
be easy, but he'd agreed to help the children, and he couldn't
do that by staying in the house all day. He had become lethargic
of late, hating the pain and effort it took for him to move
around. This was just what he needed to shake him out of his
gloom. He must never give up; never stop believing that his
condition would improve, no matter what the doctors said.

Half an hour later he was ready. Having long legs he was
able to slide the bike underneath him, but after lifting his left
leg to place it on the pedal, he felt that riding was going to
be damned near impossible. However, if he was going to have
any kind of normal life, it was essential that he got used to
doing the impossible. Since the end of the war he'd been
turned down for one job after another, and he had almost given
up hope, but his determination had returned since the visit
from the Bentley children.

He pushed off with his good leg and placed it on the pedal,
pressing down cautiously. The surge of pain that shot through
him was indescribable, making beads of sweat form on his
brow. But he was moving. The police station was only about
a mile away. He could make it!

'What the blazes do you think you're doing, Stan?' Reg Tanner,
his brother-in-law, stormed up to him as he walked into the
station.

'Coming to see you, why?'

'Don't look so blasted innocent. You came on a bike! I saw
you arrive.'

'So?'

'You can't ride with that leg.'

'Really?' Stan made a show of looking puzzled. 'Who says?'

'The doctors – everyone.' Reg studied his wife's brother

with more than a hint of respect. 'And where are your crutches?'

Stan smiled. 'They wouldn't fit on the crossbar.'

Reg lifted his hands in resignation, knowing there was little point in pursuing the subject. When Stan made up his mind about something, then nothing on earth would shake him out of it. 'Come on, you're just in time for a cuppa.'

'Good.' Stan walked ahead of Reg into the main room, the smile fixed on his face. There was no way he would allow the pain to show. He was getting expert at hiding it.

'Hello, Stan. Come to solve our cases for us?'

He gazed around the room at the men he knew so well, and his heart ached, longing to be one of them again. 'From the look of it I'd say you need help. You're never going to catch criminals by sitting around here wasting your time.'

He accepted a mug of tea and drank it gratefully. 'So, what's been happening over the last couple of days?'

'The usual,' Sergeant Baker told him. 'Burglary, domestics, and a kid went missing, but we soon found him. The little devil was only three, but he was in the park. He told us he'd been chasing a dog and he wasn't sure where his house was, but he'd have found it all right.'

He smiled at the sergeant's wry expression. 'Confident little devil then. Sounds like that family will have to keep him on a chain. Any other missing persons, or unidentified patients in hospital?'

'Nothing's come through here.' The sergeant shook his head.

Stan listened to the men talking for a while, until they began to leave to walk their beats.

'Can I stay for a while, Sergeant?' he asked. 'I won't get in the way, but being stuck at home all day is driving me mad.'

'Course you can, Stan. No luck with a job, then?'

'No, not a chance.' Stan grimaced in disgust. 'One look at the crutches and I'm on my way out the door.'

'Wish we could offer you something, but you know we can't.'

'One day you'll be able to. I'm off the crutches and riding a bike again.'

'Good. You come and see us when you can run down the street.'

'I'll do that. You keep a job open for me because it won't be long now before I'm agile enough to catch the crooks.' Stan knew that his talk was all bravado, but he wouldn't give up hope. If hope died that would be the end for him. He'd seen it in the eyes of too many ex-soldiers, and he wasn't going to allow that to happen to him.

The morning passed quickly. He talked to the policemen as they came into the station, listening to their reports. But there wasn't anything remotely connected with Mrs Bentley. He had lunch with Reg in the café across the road, and then made his way back home.

The ride back was even more of an ordeal, and by the time he arrived home he was drenched in sweat and exhausted. He dragged himself upstairs, stretched out on the bed and slept.

Stan woke so suddenly he nearly tumbled off the bed. He was searching his pockets before he was fully awake, grunting in satisfaction when he located Mrs Bentley's notebook. A possible answer to the puzzle had come to him while he'd been drifting between sleep and waking. He was eager to see if it could be that simple.

Pulling himself upright until he was leaning against the headboard, he opened the book at the first page. The highest figures were in the twenties, and there were twenty-six letters in the alphabet – each number represented a letter. It was so obvious he was disgusted with himself for not seeing it at once.

With a stub of pencil rescued from the depths of another pocket, he set to work. It didn't take him long to discover that he'd been right, and he chewed the end of the pencil as he studied the result. There were only three groups of numbers on the first page – one a surname, and the other two Christian names. Under each Christian name was a place in London – all upmarket areas. Stan was disappointed. He had been hoping for more information than this. It didn't tell him a damned thing! Perhaps he'd have more luck with the rest of the book?

He was about to tackle the next page when there was a knock on the front door. Using both banisters on the narrow staircase as support, he swung himself expertly down. Dora was on the doorstep and he didn't miss the startled look as she took in his dishevelled appearance.

'Erm . . . am I disturbing you, Mr Crawford? Only I wondered if you had any news.'

'No, nothing yet.' He reached out for the walking stick he
kept near the door and moved aside. 'Please come in. Go
through to the kitchen. I've been resting and I could do with
a cup of tea.'

Giving him a hesitant smile, Dora walked along the passage
to the kitchen. This house was exactly the same as hers, so
she knew where to go.

After Stan's morning exertions, his leg had stiffened up and
it took him longer to reach the kitchen. When he arrived, Dora
already had the kettle on to boil and cups on the table.

'Thanks.' Stan eased himself on to a chair, and looked up
to find her studying him carefully.

'I'm not sure we should have brought our troubles to you.
Have you been overdoing it, Mr Crawford?'

'I rode my bike for the first time today and my leg's sore,
that's all. I'll soon get used to riding again.' He spoke with
confidence, but his leg was telling him a different story. From
the expression on Dora's face it was clear that she didn't
believe him.

Having made the tea, she poured a cup for both of them,
and then sat at the opposite end of the well-scrubbed kitchen
table. 'You must take the bus, Mr Crawford, and tell me how
much you spend on our behalf.'

'That won't be necessary—'

'But it is!' She opened her purse and took out two shillings,
pushing the money towards him. 'You take that for a start.'

'I don't want your money, Dora!' He placed the coins back
in her hand. 'Look, I'm glad to have something to do. No one
will employ a cripple.'

'You're not a cripple!' she exclaimed. 'And you mustn't
think of yourself like that. You've got a bad leg, that's all, and
you got that fighting for this country. Where's the gratitude?
That's what I want to know. A whole generation of young
men slaughtered, and many of those who did come home are
injured or damaged in their minds. It's disgraceful that there's
no work for them. What was it all for, Mr Crawford?'

The transformation from polite, timid girl to fiery woman
was extraordinary. Stan couldn't take his eyes off her. He
knew she worked as a housemaid, but from the way she

expressed herself she'd had a decent education. He hadn't taken a great deal of notice of her before, but now he did. Dora Bentley was pretty with her cheeks flushed and eyes blazing. There was hidden fire there, and he was impressed.

She coloured even more under his scrutiny, glancing down at her clenched hands, then back at him. 'I do beg your pardon, Mr Crawford, but I get so mad when I see what's going on.'

'I know how you feel.' He grimaced. 'Whatever happened to a land fit for heroes, eh?'

Dora gave him a nervous glance, relaxing when she saw he was smiling. 'We should have put all the politicians in the trenches and see how they liked it. They might understand better and do more to help.'

'They might, but I doubt it, Dora. The war's been over for a while now, and some people have short memories.'

'That doesn't make it right though, does it?'

'No, it doesn't.' He changed the subject. 'Tell me, where did you go to school?'

'Only the local school where we lived in Limehouse, but Mum gave me lessons as well. She's very clever and always reading books.' She chewed her bottom lip in agitation. 'Where's she gone, Mr Crawford?'

'As I told you, I haven't been able to find out much today. I went to visit my brother-in-law at the police station . . .' When Dora looked at him in alarm, he said, 'Don't worry, I didn't say anything. Nothing connected with your mother has been reported, and the hospitals haven't any patients they don't have details for. But I have found the key to deciphering your mother's notebook. Is there any tea left in the pot before I tell you what I've found?'

Dora poured him another cup and sat forward eagerly.

'The book's still upstairs, but I've only worked on the first page and can remember that. The first name in the book is Duval, then Andrew, Park Lane, and then Charlie, Hampstead. Do these mean anything to you?'

'I don't ever remember hearing them before. We haven't any family. Mum and Dad never talked about their past . . . except . . .'

'Yes?'

'Well, Dad once said he'd been orphaned at sixteen and didn't have any relatives that he knew of. He always joked saying that Mum married beneath her when she took up with him.' Dora's eyes swam with tears as she looked at Stan, her expression anguished. 'She's dead, isn't she? She'd never leave us like this.'

'We don't know that,' he said gently. But she was only voicing his fears. 'Tell me about your mother.'

'Well,' Dora sat up straight and ran a hand over her eyes to clear away the moisture. 'She's always laughing and singing. She's got a good voice and Dad always said she should have been on the stage. We lived in Limehouse before coming here. It was a dump, and Mum was determined to get us out of there. She worked two jobs, in a laundry and evening wait-ress, until she'd saved enough for us to move here. Dad was a good carpenter, but he didn't earn much. They were happy together, and he said he understood her need to live in a better place. Mum had had a good education and we'd spend every Sunday afternoon doing lessons she'd worked out for us. Mum was heartbroken when Dad was killed, and that's when she started working at night – so we thought – to make sure we had a good standard of living.'

A picture of the Bentley family was taking shape in Stan's mind. The mother was evidently prepared to work hard for her children, and he felt sure that she would never have left them like this. The more he heard, the more uneasy he became.

'Mr Crawford?'

He started at the sound of her voice. 'Sorry, I was thinking. And you must call me Stan. I'll go through the notebook tonight and hope it reveals some clues. Do you know your mother's maiden name, and where she came from?'

'Sorry, and she never mentioned where she was born.' Dora glanced at the clock on the dresser. 'I'll have to go. Tom and Lily will be home from school soon.'

'I'll let you know if I find out anything.' Stan watched her walk back to her house, deep in thought. Poor little devils. They must be out of their minds with worry.

'I hope you know what you're doing!'

He turned his head and looked at his sister standing by the back door. He hadn't heard her arrive. 'Meaning?'

'You know what I'm on about. Mrs Bentley's disappear-ance should be reported to the police.'

Leaning heavily on the stick, Stan faced her. 'They've reported it to me. And how the hell did you find out? Have you been eavesdropping?'

'That doesn't matter. What you're doing is wrong! If Reg knew about this he'd insist that the police be told. That woman might be in trouble somewhere, Stan, and the police could find her much quicker than—'

'She's already dead.'

'You don't know that.'

'A loving mother doesn't abandon her three children like this. Those kids are frightened someone will come along and split them up. They've asked me for help and I've given my word. Don't breathe a word of this, Winnie.'

'I won't. I don't agree with what you're doing, but I hope you find her alive.'

'So do I.'

Four

'Don't you want your tea, Lily?' Dora sat beside her sister, concerned by how pale and unhappy she was. 'Mum wouldn't like it if you made yourself ill. Mr Crawford's started looking for Mum and I'm sure he'll find her soon. Not knowing what's happened is very upsetting, but we'll be all right, sweetie. We've got each other.'

'I've been a naughty girl,' Lily whispered. 'You're going to be very angry with me.'

'When have I ever been angry with you?' Dora teased, keeping her tone light. 'You going to risk telling me what you think you've done, eh?'

'I told June our mum hasn't come home and we don't know where she is.' Lily grabbed Dora's hand as Tom groaned. 'I'm sorry. I'm sorry! Please don't be angry with me! I tried not to say anything, but it just came out. I'm frightened! Where is she?'

When Lily's little body began to shake as the tears streamed down her face, Dora gathered her sister into her arms. 'Shush, sweetie. We're all frightened, but we've got to be brave.'

'Course we're all scared.' Tom was running his hand over Lily's back as she clung to Dora.

Lily turned her head to look at her brother. 'Nothing scares you.'

'It does, but I just don't let anyone see it.' He grinned at Lily. 'Come on, mop up the tears and eat your tea. What's done is done, and we're not going to be angry with you.'

'I told June she mustn't tell anyone.' Lily wriggled back on to her chair, darting anxious glances at Dora and Tom.

'And do you think she'll keep her mouth shut?' Tom asked.

Lily shook her head. 'She can't keep a secret.'

'That's it then!' Tom put Lily's spoon in her hand. 'Eat up, and then we'll talk over what we should do next.'

Much to Dora's relief, Lily finished every bit of her stew, and the colour had returned to her cheeks.

'Right, let's get this lot cleared up.' Tom began to scoop up the plates. 'Dora, you wash, I'll dry, and Lily can put everything away.'

As soon as the last dish was stacked, they sat around the table again.

'What do you think we should do, Dora?' Tom asked.

'Now someone knows besides Mr Crawford it changes things.' Dora squeezed Lily's hand reassuringly. 'I doubt we could have kept Mum's disappearance a secret for very long anyway, so I suggest we bring it out into the open.'

'Tell the police, you mean?' Tom looked doubtfully at Lily. 'I don't like that idea, Dora. It could cause us a lot of trouble . . . you know . . .'

Dora knew what her brother feared – that as soon as it was known that they were living here on their own, the authorities might come in and try to interfere. There was no way they would allow Lily to be taken from them, even for a short time. 'I'll be eighteen soon, and I'll fight if someone tries to come in and tell us what to do. I'm sure Mr Crawford will help us deal with the authorities, if need be.'

There was silence around the table. Dora said, 'That's my opinion. Your turn next, Tom.'

'I can see that it might be for the best, or else rumours could start to fly, and that would cause even more trouble. Stan's a nice bloke, but he's hurt bad and might not be able to manage the running around needed. You told us when we got home that he hadn't been able to find out anything today. We don't know where Mum went every night. It might be a district covered by another station, and Stan can't go to all the police stations asking questions.' Tom lifted his hands in a gesture of surrender. 'I don't see we have much choice.'

Dora turned to Lily. 'And what do you think, sweetie?'

'Dunno. What will Mr Crawford say?' Lily fixed her eyes on the floor. 'We ought to tell him what I've done.'

Dora smiled reassuringly at her distressed sister. 'I think we ought to as well. We'll go and talk to him now, shall we?'

Lily nodded, not looking up. 'Will he be angry with me?'

'No! Of course not.' Tom lifted her chin and smiled. 'You haven't done anything bad. He'll understand, and it'll probably make things easier for him now he doesn't have to keep it a secret. He wanted us to tell the police anyway, so I expect he'll be pleased. Come on, let's go and see him.'

As they walked up to Stan's front door, Tom said, 'Neighbours are going to start wondering why we keep coming here all of a sudden.'

'Let them wonder.' Dora dismissed the thought. She had enough to worry about at the moment.

After knocking they waited, expecting Stan to take time reaching the door, but it was opened quickly.

The woman standing there took Dora aback. 'Er . . . we'd like to see Mr Crawford, please. If it isn't convenient we'll come back another time.'

'No need for that. I'm his sister, Winnie Tanner.' She smiled. 'Please come in.'

Winnie didn't give them a chance to turn away, but took hold of Lily's hand and ushered them inside.

When Stan saw them he began to get to his feet. Dora held up her hand. 'Please stay where you are. We're sorry to bother you, but we need your advice.'

Winnie was smiling down at Lily. 'Hello, Lily. Do you remember me? I've seen you at the school, and June's told me all about you.'

'We're friends,' Lily whispered, glancing anxiously at her brother and sister for support.

'June likes you very much.' Winnie stooped down in front of Lily. 'She told me your mother hasn't come hone.'

'Oh . . .' Tears filled Lily's eyes as she rushed to Dora.

'It's all right, sweetie,' Dora told her. 'Don't get upset again. Everything's going to be all right.'

'Ah.' Stan stood up. 'I see what the problem is. Put the kettle on, Win. We'll all have a strong cup of tea while we talk this over.'

They trooped into the kitchen and sat around the table while Winnie and Dora saw to the tea.

'It's no good you looking at me like that, Stan,' Winnie said, ignoring her brother's pointed glances from her to the door. 'I'm staying.'

He sighed as the cups were handed round. 'Is that all right?' Stan asked. 'She already knows, and you can trust my sister.'

Dora noted the firm line of Mrs Tanner's mouth and decided

that it would be daft to argue. Brother and sister were very alike. Both determined people. She nodded.

'Right.' Stan took a gulp of tea. 'Tell me what you want to do about this.'

Dora told him about their discussion, and how they'd decided that it might be best to bring it out into the open. When she finished there was silence. 'We wanted to talk to you before we did anything.'

'Hmm.' Stan stood up and propped himself against the sink, deep in thought.

Lily became agitated again as the silence stretched. 'I didn't mean to tell. It just came out. I'm frightened. Where's my mum? Why hasn't she come home? What's going to happen to us? Where is she? I want my mum!'

Winnie was the quickest to react, gathering the distressed child into her arms and rocking her gently. 'There, there, my dear. Nothing bad's going to happen to you. We're all here to look after you.'

Seeing that Lily was clinging desperately to Mrs Tanner, Dora went and stood in front of Stan. She was shaking so badly she could hardly stop her teeth from chattering. 'We've got to ask the police to look for Mum. We can't go on like this. It's too much for Lily.'

'It's too much for all of you.' Stan held Dora's shaking hands in a firm clasp, his large hands swamping hers.

She looked down at his long fingers curled around her delicate hands, felt the strength coming from him, and was comforted. This was an absolute nightmare, but they weren't alone.

Tom had joined them, looking as pale as Dora felt. 'We were daft to think we could keep this a secret, weren't we?'

Lily's wails became louder and all attention focused on her.

Dora spun away from Stan and went to comfort her sister. 'Ah, sweetie, don't take on so. We'll tell the police and get a big search going for her.'

'Suppose they can't find her?' Lily gasped between her sobs.

'We'll find her, little one.' Stan swept Lily away from Winnie and the little girl nestled her head on his shoulder. 'We're all here for you. You're quite safe.'

'She was quite calm at first.' Tom was struggling to hide his distress.

Winnie nodded. 'The realization that her mother's missing has probably just hit her.'

Like Tom, Dora fought with her emotions. They both hated to see their sister upset, but this was a terrible crisis, and it was understandable that she was so distressed. Lily was allowing herself to be passed from one person to another, grasping at comfort wherever she could find it.

The awful sobs were fading now and Dora swept a hand over her own eyes to clear her vision. Lily was in Stan's arms, her face tucked into his neck, holding on as tightly as she could. Dora couldn't help being struck by the strength of the man comforting her sister. Lily was no lightweight, but he was holding her with ease. He was able to do this by leaning on the sink and taking the entire burden on his good leg. Her heart went out to him in sympathy. Before being injured in the war he must have been a man to be reckoned with, and a good policeman. How frustrated he must be with the restrictions he now faced. And she must face this nightmare with the same courage he was showing.

Winnie turned Lily's head until she could see her face. 'Listen, my dear, until your mother is found you can come and stay with me, if you like.'

Lily shook her head. 'Dora and Tom look after me.'

'Of course they do.' Winnie smiled at Dora. 'The offer will always be there, and you must promise to come to me if you need any kind of help. I live in the next road, number fourteen.'

'Thank you, Mrs Tanner.' Dora accepted gratefully. Stan and his sister were almost strangers – their mother had never mixed with neighbours, or encouraged them to do so – and yet they were willing to help. It was so very kind of them.

After putting Lily down, Stan sat at the table again, and Dora didn't miss the flash of pain in his eyes as he moved to the chair. She was beginning to watch him with concern. 'Can't they do something about Stan's leg?' she whispered to Winnie, as they collected up the cups.

'Only cut it off, and he won't let them do that.' There was sadness in her voice when she spoke. 'I lost one brother in that blasted war, and the other came home with his body and life shattered. But by asking Stan for help you've given him a purpose and made him feel useful and needed again. If I can ever help you in any way, Dora, then you must come and let me know.'

'I'll do that, Mrs Tanner.' Anger raced through Dora, as it always did when she thought about the blighted lives the war had caused. Young men like Stan would have to live with the consequences of that madness for the rest of their lives. 'I'm sorry about your other brother.'

Winnie nodded. 'Harry was the eldest, and we miss him so much. But you know all about loss, don't you? Stan told me your father was killed in France – and now your mother has disappeared. How terrible for you, my dear.'

'Not knowing what's happened is just awful.'

Stan put a stop to their quiet conversation by turning his head and looking at them. 'Stop whispering back there and put the kettle on again, Win, and find a drink of milk for Lily, while we sort this out.'

They settled once again, all eyes fixed on Stan, waiting.

'It should make things easier now we don't need to keep this a secret any longer. Though I understood your reasons for doing so. Your mother's been missing long enough for the police to take her disappearance seriously. We need to widen the search, and we can't do that without help.'

All heads nodded in agreement.

'What I suggest is that I report this as a concerned friend. I'll talk it over with my brother-in-law first. He's Winnie's husband and a policeman at the local station. If I can get Reg involved then we might be able to keep this low-key for the time being. He'll want to talk to you, but I'll be there when he does.' Stan glanced around at the white-faced youngsters and asked gently, 'Is that all right with you? If not we'll try to think of another way.'

Dora looked at her brother and sister for approval, but in all truth, they didn't have any choice in the matter now. When they nodded, she said, 'We agree. And thank you very much for your help and understanding. We're feeling so lost and confused that it's hard to think straight.'

'That isn't surprising,' Winnie told them. 'You can safely leave everything with Stan. You go home and try to get some rest. Lily's almost asleep.'

When they'd gone, Stan and Winnie watched them walk back to their house.

'Do you think Mrs Bentley's done a runner, Stan?'

'That was my first thought when they came to see me, but now I know more, I believe that's unlikely. She's a good mother and the children love her. She's always worked hard to give them a better life, she even taught them herself at weekends to make sure they had a good standard of education. It's inconceivable she would leave them like this.'

'She's well educated then?'

'Seems like it. Those youngsters are well spoken, and they're no fools.'

'How long have they lived here?'

'About two years.' Stan turned from the window and lurched for a chair, falling into it with a grimace. 'But we don't know anything about Mrs Bentley, do we?'

'No, she kept to herself, and she never spoke when she picked up Lily from school – except to say good afternoon politely. But this is the first time I've ever met Dora and Tom.'

Stan nodded. 'Odd, isn't it? But Mrs Bentley obviously had secrets, that's why she kept aloof from everyone. And that's what's worrying me. Once this investigation gets under way, what the hell are we going to uncover?'

'You call on me, Stan. Those poor children are going to need all the support they can get. What do you think the chances are of their mother still being alive?'

'Slim. Very slim.'

Five

'Did you get much sleep?' Tom sat at the table bleary-eyed.

'Not much. I was worried about Lily.' Dora buttered toast for her brother. 'She was exhausted though, poor thing, and slept right through the night. How about you?'

'Not a wink. What are we going to do, Dora? I know we found that few pounds, but it won't last long, will it?'

'Oh, don't worry. I've got my job, and if we're careful we'll manage for a while.'

'But what if Mum never comes back? What will we do then, Dora?'

It was obvious that Tom had been turning everything over in his mind during the night.

'We'll look for a cheaper place to rent, for a start.' Dora felt sick with worry, but tried not to let it show. Tom was grey, and Lily's outburst yesterday had shaken them both. 'We'll stay here for as long as we can though, and hope everything works out in the end. Mum could still come back.'

Tom shook his head. 'If Mum could get back she'd have been here by now. We must prepare ourselves for the worst. The uncertainty is the awful thing.'

'Yes, it is, but we've got to hang on, Tom, for Lily's sake. And we're not on our own. Stan and his sister are helping us.'

Tom nodded. 'That was a good idea of Lily's about going to see Stan. I wonder what Mrs Tanner's husband is like?'

'We'll soon find out.' Dora placed a hand over her heart as if the action would stop it racing. 'He'll be round as soon as Stan's told him.'

'No doubt.' Tom glanced at the clock. 'You'd better hurry, Dora, or you'll be late. I'll get Lily up and take her to school. Can I have some money to get something for tea?'

Dora counted out two shillings. 'Get some bread and perhaps a few biscuits as a treat for Lily.'

'I'll get the broken ones. They're cheaper, and Lily won't mind.' Tom pocketed the money.

'If you both want to stay at home today, I'll write notes for you and drop them in on my way to work.'

'No!' Tom was emphatic. 'It's better if we carry on as usual. I don't want to miss any lessons. You know how important Mum said our schooling was. So off you go.'

'Oh Tom, you're so sensible in a crisis.' Dora could have hugged her brother, but he'd never been one to show his feelings – except with Lily. 'I don't know what I'd do without you.'

He shrugged. 'We've got to help each other as much as we can. I can't let you take on the whole burden. Mum lied to us, Dora, and she was the one who always told us to be honest. I just don't understand it. Goodness knows what's going to come to light. But whatever happens, we've got to look after each other.'

Dora agreed with every word Tom said, and felt so ill she wondered how she was going to get through the day. What she wanted to do was go with Stan, but that was out of the question. They were relying on her money now, so she must just grit her teeth and get on with it.

When Dora arrived at the house she found everyone in a high state of excitement. Trunks, cases and boxes were being dragged up from the cellar, and every member of the staff was rushing around.

'What's going on, Cook?' Dora asked.

'We're moving to Scotland.'

'How long for?'

'For good. The master's inherited a place up there. A castle, I'm told.' With a disapproving snort, the cook carried on rolling out pastry for the meat pie she was making for lunch. 'Bound to be cold with terrible draughts – and what's the rush, I ask?'

Dora was so stunned by the news that her feet wouldn't move. The nightmare she was living had just got worse.

'Good, you're here.' Mrs Marsden, the housekeeper, bustled into the kitchen. 'You've heard the news, Dora?'

She nodded, speechless.

'You're a good, reliable worker,' the housekeeper continued,

'and the mistress said there's a permanent place on the staff
for you at the new residence. This house will be closed in a
week's time.'

The room swayed and Dora held on to the table for support.
Oh, dear God, she prayed silently, not this as well. Her world
was collapsing around her and turning to dust.

'What is your answer?' Mrs Marsden was obviously irritated when Dora didn't speak.

After taking a deep breath to clear her head, Dora struggled to maintain her dignity. Another thing their mother had
always impressed upon them was that they must never make
a scene in public. 'That's very kind of the mistress, but I won't
be able to leave my family.'

'That's a great pity. I shall be sorry to lose you, but you'll
be given an excellent reference.'

'Thank you,' was all Dora could manage to say. Memories
of the many interviews she'd had to go through before she
had been given this job were still vivid in her mind. Most
households wanted a maid who lived in, and that was something she couldn't do.

The rest of the day was a blur of activity. It was no small
task to move such a large house, and by the time Dora reached
home she was exhausted. But even worse, there was a feeling
of hopelessness. What were they going to do if she couldn't
get another job quickly?

'You look like you've had a rough day,' Tom remarked,
studying his big sister with concern.

Dora hugged Lily. 'How are you, sweetie?'

'All right,' Lily said with a quiver of her lip. 'I was hoping
Mum would be here when we got home, but she wasn't. Do
you think she's lost and can't find her way back? Perhaps
she's lost her memory.'

'Maybe.' Dora sat down, giving a sigh of tiredness. She
knew just what Lily was doing. The little girl was running
through every conceivable reason in her head, except the one
they were all dreading.

Tom put plates in front of them. 'I'm afraid it's only sausages and mash again. I'll need more money for tomorrow,
Dora.'

She gave a weak smile. This was Tom's favourite meal, so
they were likely to get it quite often, but he was a real treasure.

Not many young boys of his age would take over the cooking and shopping like this.

'You going to tell us what's happened?' Tom started to eat, never taking his eyes off his big sister.

'I've got more bad news, I'm afraid.'

'That's obvious from the expression on your face. Out with it, Dora.'

'I'm losing my job at the end of the week.'

'Oh, hell! What a time for that to happen.' Tom dipped his head for a moment while he took this second blow.

'Did they sack you?' Lily wanted to know.

'No, sweetie, they're moving to Scotland.'

Tom put down his knife and fork. 'Did they ask you to go with them?'

Dora nodded. 'But that's out of the question.'

'Because of us,' Tom muttered.

'No, Tom! I wouldn't have gone, anyway. London's our home and I wouldn't want to live anywhere else. We must stay here until we know exactly what's happened to Mum. Suppose she came back one day and we weren't here?' Dora reached out and touched her brother's arm. He was clearly upset. 'It'll be all right. They're going to give me a good reference, and I'll soon find something else.'

'Course you will.' Tom looked up then, a smile on his face, albeit rather forced. 'Offers of jobs will be rolling in, won't they, Lily?'

Lily nodded, her mouth full of sausage, but it was clear that the full import of the news didn't register with her.

Dora began to tuck into her meal, trying to appear unconcerned. 'We've got that money we found with Mum's things, and I've still got a bit put by. Then there's my pay at the end of the week. So we'll be all right for a while.'

'Nothing to worry about then, eh?' Tom said, keeping his tone cheerful. 'Wonder how Stan got on today? He wasn't in when we came home.'

'He'll let us know.'

They had just finished clearing up when Stan arrived, only he wasn't alone, he had a uniformed policeman with him.

'This is my brother-in-law, Reg. He needs to ask you some questions.'

'Erm . . . yes, of course.' Dora was flustered and apprehensive when she saw the stocky man with Stan. She stood aside while Tom showed them into the front room. 'Please sit down. Would you like tea?'

'No thank you.' Reg smiled, and both men waited for Dora to sit before they did the same.

Lily's eyes were wide with fright, so Tom pulled her towards him, whispering in her ear, 'He's not going to eat you.'

Reg chuckled as Lily continued to stare at him. 'She doesn't believe you. Do you want to put her to bed before we start?'

'No.' Dora spoke firmly. 'This concerns all of us, and Lily stays. You can speak freely in front of her, sir.'

'Have you found our mum?' Lily asked, looking braver now her brother had a protective arm around her.

'Not yet.' Reg opened his notebook and read something written there. 'Stan's told me about the book you found. He's finished going through it, but there doesn't seem to be anything in it to help us. It's just a series of names and places.'

'Then why did Mum hide it if it wasn't important?' Tom frowned.

'It might well be important, but until we find out what she's been doing for the last two years, it means nothing to us.' Reg paused and looked at them all in turn. 'I want you to tell me everything.'

'But Stan's already told you, hasn't he?'

'Yes, Dora, but I'd like to hear it in your own words, please.'

It didn't take Dora long to relate what had happened, with Tom and Lily joining in now and again.

Reg had written quite a lot down in his notebook, and when he stopped writing, he asked, 'Stan said you found some letters. Would you let us see them?'

When Dora hesitated, Stan said, 'We need to build up a picture of your mother, What she liked doing, places she liked to visit, things like that. Letters can often help us do that.'

'There's no harm in letting them see them.' Tom was already on his feet. 'I'll get them, shall I?'

'All right,' she agreed reluctantly. They had been brought up never to read anything addressed to their parents, and it was hard to break that rule, even in these exceptional circumstances.

Tom soon returned, and Stan and Reg settled back to read. Dora decided to make a pot of tea, more for something to do than from the need for a drink.

'Do you know anything about your mother's family?' Reg asked suddenly, making Dora jump as she was pouring the tea.

'She never talked about them. I don't think she had any family.'

'We never met any grandparents, so we don't think Mum or Dad had any family,' Tom told them, looking puzzled. 'This can't have anything to do with Mum's disappearance, surely?'

Reg just smiled. 'We need to look at every angle in the hope that it might produce a clue. Can we see your mother's room now?'

'Er . . . is that necessary?' The thought of strangers going through her mother's things did not sit well with Dora. 'We've already searched every inch.'

'Dora,' Stan said. 'We might find something you've missed. Something that looks out of place, but so ordinary that you wouldn't think it important.'

'Let them do it,' Tom said. 'There might be something we didn't notice.'

'Yes, of course you're right,' Dora agreed reluctantly. 'The only important thing is to try and find out what's happened to Mum. Were the letters any use?'

'Not at first glance.' Reg tied them together again. 'Would you let us keep them for a while, so we can go through them again? You can have them back in a couple of days.'

'We'll take good care of them,' Stan assured Dora, 'and I promise no one else will see them.'

'Very well.' She gave Stan a brief nod. 'I know we can trust you.'

'Good, thank you.' Reg stood up. 'Will you show us your mother's room now?'

Tom led the way up the stairs, followed by Reg and Stan, with Dora and Lily behind them.

Stan had left his stick at the bottom of the stairs, and was using the banisters to swing himself up. Dora knew he would need it when he got to the top, so she took it with her, and handed it to him on the landing.

Tom opened their mother's bedroom door and stood back to allow them to enter first. The three of them stood by the door and watched Reg and Stan search. Dora felt very uneasy as each item was examined and put back in the drawers or wardrobe. Occasionally they showed each other a pair of shoes or piece of clothing, but they said nothing, and their expressions gave nothing away.

'What're they finding so interesting?' Tom whispered, when they had spent a while studying a frock.

Dora shrugged, just as puzzled.

After what seemed like an age, Reg looked across at them. 'Do you know if any of your mother's clothes are missing?'

'No, sir,' Dora replied. 'They're all there, except the things she was wearing.'

'I understand that you found the letters and notebook hidden in the bed. Was there anything else?'

'No, that's—'

'There was the necklace,' Tom interrupted.

'What necklace?' Both men spoke at once.

'Oh, it's only a cheap thing. Something Mum kept for sentimental reasons, I expect.'

'Can we see it, Dora?' Stan asked.

Tom was already lifting the mattress, and when he'd retrieved the box he handed it to Stan, who removed the necklace and held it up to the light.

'Oh, that's pretty!' Lily hadn't seen it before, and forgetting her shyness of the man in uniform, she rushed forward. 'Let me see it, please.'

Stan held it out for her. 'See how it shines?'

'Dora, look!' Lily bounced with excitement, her expression animated.

Dora was so pleased to see her little sister smile again that she took the necklace from Stan and fixed it round Lily's neck. Then she stood her in front of the mirror on the wardrobe door. 'There, don't you look beautiful.'

Lily giggled. 'Look, Tom, look!'

He shaded his eyes as if blinded by the brilliance. 'Who's this dazzling girl? I don't recognize her.'

Giving a shriek of delight, Lily launched herself at her teasing brother. 'It's me, silly.'

Tom lifted her up. 'So it is.'

It was wonderful to hear laughter and see her brother and sister fooling around again. The scene brought a lump to Dora's throat. And she couldn't help noticing how big and strong Tom was now. He seemed to be growing every day. He was going to be a fine-looking man.

The search finished, and they let Lily keep the necklace on as they all went downstairs again.

'Did you find anything to help you?' Dora asked.

Reg tucked his notebook into his top pocket. 'Hard to say yet. We'll have to go through my notes at leisure, but thank you for allowing us to do this tonight. I realize how upsetting it's all been. Everything will be done to find your mother.'

'Thank you, sir.'

'The name's Reg. We'll let you know the moment we have any news.'

Six

The moment they were back in Stan's house, Reg swore, 'Who the hell is Harriet Bentley? I've got a nasty feeling about this, Stan. I'll see that Win keeps an eye on those youngsters. Can you believe it? They're polite, well spoken and completely innocent. They'll never cope if we uncover anything unsavoury.'

'Don't be too sure about Dora.' Stan sat down and gave a quiet groan, rubbing his leg. 'She might seem shy, but there's fire underneath that unworldly exterior. She cares deeply about some things, and shows it when she talks about them. But I agree that as far as the world goes they are innocent.'

'Now you come to mention it, I did see her eyes flash in disapproval now and again. She hated us poking around her mother's things, didn't she.'

Stan nodded. 'But she also knew it had to be done. Now about the mother. The letters didn't give much away, but I got the impression there was something in her past. The man she married knew about it but loved her too much to care. Dora told me their parents had been happy together, and that Mrs Bentley was devastated when her husband was killed in the war.'

Reg paced the room. 'And it looks like that was when she started lying to her children. I don't suppose they noticed that some of their mother's clothes were expensive. I'd swear one of her nightgowns was pure silk, but the label had been carefully removed. I wish we could have borrowed that necklace, but I didn't like to make too much of it. They think it's glass . . . Hell, I'm no expert, but I'd like to show it to someone who is.'

'I've made a note of the name and address of the jeweller. It was in the lid of the box, and . . .' Stan removed a sheet of paper from his pocket, 'while they were fooling around with Lily, I made a sketch of the necklace.'

'I didn't see you do that.' Reg sat beside Stan and studied the drawing.

'I'm not surprised. You couldn't take your eyes off the necklace.'

'Hmm. That's very good. What are you going to do with it?'

'Visit the jeweller tomorrow, see what kind of a place it is and ask if he recognizes it. Of course, it might be a cheap thing and been put in an expensive box, but I don't think so somehow. It fitted perfectly, as if the box had been made for it.'

'I agree.' Reg stood up and tucked the bundle of letters in his pocket. 'I'll go through these again tonight in case we missed something. You take it easy tomorrow.'

Stan pulled a face, making Reg laugh. 'Daft thing to tell you, isn't it?'

The next morning, Stan was ready early for his visit to the jeweller's in Bond Street. He would have to go by train, and the journey would be impossible using just a stick. Loath as he was to use the crutches, he knew he didn't have any choice. His leg would never stand up to everything he wanted to do today. He would have to keep as much pressure off it as he could, and that would mean using the blasted things. The problem was that they put a strain on his back, but he'd just have to put up with that.

He retrieved them from the shed and set off for the station.

'Watch it!' Stan swayed and nearly lost his balance when a young boy of around seven ran straight into him. He struggled to stay upright and avoid the indignity of ending up flat out on the pavement.

'Jimmy!' A woman rushed up and grabbed hold of Stan to support him. 'Come here and apologize to the gentleman.'

The boy crept back, looking downcast. 'Sorry sir, I wasn't looking where I was going.'

'You all right?' the woman asked. 'I hope my boy didn't hurt you?'

'I'm fine, thank you,' Stan lied. The boy had given his injured leg a sharp kick as he'd sped by, and the pain was excruciating. He gritted his teeth and continued up the road. Nothing was going to stop him doing what he'd planned today. Nothing!

By the time he reached the station and bought his ticket, the pain was bearable. He found a bench and sat down to wait for his train. The platform was quite crowded with men going to work, women with children, and young girls. There weren't many young men, as nearly a whole generation had been slaughtered in the war. As Stan watched people laughing and talking, he was suddenly overcome with a feeling of loneliness. He was still a young man, but what kind of a life did he have in front of him? No girl in her right mind would want to marry him. He would never be able to take her out walking or dancing – never have a family of his own . . .

As the feeling of emptiness engulfed him, he swore under his breath, took out a cigarette and lit it, drawing on it deeply and blowing the smoke into the air. Damn it! He'd accepted all this. Why did the regrets have to rear their ugly head again? When he'd first returned home he'd tried to drown the pain and hopelessness in whisky, but had soon found out that it didn't help – only made him feel worse. He'd come to terms with the restrictions by reminding himself that he was alive and a lot better off than many other poor devils, and that included his older brother. God, that still hurt, but he was damned if he was going to allow himself to become a bitter man, and a burden to his family.

The train puffed into the station, and Stan hauled himself up.

'You need a hand?' a middle-aged man asked.

'I can manage.' But Stan smiled his thanks when the man held the train door open for him.

Stan was about to sit down when he saw a young man having difficulty getting into the carriage. He recognized the condition immediately, and holding the door he reached out. 'All right, mate. You take your time.'

With the help of the middle-aged man, they pulled him in and settled him in a corner seat so he could look out of the window. Stan sat beside him, lit a cigarette and placed it in the young man's mouth.

'Shell shock,' the other man muttered grimly. 'Bloody war. What about you, son? Have you lost your leg?'

'No, I've still got it, but it's not much use.' Stan turned to the young man. 'Where you going, mate?'

With a great deal of difficulty the young man took a piece of paper out of his pocket. It bore the address of the Royal London Hospital, Whitechapel, and a doctor's name.

The other man leant across so he could read it as well.

'He's got to change trains. He's never going to get there on his own.' Stan was furious. 'Why isn't someone with him? I'll take him myself.'

'No need for that, son. I work there. I'll see he gets to the hospital all right. I'm Doctor Burridge.' He held out his hand. 'If you ever need another opinion on your leg, come and see me at the hospital. No need to make an appointment.'

'Stan Crawford.' He shook his hand and gave a grim smile. 'They've said there's nothing they can do for me. You hard up for patients, Doc?'

'Wish I were, but our methods are improving all the time. God knows we're getting enough practice.'

'I don't doubt it.' Stan looked at the silent, shaking man beside him and counted his blessings. He might be in constant pain, but at least he was in his right mind. He laid his hand on the young man's arm and smiled. 'This man's a doctor and he's going to take you to the hospital.'

The young man managed to nod to let him know he understood, then Stan turned his attention back to the doctor. 'Who's the doc this man's going to see? Is he any good?'

'The best in his field. The poor devil will get proper help. My line of work is putting shattered bodies back into some kind of working order.' Dr Burridge took a card out of his pocket and signed the back. 'Come and see me, son. Just show this card and they'll call me.'

Stan tucked the card into his pocket, knowing it would take something extraordinary to get him near a hospital again. 'Thanks.'

Bond Street was crowded and Stan had to walk quite a way before he found the jeweller's he was looking for. He whistled softly under his breath when he saw the shop. That necklace couldn't have come from here. He was probably wasting his time, but he'd come this far and might as well go in.

The inside was fitted with plush carpets and upholstered chairs in dark blue. The customers who came in here obviously expected comfort while they spent their money.

'May I help you, sir?' A short man in a dark suit was eyeing him with more than a hint of suspicion.

Stan decided that it wouldn't take much for them to show him the door. He decided to bluff it out. 'I'm Sergeant Crawford from Kilburn Police. Mind if I sit down?'

The assistant held a chair for him and Stan propped his crutches against a display cabinet.

'Had an accident, sir?' the assistant asked as he went back to the other side of the counter.

'Tripped over chasing a thief.' Stan gave him his most ironic smile.

'I see, sir.'

Liar, Stan thought, you don't know whether to believe me or not, but you're too polite to say so. He removed the sketch from his pocket and laid it on the counter. 'We're trying to find out about this necklace. It was in one of your boxes.'

'Really?' Now the man was interested. 'Hmm, you don't have the jewel with you?'

'Sorry, this is all I've got. The chain is silver and the stones colourless. There are small stones along the chain at intervals of about an inch, and larger stones in the three daisy-shaped flowers in the centre. Can you tell me if it's one of your designs?'

'I'll ask the owner.' The assistant beckoned over a young lad. 'Get Sergeant Crawford a cup of tea, Edward. I'll be just a moment, Sergeant.'

Stan stifled a sigh of relief. It looked as if he was getting away with his subterfuge. He shouldn't be doing this, but this was the only way anyone in a place like this was going to talk to him.

The lad came back carrying a cup of tea on a silver tray. Stan had never seen such delicate china.

'Thanks.' He needed this. His leg was still hurting after the kick it had received, and the journey on and off trains had not helped.

The lad was about to say something, but the assistant returned with the owner. He was past middle age, Stan guessed, tall and with a shock of white hair.

He didn't waste time. 'May I ask what your interest is in this item?'

'We're trying to trace a missing person, and the necklace belongs to her.'

'I would have to see it before I could make a positive identification, but according to our records, a necklace similar to this design was made here.'

'When?' Stan took out a police notebook Reg had given him.

'December 1900. But I couldn't say for sure this is ours without examining the workmanship.'

'Twenty years ago? Can you tell me who might have bought one like this?'

'I'm afraid I can't divulge that information, Sergeant Crawford. Our transactions are confidential.'

That was only what Stan expected, and he had no power to push for answers. But he'd try one more question. 'If this is the real thing, is it valuable?'

'If it is one of ours then the setting would be platinum, diamonds of the finest quality, and it would be worth a considerable amount.' The owner hesitated, then continued, 'But unless the missing lady is from – shall we say – a fine family, then it is unlikely to be genuine.'

'Have you ever made a copy?'

'No, Sergeant! Our jewels are exclusive.' The man looked offended.

He drank the tea in two mouthfuls and replaced the cup on the tray, then he stood up, knowing that he had all the information he was going to get. The necklace in Dora's possession must be a fake, but the mystery of Harriet Bentley deepened.

Resting on his crutches, he nodded to the two jewellers. 'You've been very helpful. Thank you for your time.'

He had arranged to meet Reg for lunch in the café opposite the police station. His brother-in-law was already there, and surged to his feet when he saw Stan. 'Good Lord, man, come and sit down before you fall down.'

Slumping into a chair, he closed his eyes and breathed deeply, trying to let the pain flow out of him. There had been times during the journey when he'd doubted he was going to make it. This was the most he had tried to do since he had been injured, and it made him aware of the poor state he really was in. Sweat was pouring down his face, and he was having difficulty focusing.

'Give this to him, Reg.'

Dragging his eyes open, Stan saw the café owner by the table with a glass in his hand.

'Cheers, Len.' Reg took the glass and wrapped Stan's fingers around it. 'Knock that back. It'll revive you.'

Stan had to use both hands to bring the glass to his mouth. He was shaking nearly as badly as that poor devil on the train. That scared him, and he gulped down the brandy. The fiery liquid did its job and jolted him back to life.

'Thanks, Len.' He handed back the glass, relieved to see that his hands were almost steady again. 'That's strong stuff.'

Len winked. 'I keep it for emergencies. What you need now is a good meal. I've got a steak and kidney pudding. That should put a bit of strength back in you.'

As the café owner went away to get their meals, Reg was clearly concerned and furious with himself. 'I shouldn't have let you do that journey today. You frightened the life out of me when you came in, Stan. You were grey and you could hardly stand. Thank God you had the sense to use crutches.'

'Sorry about that. I didn't realize just how hard it would be.' Stan pulled out a handkerchief and wiped his face, hating to appear so weak. He had always been strong and vigorous, excelling in many sports. Now he was just a shadow of his former self, and it was hard to take. In his mind he was still that fit active person, but his body didn't agree. Not only had his leg been shattered, but they'd also spent days digging bits of shrapnel out of his back, and even that was hurting now. In fact, he couldn't find a part of him that wasn't sore.

'You've got a bit of colour back now.' Reg was studying him intently. 'For goodness sake don't tell Win about this or I'll never hear the last of it.'

Stan grimaced. 'Neither will I.'

Two plates were put in front of them, piled high with food. 'You need another brandy, Stan?'

'No thanks, Len. A good strong cup of tea would go down well, though.'

'Coming right up.'

They ate in silence, and Stan was glad of the quiet as it was giving him the time to recover.

When they'd finished eating, they lit cigarettes and relaxed. 'Feel up to telling me what you found out?'

Stan drew deeply on the cigarette, and then told Reg about

his visit to the jeweller's. When he'd finished his brother-in-law swore fluently. 'You impersonated a police officer?'

'I didn't think they'd talk to me otherwise.'

'You were lucky they didn't ask you for proof.'

'Wasn't I.' Stan grinned, feeling much better now. 'Anyway, what do you think about the necklace?'

'Oh, it can't be real. We'd have to borrow it if we wanted to get it verified, and I don't want to do that at the moment, because I don't think it's going to help us find Mrs Bentley. Don't say anything to Dora. We'd better forget about it for the time being.'

'I agree. Had any luck with your enquiries so far?'

Reg shook his head. 'We're still waiting to hear from some area stations. And I must get back.'

Stan propped himself up on his crutches and followed Reg, who stopped suddenly in the middle of the road.

'Your bus stop is on the other side of the road.'

'I know, but I'm coming with you to see if there's any news.'

Giving a gusty sigh, Reg glared at him. 'You need to go home and rest. Any good me arguing?'

'None at all.'

Seven

It was after six o'clock, and Dora stood by the window watching anxiously for Stan to return home. When she saw him making his way along the road, it made her gasp in shock. He looked dreadfully ill, and in so much difficulty she expected him to topple over before he reached his gate.

'Tom, look after Lily for me. Stan's just arrived and he needs help.'

Dora rushed out of the house and reached Stan's gate just before him. She held it open, waited while he opened the front door, and followed him into the front room. He didn't say a word as he collapsed into an armchair, the crutches clattering to the floor.

Dora picked them up and stood them against the wall within his reach. Then she stooped down in front of him, deeply concerned. 'Do you want me to get a doctor for you, or ask your sister to come?'

'No, I don't! And what the hell are you doing here?' he growled.

Although she was taken aback by his sharpness, she chose to ignore it. 'I came to help,' she said gently. 'You rest and I'll get you something to eat.'

'Go away, Dora!' He laid his head back and closed his eyes.

Inside Dora there was a stubborn streak. It didn't often surface, but now it did. Finding a stool in the corner of the room, she put it by his feet and carefully lifted his leg to rest on it. 'There, that will be more comfortable for you. I'll make a pot of tea.'

'I told you to clear off!' His eyes were now open, and furious. 'I don't want your help, so just mind your own bloody business.'

That was it as far as Dora was concerned. She cried out, 'Don't you talk to me like that! You're worn out, and whether you like it or not, you need help. That's what I came to do, and don't you dare throw it back in my face. I understand that you don't want people to see you like this. You're hurt and frustrated because you can't do what you used to. I wish I could change that for you, but I can't! I wish I could change what's happening to my family, but I can't! However much we dislike the situation we're both in, we're stuck with it! What's done is done! But it's clear to me now that we shouldn't have come to you for help. It's obviously too much for you, and I'm sorry we've bothered you with our problems. But we didn't know what else to do, and I've got enough to put up with, without receiving the sharp end of your tongue. My mother's disappeared. I've got Tom and Lily relying on me and I've lost my job. How am I going to manage, I ask you? How am I going to keep my family together . . . ?'

Tears of rage and despair began to gather in her eyes, so she spun away from the ungrateful man before she disgraced herself by sobbing.

As she reached the door strong hands rested on her shoulders, stopping her flight.

'I'm sorry. Please forgive me. You don't deserve to be treated like that. You were right to come to me, and I'm glad you did.' Stan tightened his grasp and turned her to face him. 'What do you mean, you've lost your job?'

'They're moving to Scotland at the end of this week, on my eighteenth birthday would you believe, and I don't know what I'm going to do. Most households want maids who live in, and I can't do that.'

'You're an intelligent girl, you can do something else.'

'What? Looking after other people is all I've ever done. I won't be able to pay the rent on our house for long. We'll have to move to a cheaper place.' All Dora's suppressed fears were tumbling out. 'Mum worked hard to get us out of the slums and we could end up back there again. I don't want that for Tom and Lily. I've *got* to find another job. I must, but what am I going to do? Don't shout at me, Stan. I can't take any more.'

'I won't, I promise.' Stan propped himself against the door-frame and gathered Dora into his arms. 'You must be out of your mind with worry, but we'll work something out. It'll all come right in the end, you'll see. If the worst comes to the worst you can move in here, and I'll inflict myself on Win and Reg.'

'Oh, you can't do that.' Dora lifted her head, eyes troubled. 'I wouldn't allow you to give up your home. It wouldn't be right. I'm letting my fears run away with me. I'll soon get another job. I can be very determined when I have to be.'

'I'm already finding that out.' He brushed his lips over the top of her head. 'I think you said something about a pot of tea?'

She nodded, and helped him back to his chair, wondering how on earth he'd managed to get across the room without support. Then she noticed the grim set of his mouth, and knew he'd reached her at some cost to himself. She placed his leg carefully back on the stool and stood back, feeling breathless. He was quite a disturbing man to be close to. 'Have you changed your mind about something to eat? It wouldn't take me long to prepare a meal for you.'

'That's kind of you, Dora, but I had a huge lunch with Reg.'

'Just tea then.'

Stan took hold of one of her hands as she went to turn away, brought it to his mouth and kissed it gently. 'I really am sorry. I've overdone it today and it's no one's fault but my own. I'm inclined to snap and snarl with frustration at times.'

'So I've discovered.' She removed her hand and smiled. 'I'll make that tea.'

Alone in the kitchen, Dora rested her hands on the sink and bowed her head. One large tear trickled down her cheek. She was so frightened, but had managed to keep it under control until Stan had snapped at her. Then every worry had come to the surface. Her fears had all been for Tom, Lily and herself, but now Stan had been included. He was pushing himself too much for them, and he just wasn't fit enough. Thank goodness the police were now involved. She must get him to leave it to them. That thought made her pull a face. He would probably shout at her again for trying to tell him what to do, but it was a risk she would have to take. She cared about him.

With the tea made, she put it on a tray and took it into the front room. Stan hadn't moved. He smiled when she handed him a cup, but it couldn't erase the lines from his face, or the look of sadness from his eyes. He'd lost a brother, seen goodness knows what horrors, and been injured. He had suffered, and was still suffering from the madness of war, but like other ex-servicemen, he never spoke about it. How she wished she could help . . .

'What are you thinking?'

The sound of his voice brought her out of deep thought. 'Oh, nothing worth mentioning,' she said, refilling his cup. 'Did you find out anything today?'

Stan took a mouthful of tea, swallowed, and then shook his head. 'Nothing yet, I'm afraid, but Reg is widening the search. He'll let us know immediately there's news.'

'How can someone just walk out of the house and disappear, Stan?'

'There are many reasons, and some of them don't want to be found.'

'Mum would never leave us like this. And she certainly wouldn't go without her clothes. She was always particular about looking smart.'

'I agree. Your mother was always smartly turned out.' Stan sighed quietly. 'We won't give up until we know what's happened to her. That's a promise, Dora.'

'Thank you, and you must promise not to overtire yourself again.' She clasped her hands together tightly as he nodded his head. 'In the meantime we've got to deal with the situation we find ourselves in. You must rest more, and I must find myself another job.'

'Don't only look for a position as a maid, Dora. You might be able to find work in a shop, or something like that.'

'I'll try anything.' Dora put the cups back on the tray and stood up. 'I'll wash these, and then I must get back to Tom and Lily. They'll be anxious to know if there's any news.'

'Tell them everything possible is being done.' Stan glanced casually at Dora. 'How's Lily? Did you manage to get the necklace off her last night?'

The tension lifted from Dora's face as she smiled fondly. 'She wanted to sleep in it, but I told her it would break. I've put it back where we found it, and said she could have it when she was older.'

Stan merely smiled.

While she was washing up, the back door opened and Winnie walked in.

'Hello there.' She greeted Dora in a friendly manner. 'I see you've beaten me to it with the tea. Is he all right?'

'He seems to be now.'

Winnie frowned. 'Now? What do you mean?'

Dora told her what had happened.

'I thought Reg was holding something back.' Winnie was clearly worried about her brother. 'If he keeps pushing himself like this, I'm frightened he might shorten his life. The strain on him is immense. He's got other injuries as well as the leg.'

'Oh, I didn't know that.' Dora was shocked.

'The doctors told me they couldn't be sure they'd removed all the shrapnel from his body.' Winnie sat on a kitchen chair. 'I've lost one brother and I don't want to lose this one. He's such a special man.'

'Yes, I think he is,' Dora agreed, and sat beside her. 'I haven't known him very long, but I've found out one thing about him. No matter how severe his injuries, he isn't the kind of man who could live a half-life. I think he'd rather have a shorter, active life than a longer, lingering one.'

Winnie stared at Dora in amazement. 'My word, you have worked him out, haven't you? You're so observant. You've caught my brother's character perfectly. I shouldn't fuss, he hates it. But I love him, and I'm being selfish by trying to curb what he does.'

'Well, I'm just as bad.' Dora stood up to stack away the cups. 'I've made him promise not to overdo it, but I expect I'm wasting my breath. He's going to do whatever he wants, no matter what anyone says.'

'How right you are.'

'Tell you what,' Dora whispered in Winnie's ear, 'we'll leave him in peace for the moment, but soon we'll gang up on him and get him to see a doctor again. Things change, and they might be able to do something for him by now.'

'He's never said, but I think he had a rough time. He's reluctant to go near doctors again.' Winnie looked doubtful. 'I've tried several times already, but he either ignores me or explodes.'

'Ah, but he'll have two of us to cope with from now on.'

Dora and Winnie walked into the front room, looking like a couple of smug conspirators.

'You two look suspiciously pleased with yourselves. What are you up to?'

'Nothing you need worry about.' Winnie winked at Dora.
'Yet.'

Dora took her leave in a hurry. Hatching that little plot with
Winnie had lifted her own worries a little, but as soon as she
stepped in the house they came crashing down on her again.

'Any news?' Tom asked, when she walked in.

'Nothing, I'm sorry to say, but they're widening the search.
They'll let us know as soon as they have anything to report.'

Tom drew Dora away from Lily, who was busy drawing at
the kitchen table. 'Nothing was said about someone coming
round to see if we're all right, then?'

'It wasn't mentioned. Reg seems to be handling the investigation, and he knows us, so I'm sure he'll tell everyone
that.'

'I expect so.' Tom looked relieved. 'You rushed off to help
Stan. How is he?'

'Exhausted.' Dora told her brother what had happened, and
what Winnie had said about Stan's injuries.

'That's bad news, but I'm sure he's pleased to be doing
something useful. We'll just have to hope we haven't asked
him to do too much for us. Shall I pop in and see him now?'

'I wouldn't, Tom. He needs to rest, and he isn't in the best
of moods. You and Lily go and see him in the morning before
you go to school. He seems to like her.'

'Good idea, and perhaps I can drop a hint about him taking
it easy.'

'You can try.'

Tom frowned as he thought over what he'd just been told.
'We mustn't be selfish and expect him to do any more for us.
I'll ask him if he needs any shopping. I can get that along
with ours on my way home from school.'

'I'm sure he'll appreciate that, Tom.' Dora had always known
that Tom had a kind nature, but since their mother had disappeared he had become a caring young boy. This crisis was
making him grow up quickly.

'We'd better get Lily to bed.' Tom lifted her off the chair,
making her squeal, and started up the stairs with her.

Once the little girl was tucked up in bed, Dora held on to
Tom, making him stay. 'We'll all say our prayers together
tonight, and include Stan in them.'

Lily had fallen asleep quickly, and they went back to the

kitchen to make themselves a cup of cocoa. Then they sat down to talk things over.

Dora stared at her hands wrapped around the cup. 'Tomorrow I'll ask Mrs Marsden if she knows of a family who need a daily maid. If she doesn't then I'll take a couple of hours off and visit a few shops and apply as an assistant. They've said I can do that if I need to.'

Tom nodded. 'You take all the time you need. I'll see to Lily and get the dinner ready.'

'Thanks, Tom.'

'How long can we afford to pay the rent, and buy enough food for us? And Lily's growing out of her shoes.'

'I know she needs new ones.' Dora opened her purse and tipped the contents on the table. 'I've put aside the money we found. That'll take care of the rent for a little while, but Lily must also have her shoes. Then there's our bus fares . . .'

'If you can't get another job our money isn't going to last long, is it? I don't want to move from here, Dora. Lily likes her school, and so do I. But we've got to face the fact that Mum isn't coming back, haven't we?'

Dora's insides heaved with grief and worry. Tom was voicing her own conclusions. Something dreadful must have happened. But what? She gazed at her brother, deeply troubled. 'I think we must plan as if she's gone for good. We've got to keep us together. It isn't going to be easy, but we'll find a way. Between us we'll do it, Tom.'

'Of course we will.'

Eight

That was the best night's sleep he'd had in a long time. But it was hardly surprising; he'd been exhausted. Stan stretched cautiously, aching from head to toe, and wondering if he was going to be able to get out of bed.

Pushing back the covers he eased his legs out and sat on the edge of the bed. So far, so good. His leg was badly bruised where the young lad had kicked him but, as far as he could see, no other damage had been done. Reaching for the stick he kept beside the bed, he braced for the effort of hauling himself to his feet. After the third attempt he was standing.

'Attaboy, Stanley,' he muttered. 'Now all you've got to do is move.'

It took him nearly an hour to wash, shave, dress and get down to the kitchen. He was breathing hard by the time he slumped on a chair, but he was well pleased with himself. After what he had put himself through yesterday, he'd had grave doubts that he'd be able to get out of bed this morning.

'Ah, you're up then,' Winnie said as she came in the back door.

'Of course.' Stan raised his eyebrows. 'What are you doing here so early?'

'Thought you might like breakfast in bed.'

Stan sighed. 'You know I never do that.'

'No, well . . .' Winnie looked slightly uncomfortable. 'I was worried about you—'

Stan caught hold of his sister's arm. 'You've got to stop this, Win. You've got enough to do looking after your own family. I'm fine. For the first time since I came home I have something useful to do – something to take my mind off my own problems. The three Bentley children need me, and that makes me feel good. We've got to find out what's happened to their mother, and when we do, it won't end there. I have a nasty feeling there's going to be an almighty mess to clear up. Mrs Bentley was obviously living a secret life, and if it turns out to be something shady, then those children are going to be hurt.'

'You can't be sure about that, Stan.' Winnie sat down and poured them both a cup of tea from the pot she had just made. 'There might be a perfectly reasonable explanation for lying about the job she was doing. Perhaps she was working in a club or something, and didn't want her children to know?'

'You might be right. Dora did tell me her mother took any kind of job so she could move them to a better area. After her husband was killed, she might have had to earn as much as she could to keep them here. But whatever it was, I'm going to see this through. If that means pushing myself hard, then that's what I'll do.'

Winnie gazed at her brother with love and admiration. 'Of course you are. If I stop fussing over you, will you promise me something?'

'If I can.'

'When this is all over you'll go and see the doctors again?'

'It'll only be a waste of time, but I promise to do that. Just to please you though – and stop you fussing.'

Smiling with relief, Winnie opened the kitchen table drawer and took out a pencil and paper, then she slid it towards him. 'I'll have that in writing, please.'

'You're pushing your luck, Win.' But Stan was chuckling as he wrote down the promise. 'Now, as you're here, you might as well cook me a nice big breakfast. I'm starving.'

After finishing off eggs, bacon, sausages, fried bread, two slices of toast and three cups of tea, Stan sat back and lit a cigarette.

'My goodness!' Winnie exclaimed. 'You are feeling better. That's the most I've seen you eat in a long time.'

'I was exhausted at the end of yesterday, but it did me good.' Stan's expression sobered as he took out his wallet and handed Winnie ten shillings. 'It's Dora's eighteenth birthday on Friday, so would you buy her something from me? It's also the day she loses her job.'

'Oh, poor thing.' Winnie put the money in her purse. 'We'll give a little party for her. Not that she'll feel like celebrating . . . but I'll bring Reg and June with me, as well.'

'Thanks Win, that's a kind idea.' Stan stood up. 'Now I must get going.'

'Where are you off to?'

'I'm meeting Reg at the station. They're letting me hang around in case anything comes up, and they thought that as I know the family I might be able to spot something they'd missed.'

'How are you going to get there?'

'On my bike.'

'Stan!' When she saw the expression on his face, she held up her hands. 'Sorry, sorry. I promised not to fuss.'

'That's right.' He grinned. 'I think signing that paper was a good idea.'

At that moment there was a knock on the front door. When Winnie opened it, Tom and Lily tumbled in, all concerned.

'Where's Stan? Is he all right? Dora said he wasn't too well last night. Is he still in bed?' Tom was already heading for the stairs.

'I'm here, Tom.' Stan stood in the hallway.

Tom spun round, studying Stan intently. 'Oh, good, you're up. You feeling all right now?'

'I'm fine.' Stan was touched that the youngsters should be worried about him. They had enough troubles of their own, for goodness sake! 'As you're here we might as well tell you what we've planned for Dora's eighteenth birthday.'

Winnie explained about the party.

'Oh, thanks.' Tom looked from Stan to Winnie, his face glowing with gratitude. 'Eighteen's a big birthday and we ought to mark it. I'm sure Dora will be pleased.'

Lily tugged at Stan's arm, her eyes bright with unshed tears. 'Mum told me she was going to give Dora a big cake and jelly and stuff. She said it must be special because Dora would be all grown up then. She told me not to say anything as it was going to be a surprise. Can you find Mum so she can come to the party?'

Stan bent slightly to look into Lily's bewildered eyes. The poor little thing just couldn't understand what was happening. 'We don't know, Lily, but we'll try and make it special for your sister, shall we?'

'Yes, please.' Her little mouth trembled. 'I love Dora. She's nice – and Tom as well, of course.'

Tom pulled a face and took hold of his sister's hand. 'I think I came as an afterthought. Come on, urchin, it's time we were at school. Take it easy today, Stan, and I hope you find something soon. Do you need any shopping or anything? I could get it on my way home from school.'

'I've got everything I need, Tom, but thanks.'

'You sure?' Tom hesitated by the door, and when Stan nodded, he said, 'You just ask if you need anything.'

The children left, waving as they walked up the street. Winnie turned away from the window, her eyes filled with sadness.

'Find that woman, Stan! If she's dead then let those sweet kids bury her and move on with their lives. I'll take them on myself if they haven't got anyone else. I won't see them struggling to fend for themselves.'

'We'll do our best, Win, but this is a damned strange case.' Stan placed an arm around his sister's shoulder. 'Whatever Mrs Bentley's done, you have to admit she's made a good job of bringing up her children.'

'Yes, she has, and I can see now she wouldn't have left them like this. When I first heard the story I had my doubts about her, but seeing how her children love her and how she's obviously cared for them, I'm not sure now. I think she must be a decent woman doing the best she can for her children.' Winnie gave a troubled sigh. 'And that means she's being held somewhere and can't get away, or she's dead.'

'Let's hope it's the former.'

'Oh, I do hope so, Stan. But all this speculation isn't getting us anywhere, is it? It's a complete mystery.' Winnie shook herself as if to push away the unpleasant thoughts. 'I must get a move on. I've only got two days to make a cake and arrange a party.'

'I'm having second thoughts about the party. Don't you think it's a bit insensitive at a time like this, Win?'

'Some might see it that way, but I don't. Dora's carrying a heavy burden on her slender shoulders, and I think we ought to try and give her a treat on her eighteenth birthday. Tom and Lily think it's a good idea.'

Stan nodded and watched his sister hurry off. Then he went to the shed, tied his stick on the crossbar of the bike, and set off for the police station. He pedalled along cautiously at first, and then more confidently. He was stiff, but it wasn't nearly as painful as the first time he'd ridden the bike. He grunted in satisfaction. So much for the doctors' predictions that he was going to be confined to a wheelchair if he didn't have the leg amputated. What did they know?

Stan was disappointed when he saw the superintendent as he walked into the station. Most of the others knew him when he'd been one of them, but the super was a stranger to Stan. He could be ordered out of here, and he desperately wanted to stay. If any information came in, he needed to see it. He couldn't sit at home and wait. It would drive him crazy.

Reg introduced him to Superintendent Greenwood and explained the case they were working on.

'Neighbours of yours, are they?'

'Yes, sir,' Stan replied smartly. 'Nice family, and I'd like your permission to stay here and see any information that comes in. I was a policeman at this station, so I know the ropes.'

The superintendent cast a glance over Stan, noting the stick. 'Get that injury in the war?'

'Yes, sir.' Stan was almost afraid to breathe. He hadn't been ordered out yet.

'Permanent, is it?'

'So they say, but I've got my own opinion about that!' Stan spoke forcefully.

The super's stern expression relaxed. 'I expect you have. Stay if you wish. You know the family and might be able to help.' With a nod to the room, he strode out.

Reg slapped Stan on the back, grinning. 'You handled that well. He obviously liked your determination. Now, to work. You can share my desk. The reports will be handed to you to see if there's anything that might connect with Mrs Bentley, no matter how unlikely.'

It was a couple of hours later when something occurred to Stan. 'Reg, all these reports are from the poorer areas of London. Do you remember those expensive items Mrs Bentley had in her wardrobe?'

Reg sat back thoughtfully. 'You think we ought to look at the West End?'

Something was niggling at the back of Stan's mind. He'd always been known for his uncanny intuition. It was one of the qualities that had made him a good policeman. 'And places like Park Lane.'

'What?' Reg looked astounded, then gazed around the room. In the silence all eyes were fixed on Stan.

The sergeant heard and came to sit on the edge of the desk. 'What makes you think the woman might be in the classy parts of London?'

'Just a feeling, and there's nothing here.' Stan tapped the pile of reports he'd been reading.

The sergeant gazed into space for a while, then stood up. 'Right, let's do it. We need names of any deaths, murders or otherwise, missing persons, and any unusual goings on.'

'That'll take time,' one of the constables pointed out.

'Then the sooner everyone starts, the sooner we'll have the information.'

Stan watched as the men were given their assignments, wishing desperately that he could get out with them, but he'd never be able to keep up. He was being allowed to play a small role in the investigation, though, and he was grateful for that.

Reg wasn't around at lunchtime, so Stan went to the café on his own. It was late afternoon before the men began to return. They all had the same to report. The other stations had agreed to compile the reports, but it could take a couple of days.

'You might as well go home, Stan.' Reg sat down wearily. 'I've walked miles today, but there's nothing more we can do till tomorrow.'

It had been a frustrating day, and Stan was glad to be home. He was just wondering what to get himself to eat when there was a knock on the front door.

At first Stan didn't recognize the fashionable girl standing on his doorstep. She was dressed in a dark blue coat, and a hat in the latest fashion which he had likened to a pudding basin. But it suited her beautifully, and so did the black shoes with a silver buckle on them. 'Dora!'

'I hope you don't mind me calling, Stan? I knew you were here because I saw your bike round the side. Lily and Tom aren't home yet so I thought I'd pop in and see if you had any news.' She began pulling off her gloves nervously.

'There isn't any, I'm afraid, but come in.' Stan stepped aside. 'Don't look so doubtful. I won't shout at you again.'

She walked straight into the kitchen, removed her coat and

draped it over the back of a chair. The dress she was wearing was of a lighter blue, and had a delicate lace collar. Stan couldn't take his eyes off her. She looked lovely – and grown up.

'That's a smart outfit you're wearing.'

'It's Mum's, we're about the same size. I've been looking for a job in a shop and I thought I might stand more chance if I was well dressed.'

'Any luck?'

'Nothing definite. A couple of shops said they'd let me know, but I don't suppose I'll hear from them. There are so many people looking for work.' Dora filled the kettle to make tea.

She looked so dispirited that Stan wanted to reach out, take her in his arms and tell her that everything would be all right in the end. He'd take care of her, and her brother and sister. He recognized the danger at once and slammed his mental door shut, sliding the bolt in place. What he was feeling rocked him. My God, he was attracted to her! He had to get any such thoughts out of his head. Dora Bentley already had more than enough to cope with. And if he allowed his admiration for her to turn into something stronger, then he was in for rejection and pain. And he had enough of that already. No, no, he mustn't go along that route – for all their sakes.

Much to his relief Tom and Lily arrived at that moment, and ran into the kitchen to see him, their expressions eager. They became subdued when he told them there wasn't any news, and Dora said she hadn't been able to find a job.

Lily soon recovered. 'I'm hungry, Dora. Can Stan eat with us tonight?'

'Of course, if he'd like to. Why don't you ask him?'

'Please come and have tea with us tonight.' Lily gazed up at him, pleading.

It was on the tip of his tongue to refuse, but how could he? 'Thank you, I'd like that very much.'

Dora nodded in satisfaction. 'Come round in an hour.' Then she hustled the children out, leaving him to drink the tea on his own.

Stan felt he shouldn't have accepted, but one look at their faces and only a heartless man would have refused. And he was beginning to realize that he did have a heart after all. He thought it had died in the trenches.

Nine

The Barrington house was in chaos, and Dora could understand why the family had already left for Scotland. They
were quite happy to let their staff deal with the moving. Quite
a lot of the furniture was already on its way to Scotland, and
more was going out the door. All thought of separate duties
had been abandoned and Dora was helping with anything. The
turmoil mirrored her own, and she was glad to be kept busy.
This was her last day here, and also her birthday. At breakfast this morning, Lily and Tom had given her cards they had
made themselves, and she'd had a job to speak. It was touching
that they had bothered, considering the frightening situation
they were in. The fact that it was her eighteenth birthday had
only heightened the feeling of desolation and worry for the
future that was taking a firm grip on her. The police didn't
seem to be getting anywhere, and fear of what might have
happened to their mother was tearing her apart.

Cook caught Dora's arm as she hurried past. 'Stop, my girl.
Take a break. You look done in.'

A cup was put in her hand and she drank the tea gratefully.
'Thanks, Cook.'

'Sad day for you. But don't you look so worried. You're a
good girl and a hard worker. You'll soon find another position.'

'I hope so.' Dora finished the drink, put the cup in the sink
and forced a smile. 'I'm going to miss you all. And I'll miss
your plum duff.'

Cook was clearly pleased with the compliment. 'Go on with
you. I bet your mum's is just as good.'

Dora shook her head. She hadn't said anything about the
disappearance. 'No one cooks like you. Just wait till you get
to Scotland. I bet you'll be able to teach them a thing or two
about good food.'

'Humph!' Cook scowled. 'I don't want to leave London, but I'm too old to start with another household.'

'I expect you'll soon get used to it, and they say the scenery is beautiful.' All Dora heard as she hurried back to work was another 'Humph!'

At the end of an exhausting day it was hard saying goodbye, but in a way she was glad when it was all over and she was on her way home. The mistress had been kind and added another two and sixpence to her wages in recognition of her hard work over the last two years. Dora had got the job a month after they'd moved to the house in Kilburn. The work had been hard and the hours long, even working on a Sunday when the mistress had visitors staying, which was often. Then she had been elevated from housemaid to serving upstairs. It hadn't left much time for herself, but Dora had been content; hard work had never worried her.

Now all the security in their lives had gone with the disappearance of their mother and the loss of her job. She was so tired, struggling all the time to stay in control, but it was a week now, and each day became harder. If it hadn't been for Lily and Tom, she was sure she would have crumbled under the strain.

What a terrible birthday, she thought, as she walked in the house.

Lily rushed up to her. 'You're late! Hurry up and put on a pretty dress.'

'What for?' she asked.

'We're going out.'

'Oh, sweetie, I'm too tired. I don't think—'

'Don't argue, Dora,' Tom told her firmly. 'Once you're washed and changed, you'll feel better.'

'Dora, you must come, mustn't she, Tom?'

Lily was beginning to look worried, so Dora knew she would have to go along with their plans. Whatever they were . . .

In thirty minutes she was ready and wearing her Sunday best dress. It was dark red and suited her colouring perfectly.

'Wear Mum's necklace,' Lily urged. 'She'd like that.'

'I'll get it.' Before Dora could object, Tom had raced up the stairs. After much thumping about, he returned with the necklace dangling from his fingers.

Dora had to admit it did look nice with the dress, and well, it was her eighteenth birthday, so why not wear it?

Lily clapped her hands. 'That's pretty. Come on, let's go. We mustn't be late!'

They hustled her out of the house, but instead of heading for the bus stop as Dora had expected, they turned the other way.

'Where are we going?'

Lily giggled as Tom held open Stan's gate. 'We're there!'

The front door was already open, and when they walked into the front room, she stopped in amazement. Winnie, Reg, June and Stan were there. On the table by the window was an iced cake with a single candle already alight. There were also sandwiches and other tempting-looking things to eat. Overwhelmed by such kindness, it was hard to keep her emotions in check, but it would only upset everyone if she broke down.

'Here's the birthday girl!' Winnie handed her a parcel. 'Open that first, and then you must blow out the candle.'

Dora's hand shook as she looked at the gift in her hands, and she was so relieved they hadn't wished her a *happy* birthday. But she was beginning to see that these people were not that insensitive.

'Open your present,' Lily said, excitement in her voice. 'See what you've got.'

'Oh yes, of course.' Dora forced herself into action, managing a smile. 'This is such a surprise.'

The parcel contained a brightly coloured scarf from Winnie and Reg, a pair of leather gloves from Stan, and a pretty handkerchief from June.

She had to clear her throat before she could speak, and then the words only came out in a whisper. 'They're all beautiful. I don't know what to say. Thank you seems so inadequate.'

'Thank you will do.' Stan stepped forward and smiled in encouragement. 'Now you must blow out your candle and cut the cake.'

'You've got to make a wish,' June told her. 'But you mustn't tell us what it is.'

Dora smiled at the little girl, so like her Lily. 'Do you think it would be all right if I made two wishes?'

''Spect it will be.' June glanced at her mother. 'Will it be?'

'Of course it will. You make as many wishes as you like.'

Taking a deep breath, Dora blew out the candle, then closed her eyes and wished silently. *Wherever you are, Mum, I want you to be safe and come home to us soon. And make the doctors be able to do something for Stan, so he can live without so much pain.*

Opening her eyes again, she picked up the knife and cut the cake.

They all cheered, and then settled down to enjoy the food Winnie had so generously provided.

While they were eating and talking, Winnie was staring at Dora in a curious way. 'That's a lovely necklace.'

'It's Mum's, but Lily insisted I wear it tonight. It's only a piece of cheap jewellery, but she thinks it's pretty.'

'She's right, and it suits you.' Winnie smiled then. 'I'd better make another pot of tea.'

No one tried to pretend that this was a time for a lively party, but Dora was grateful for the kindness of Stan's family. The subject of their mum's disappearance was not mentioned, and for a short time they could try to pretend that their life was normal. Lily and Tom hadn't looked this relaxed since their mum had failed to come home. As she gazed round the room, it felt as if they had found another family. It was at that moment it struck her how isolated their lives had been. As far as she knew, they had no other relatives, and their mother had not been one to make friends. They had lived in this street for two years and yet they didn't know anyone. All they had ever done was smile and nod at neighbours. Why had she never thought that was strange before?

Dora glanced at Lily and saw her yawn. The time was eight thirty by the clock on the mantelpiece. They'd been here for over two hours. 'My goodness!' she exclaimed, standing up. 'Where has the time gone? It's your bedtime, Lily.'

After saying thank you, they left, with Lily carrying the remains of the cake.

Winnie sat beside her brother and spoke quietly. 'Stan, that poor girl is close to breaking. She's making a valiant effort to hide it, but the signs are there, and it won't take much to tip her over the edge. Keep an eye on her and call me if she needs help.'

'I'll do that, Win, but I believe she'll cope with this disaster because she needs to for the sake of her brother and sister.'

'I hope you're right.' Winnie looked doubtful, but changed the subject. 'That necklace Dora was wearing didn't look like cheap jewellery to me.'

'I agree.' Stan told his sister about his visit to the jeweller's. 'They only had my rough drawing to go by, and although they thought it looked like one of their designs, they couldn't say more than that without examining the original. There were bits of jewellery on Mrs Bentley's dressing table but none of it was worth anything. It's unlikely that someone of modest means like Dora's mother would have anything of great value.'

'I suppose so.' Winnie stood up. 'Come on, June, time you were in bed as well. You coming, Reg?'

'No, I'll stay for a while.'

'All right, but don't the two of you spend half the night talking, will you?'

Once they were on their own, Stan produced a bottle of whisky, and they settled down with a glass and a cigarette each.

Reg sipped his drink and gazed into space. 'I don't understand why we haven't found any trace of her. I know people do just disappear and are never heard of again, but this is a mother of three children. They care a great deal about her, so she must have been a good mother. Why haven't we been able to find her, Stan? There isn't a whisper about her anywhere. It's almost as if she didn't exist.'

'The whole damned business is odd.' Stan stubbed out his cigarette in the ashtray balanced on the arm of his chair. 'I think I'll go to that factory in the morning. There must be a reason she told her children she worked there.'

'Hmm.' Reg eyed Stan with suspicion. 'You're not to pretend you're a police officer again. If you do I'll have to arrest you.'

Stan grinned. 'Can I tell them I'm making enquiries for the police?'

'As long as you make it clear you're not in the force.'

Stan picked up his stick and waved it at his brother-in-law. 'Do you think they'd believe me if I did?'

'You got away with it before, and that time you were on crutches.' Reg frowned. 'I never did ask you how you got round that.'

'Told them I tripped over chasing a thief.'

Reg couldn't help laughing. 'You've got a nerve, Stan, but it's good to see you more like your old self.'

'It's good to feel useful again.' Stan hauled himself to his feet. 'I'll get you another drink while you tell me about your plans for tomorrow.'

While the men talked over the case late into the night, Dora was in bed, her face pushed into the pillow to muffle her sobs. This was the first time she had allowed her grief to come to the surface, but today had just been too much.

Ten

During the night Stan had been reading through the notebook again in case there was something he had missed. But no matter how many times he studied it, nothing new struck him. It was just a series of names, repeated at intervals. The only name to appear once was the first entry. There didn't appear to be any rhyme or reason to the notebook, and yet Mrs Bentley had bothered to hide it, so it must be important.

Eager to get going, he was up as soon as the birds began to sing. He was waiting outside the factory gates when they opened, but stayed back until all the workers had gone in. Then he followed them.

''Ere!' The gatekeeper stopped him. 'I ain't seen you before. You don't work here.'

'I've come to see the manager. Tell him I'm here please.'

'Expecting you, is he?'

'No, but this is a police matter. He'll see me. My name's Crawford.'

'Ah, that's different. You'd better come with me.' The man set off at quite a pace, but when he noticed that Stan couldn't keep up with him, he slowed. 'How'd you get that?' he asked, pointing to his leg.

'Some bugger dropped a shell right beside me.'

'Bloody war. My sister lost her eldest. Broke her heart. Good boy he was. What a bloody waste!' The gatekeeper's surly manner had disappeared, and he even smiled at Stan as he held open the door for him. 'Wait here, mate. I'll tell Mr Grant you wants to see him.'

Stan knew there was always the chance that he would be sent on his way when the manager found out it wasn't a police officer wanting information. He had to be careful not to get Reg into trouble, so he was going to have to be honest this time. He'd got away with impersonating a police officer once – twice would be pushing his luck!

The door opened and an elderly man came out. After shaking hands with Stan, he asked, 'How can I help you, Constable?'

'I'm making enquiries about a missing person, sir, by the name of Bentley.'

''Ere.' The gatekeeper was hovering. 'A young girl was asking about her. A week ago it was. You remember, Mr Grant, I told you about it?'

'Ah, yes, and we couldn't help, I believe.'

'That's right, sir.'

Stan shifted to ease the weight on his leg, making the stick take more of his burden.

The manager noticed. 'Come into my office and sit down. Dave, have some tea sent in.'

'Right away, sir.'

Stan took this chance to set the record straight. 'Before we go any further, sir, I must explain that I'm not a police officer. I was before the war, but injury has stopped me joining the force again. However, the local station lets me help out now and again.'

'I understand.' Mr Grant nodded in sympathy. 'Tell me what this is all about.'

Stan explained, keeping it brief.

Mr Grant sat back and frowned. 'It's true we don't have a night shift now, but we used to. We stopped it a couple of months after the end of the war when the demand for buttons eased off. We had to supply the forces during the war.'

The tea had arrived, and Stan took the cup offered to him. 'Then it's possible that Mrs Bentley could have worked here for a while. Do you still have a record of your employees at that time?'

'Of course. Would you like to see it?'

'If I may, sir.'

Mr Grant stood up and removed a large book from the shelf behind his desk, handing it to Stan. 'The employees are listed in alphabetical order.'

First Stan checked the names under B. Finding nothing, he started again at the top in case the name was listed out of order. He gave a sharp intake of breath, his finger resting on one name.

'Have you found her?' Mr Grant asked.

'Not Bentley.' Stan pointed to the name that had caught his

attention. 'Do you know anyone who worked here at the same time as this person?'

'Duval? Our foreman, Jim, worked on nights. Let's go and see if he remembers her.'

The factory was noisy so Mr Grant beckoned Jim over and they moved to a slightly quieter corner. He showed him the name in the book. 'Do you remember her?'

'Not off hand. It was some time ago. Do you know her Christian name?'

'Harriet.' Stan could hardly contain his excitement as he removed the photo from his pocket. 'This is her.'

The foreman studied it for a few moments, then handed it back. 'She looks familiar, but I can't say for certain that the woman in the photo worked here. We employed a large work-force then – all women. Once the war ended most of them packed it in and went back to their families. I honestly can't help you. Sorry.'

Stan knew the photo he had wasn't very clear, but that surname cropping up again was too much of a coincidence to be ignored. He continued pressing the foreman. 'Do you know who might remember her?'

Jim shook his head, looking uncomfortable.

As luck would have it, at that moment Mr Grant moved away to talk to someone else. Stan took the opportunity to probe. Jim obviously had something to say but didn't want to be overheard. 'You sure about that?'

'Well, Mr Grant's son, Roger, was very friendly with some of the women – if you know what I mean.' Jim cast his boss an anxious glance. 'Don't say anything. It was only gossip.'

'I'll keep it to myself. Thanks Jim, you've been a big help.'

'Can I ask why you want to know about her?'

'She's disappeared.'

Their conversation was cut short when Mr Grant returned to them. 'Has Jim been able to help you, Mr Crawford?'

'Yes, sir.' Stan held out his hand. 'Thank you for seeing me, Mr Grant, and allowing me to talk to Jim.'

'Least we could do. I hope you find this woman soon.'

'Let's hope so.' With that Stan left, eager to see Reg.

As soon as he walked into the station, Reg came towards him. 'From the expression on your face, I'd guess you've found out something.'

Stan stopped to get his breath after the rush to get there, ignoring the throbbing in his leg. 'We might be looking for the wrong woman!'

'What?' Reg pushed him on to a chair and perched himself on the edge of the desk. 'Explain that strange remark, Stan.'

'There's a possibility she's using another name.'

There was a stunned silence before Reg spoke. 'Why the hell would she do that? Are you sure?'

'No, not sure, but I think it's worth looking into.' Stan removed the notebook and photo from his pocket. 'The factory did have a night shift during the war. There's a name on the list of employees that's in Mrs Bentley's book. The foreman thought the woman in the photo was familiar but he couldn't be sure it was the same one. But he did hint that if anyone remembered her it would be the son, Roger Grant. He was evidently friendly with the women.'

'Hmm.' Reg folded his arms. 'That's a bit flimsy, Stan. Did you see this Roger Grant?'

'No, I thought I'd better leave that to you. But it's more than we've had up to now. Let's at least check the reports again for the other name. We were only looking for Bentley the first time and could easily have missed it.'

'All right. What is it?'

'Harriet Duval.'

An hour later Stan sat back disappointed. 'Damn it. Nothing!'

'Don't tell the children about this, Stan. It's unlikely, but if the mother was working under a different name, then there's something very wrong here. It might mean she didn't want anyone to know who she was. There could be several reasons for that, and all of them unpleasant.'

Stan ran a hand over his eyes. 'I agree we keep this to ourselves for the time being. Duval could turn out to be a different woman and the name in the notebook might be just a coincidence. But it isn't a common name, and I've got a strong feeling they're one and the same. I hope to God I'm wrong!'

'I agree with you though, it can't be ignored. What was Mrs Bentley like?'

Stan thought for a moment, trying to picture the woman. 'I only saw her walking past the house. She was always smartly dressed, and she had an air about her that made her seem unapproachable.'

'I never met her.' Reg gazed into space thoughtfully. 'I'll tell you one thing, the more I look into this case the less I like it. I'm tempted to stop the investigation and leave it unresolved.'

'Dora would never accept that.' Stan spoke with certainty. 'And neither would I.'

'I know, and I doubt if I could walk away from it now either.' Reg grimaced. 'Those poor little blighters!'

'The one I'm most worried about is Lily. She seems rather emotional and delicate. Tom's a strong lad, even if his temper is a bit suspect, but he'll fight for his sisters. Dora has a determined streak and she'll keep the family together whatever it takes. She's a young woman of eighteen now, and from what I've seen of her so far she's a very capable one.'

'And lovely when she pushes aside her worries enough to smile.' Reg gave Stan a speculative look. 'She's a nice girl too. She'll make some man a good wife one day.'

'I agree with everything you say, but don't look at me. I wouldn't burden any girl with me for a husband. I'm not a fool, Reg. I know my future outlook isn't good.' Stan smiled grimly and changed the subject. 'So, what are we going to do next?'

'Start again, only looking for two women this time. What we badly need is someone who knew Mrs Bentley well.'

'She didn't seem to have any friends. She was always alone when I saw her. And not even her children know that much about her.'

'That's how it seems.' Reg patted Stan's shoulder. 'Nothing more you can do today, so go home. You look worn out.'

Without a word of protest, Stan left the station, regretting he hadn't come on his bike. It would have been easier than getting on and off the bus. How he hated this constant struggle to do even the simplest things in life. But that was how things were, and he had to get on with it.

He had reached his house when Lily came tearing towards him, and he could see immediately that she was distressed again. Tom and Dora were right behind their sister.

'Have you found my mum?' Lily was gazing up at him with pleading eyes.

'Not yet—'

'Why? Why?' Tears began to flow down her cheeks, and she waved clenched hands at him. 'I told Dora and Tom you'd find her for us. But you haven't! You're not trying hard enough!'

'Lily!' Dora caught hold of her sister. 'You mustn't talk to Stan like that. He's out every day with the police, and you know it isn't easy for him. Say you're sorry for being so rude.' When Lily just stood there, Dora stooped down. 'Sweetie, if it wasn't for Stan and his family, we'd be completely on our own, and even more frightened than we are. They're being very kind to us. Now, I want you to say you're sorry.'

Lily wiped her hand across her eyes, and looking down at her feet, touched his hand gently. 'I didn't mean it. I'm sorry. I want my mum to come home.'

Stan felt as if the heart was being ripped out of him. He remembered fear, confusion and the feeling of utter helplessness he had experienced in the trenches, and knew that these youngsters must be feeling something like that now.

Without thinking what he was doing, he swept Lily up in one arm, leaning heavily on the stick to keep his balance. 'Shush now, I understand. We'll never give up trying to find her, no matter how long it takes, Lily.'

'Thank you,' she muttered, her head tucked into his shoulder.

'Now, let's go indoors and have a cup of tea together.'

Lily nodded and allowed Tom to take her from Stan. It was then he realized that Dora was supporting him.

'Give Tom your door key, Stan,' she said firmly.

'Right jacket pocket.' He spoke through clenched teeth.

Dora found the key and gave it to her brother. 'Take Lily inside, Tom, and put the kettle on.'

There were beads of sweat running into Stan's eyes, and he didn't think he would be able to move.

'Take your time. Would you like me to get your crutches for you?'

'No!' Stan spoke more sharply than he meant to, but he didn't like them seeing how weak he was. Pride, he supposed, but that was all he had.

'You shouldn't have picked Lily up. She's too big and heavy.'

'She's also upset – you all are –and I hate to see it.' Stan drew in deep breaths in an effort to override the pain, and began to move forward.

'You need to rest.' Dora placed an arm around him.

At that moment, Tom rushed out of the house and held Stan from the other side. As much as he hated doing it, he had to let them help him inside.

As soon as he was sitting down, Tom handed him a cup of tea. While he drank it, he tried to decide whether to tell them anything about his visit to the factory. Lily was still upset, and staring silently out of the window. He knew that all the Bentley children were desperate for some news, however small. Perhaps he could tell them a little . . .

'I went to the factory today and spoke to the manager.' They were immediately alert, and he could feel three pairs of eyes looking at him hopefully. 'It seems they did have a night shift there, but it finished a few months after the end of the war.'

Dora leant forward in her chair, waiting for him to continue.

'I showed the foreman your mother's photo. He thought she looked familiar, but he couldn't say for sure that she'd worked there.'

Tom turned to Dora. 'But if she had been there, then she didn't lie to us. She could have worked there – for a while, anyway.'

'It's possible,' Dora agreed. 'But why didn't she tell us when she left?'

'Perhaps she didn't want to worry you,' Stan offered.

'Hmm, it was towards the end of the war that Dad was killed, and she was terribly upset, so she could have just forgotten to mention it.' Dora still looked doubtful.

Lily was listening intently to all of this. 'Mum was always telling us that we wasn't to worry.'

Stan felt it was time to change the subject before he revealed more than he wanted to. 'Have you had any luck finding a job, Dora?'

'No, but I'll try again on Monday.' She went to the table by the window to collect the teapot, and saw the rent man coming down the street. 'We'll have to go now, Stan. Thank you for telling us about the factory. Will you be all right now?'

'I'm fine, and Winnie will be here soon.'

'You take care now and rest.'

Stan watched them leave and then laid his head back, closing his eyes. He'd taken to these youngsters from the moment they had come to him, and prayed for a happy outcome for this, but that hope faded with each day that passed.

Eleven

'Come and sit down. We have to talk.' After another fretful night, Dora had come to a decision. They couldn't go on like this. Tom and Lily looked just as weary when they settled down to see what she had to say.

Dora didn't waste any time. This was going to upset them, but it had to be faced, and the sooner the better for all their sakes. 'It's just over a week now and there's no sign of Mum, so we've got to start thinking about ourselves. We don't know what's happened to her, and we must accept the fact that we might never know.'

Lily made a sound like a stifled sob, and Dora grasped her hand. 'We need you to be brave, sweetie.'

When Lily nodded, Dora continued. 'We've also got to admit that we didn't know her as well as we thought. She had secrets, and I think Stan knows more than he's telling. It looks to me as if he's trying to protect us from something.'

'I thought that, too,' Tom admitted. 'He's a good man, but I'd rather know the truth than go on like this.'

'We all would. And until the truth comes out we've got to get on with our lives.' Dora hesitated. 'We've got to assume that Mum isn't coming back.'

'Never?' Lily whispered.

'Yes, sweetie.' Dora didn't know how she was managing to sound so calm. 'If she could, or wanted to, she would have come home by now. She's either left us . . . or she's dead. Whatever's happened, we've got to look out for ourselves.'

'Dora's right, Lily.' Quiet tears were rolling down the little girl's face and Tom handed her his handkerchief. 'Stop crying, and let's see what Dora thinks we ought to do.'

Lily obediently mopped her face and blew her nose, then gave her brother back his handkerchief. 'I'll be brave.'

'We know you will.' Tom ruffled her hair. 'We'll be all right. We've got Dora, and she has all the brains in this family.'

Dora felt herself sag slightly. The burden had just been placed firmly on her shoulders. That was only to be expected because she was the eldest, and she was determined not to let her brother and sister down. 'Is it agreed that we don't want to move from here?'

She received vigorous nods. 'Right. I must concentrate on finding a job, but it might take a while. I've worked out that we have enough money to last another two weeks if we're careful, but when that's gone there are things we can pawn. Once I'm working again we might be able to redeem them.'

'That won't matter,' Tom said. 'There are plenty of things we can do without. Mum's bits and pieces can go first.'

'Agreed, but let's hope it doesn't come to that. Now, the other thing worrying me is Stan. We're putting a great strain on him. I suggest we stop pestering him and allow the police to get on with their work.'

'I didn't mean to shout at him.' Lily was looking upset again.

'We know that.' Tom patted his sister's hand. 'And Stan understood, so don't you fret about it. But Dora's right, we've got to leave him in peace. He isn't strong enough, and he's wearing himself out by running around for us.'

'I won't do it again, but can we see him sometimes? I like him.' Lily was clearly worried about this.

'Yes, we'll see him about once a week and ask if there's any progress in the investigation.' When Lily accepted, Dora started to relax. She had been dreading having this conversation, but keeping her family together was all that mattered to her now, and she would do whatever was necessary.

She sat back as the tight knot inside her eased. 'If either of you have any worries, or ideas how we can manage better, I want you to say so. We'll sit down every evening and talk things through.'

'Good idea.' Tom smiled easily for the first time in days.

When Lily did the same, Dora knew she had been right to make them face the loss of their mother. 'It's a nice day, so I suggest we go out somewhere. We'll take sandwiches and make a day of it, shall we? Where would you like to go?'

'To the park with the lake in it.' Lily grabbed hold of Tom's arm. 'Have you still got that boat? We could sail it.'

'It'll probably sink.'

Lily giggled. 'Then you'll have to go in the water and get it.'

Dora never ceased to marvel at the rapid changes in her sister's mood. One minute she could be crying and the next, laughing. Lily had a much more emotional nature than either herself or Tom. 'Is Regent's Park all right with you, Tom?' she asked.

'Perfect on a day like this.' He turned his attention back to Lily. 'Come and help get the sandwiches ready. What do you want in them? Or is that a silly question?'

'Jam!'

Tom sighed. 'It was a silly question. Better take a wet flannel with us, Dora. Or we could always dip her in the lake to get rid of the sticky mess.'

With a shriek, Lily attacked her brother, laughing as he fended her off.

'Stop fighting, you two,' Dora ordered, trying to keep her expression stern. This day out had been a good idea. It was already taking their minds off the distress they were suffering. It was only a temporary relief, but welcome nonetheless.

An hour later they set off with a variety of sandwiches, and the wooden sailing boat rescued from the cupboard under the stairs. There wasn't a cloud in the sky, and they were looking forward to a day in the park.

There were quite a few people about, but they found a spot by a tree where they could watch everything going on around the lake. The warmest day in May so far had brought families out with children and grandparents. There were also a few young men who had been disabled during the war. It always tore Dora apart when she saw them.

One young man came and sat quite near them. He had lost a leg and a hand, and he was on his own. Dora smiled at him. 'Lovely day, isn't it?'

He seemed startled that she should speak to him, but he smiled back and nodded.

'I'm hungry, Dora!' Lily yelled as she raced back from the lake where she had been playing with Tom.

'So am I.' Tom was right behind his sister.

Dora opened the bag with the food in it, and gasped. 'My goodness! You've made enough for dozens. Lily, go and ask that young man if he'd like to help us eat this lot.'

Without protest, Lily went and sat on the grass next to him. Dora said softly, 'Go and give him a hand if he needs it, Tom, but be careful. You know how independent some of them can be.'

'Like Stan. He hates feeling so helpless, doesn't he?' Without waiting for an answer, Tom joined Lily, who was chattering away to the man.

It looked as if he was trying to refuse, but Lily and Tom were having none of it. In the end he pulled himself up and came over to where Dora was setting out the picnic.

'This is very kind of you. My name's Alan,' he said, introducing himself politely.

Tom took over. 'This is our sister, Dora, the chatterbox is Lily, and I'm Tom. Sit down, Alan, and let's see if we can work our way through these sandwiches.'

Tom was growing up fast, and becoming a real gentleman, Dora noticed. There was a confidence about him as well. But they all needed to be like him if they were going to survive this crisis.

Alan rested his crutches against the tree and sat down. He carried out the tricky moves very well, and they hadn't felt the need to interfere.

'I'm having jam,' Lily announced, 'but there's other things like cheese, cold meat or tomatoes. What you going to have?'

Alan frowned in concentration. 'Oh, such a choice, but I think I'll have cheese, please.'

Lily handed him the cheese packet so he could take one. 'Our neighbour, Stan, walks with crutches, or a stick sometimes. He was hurt bad in the war, too.'

'Lily!' Dora stopped her sister. She knew that most of the ex-servicemen didn't like talking about the war.

'It's all right,' Alan told Dora. 'It's refreshing to find someone who doesn't shy away from the subject. Do you know, some people I've known for years actually cross the road so they won't have to speak to me.'

'That's disgraceful!' Tom exclaimed. 'They ought to be ashamed of themselves!'

'I can understand it. Many just don't know what to say when they see me like this.'

'Well, I don't understand it!' Dora said indignantly. 'You're still the same person you were before the war. Stan's in almost constant pain, but that doesn't change the man he is inside. And your injuries don't change the man you were born to be.' She stopped talking, looking embarrassed. 'Oh, I'm sorry. There I go again. I'm not making sense, am I? I know what I mean, but it's hard to put it into words.'

'You're making perfect sense. I wish more people could see it that way.' His smile was grim. 'But I must correct you on one point. Those of us who've survived the horror of the trenches will never be quite the same.'

'No, some of you will be stronger, others will always be damaged.' Dora gave a hesitant smile. 'Please forgive me, Alan. I get so mad about how little's being done to help those in great need.'

Tom grinned. 'If Dora could she would have put all the politicians and generals in the trenches and made them wade around in waist-deep mud while the enemy fired at them.'

'That did cross my mind from time to time.' Alan turned his attention back to Dora and studied her intently, respect showing in his grey eyes. 'I think you're a remarkable young woman.'

'There's nothing remarkable about me,' she laughed. 'I've always been told I think too much, especially for a female, always wanting to know the reason for everything.'

'That's good, don't change. What do you do with yourself, Dora?'

'Do?' She was puzzled for a moment. 'Oh, I work, of course. Only I haven't got a job at the moment. I have to find something.'

'What kind of work?'

'I was a daily housemaid.'

Alan grimaced in disbelief. 'What a waste! You're obviously intelligent. Surely you could get something better.'

'Work's hard to come by. I'll take anything I can get.'

He fished in his pocket, brought out a small notepad with a pencil tied to it with string. He opened the pad with his mouth, rested it on his knee and began to write laboriously.

Noting his struggle, Dora said softly, 'You were right handed.'

'Yes, but I'm getting used to using my left hand for most things. Writing's still awkward, though.' He looked up. 'But I'm one of the lucky ones. I've only lost my right leg from below the knee. I'll soon have a false one, thanks to a fine doctor I know. He reckons I'll be able to walk well once I get used to it, and they're giving me a hand as well, so I should look almost normal. From a distance, anyway.'

'That is good news.' Dora was so pleased for him.

Alan finished writing and held the pad towards her. 'Tear out that page. It's the address of a centre for ex-servicemen who've lost limbs. A Doctor Burridge has set it up, and they're always desperate for help. Go and see them, Dora.'

'Thanks.' Dora put the note in her purse. 'Can I say you sent me?'

'Of course. My name's Alan Harrington.'

Tom and Lily had been quietly eating, more interested in what was going on around the lake than the conversation Dora had been having with Alan. Now she was full, Lily was eager to get back to the water.

'Let's sail the boat again, Tom. You come too, Dora, it's good fun.'

'You go, I'll just clear up this mess and be with you in a minute.'

Alan stood up and settled on his crutches again. 'I have to go now, but thank you for the sandwiches. It has been interesting talking to you.'

'Thank you for joining us,' Tom said politely.

'Yes, we've enjoyed your company.' Dora meant it. Alan seemed a nice young man.

'Bye bye,' Lily waved, and began to drag her brother towards the lake.

'I hope everything works out well for you.'

'Thank you, Dora.'

She watched him make his way across the park, and could picture him without the crutches, walking normally. She hoped she would see him again . . .

'Dora!'

'I'm coming, Lily.'

Twelve

They had worked out a routine. Tom took Lily to school and collected her afterwards, but now Dora wasn't working she took over the shopping, relieving Tom of that chore. She knew he disliked shopping for food, although he never complained. It worried her that he was no longer playing with friends after school, but since their mother's disappearance he had let that activity drop. The three Bentley children had drawn close in this terrible crisis, protecting each other. When she had mentioned this to her brother last night, he had just waved away her concerns for him, saying that they would sort themselves out when this was all over.

Dora's thoughts turned to their day in the park. Their mother had always insisted upon good manners, and that teaching had been very evident in the way her brother and sister had dealt with Alan. Even Lily, young as she was, couldn't have been faulted on her conduct.

After clearing away the breakfast things, Dora chose clothes from her mother's wardrobe. She'd never bothered about what she wore as long as she was clean and tidy, but things were different now. She was eighteen, and had begun noticing couples together with their children. Not that there was much chance of her marrying. Women far outnumbered the men after the slaughter of the war. Like many young girls she was probably destined to remain a spinster. Still, Lily was only six, and would need her for some years. Tom at twelve would soon be a young man, and it wouldn't be long before her brother was being pursued by hordes of girls.

The outfit she chose was perfect, smart without being showy. She hadn't realized that her mother had such nice things, and all matching. It was important to be well dressed, because she was off to Wandsworth today in the hope of getting a job at the address Alan had given her.

With a final adjustment to the hat, Dora set off for the train station. If they didn't need anyone at this place, then she would spend the day searching for a job. She didn't want to go home tonight without some good news. It was now up to her to take over the role of mother to Tom and Lily.

The house was easy to find. It backed on to Wandsworth Common, and was very large. Dora stood by the gate and took in the scene. It had once been a grand house, but now it was sorely neglected. A coat of paint would do wonders, though. The garden was also overgrown, but that could be put right with a bit of effort.

The front door was open when she reached it, and when she knocked a sliver of dark red paint fell off. Her hopes of finding a job here disappeared. It didn't look as if they had enough money to employ staff. The building was falling down around them. Dora couldn't think why Alan had urged her to come.

Ah well, she was here now and might as well talk to someone. She tapped more cautiously this time. 'Anyone there?' she called, stepping just inside the door.

A head appeared from a door on her left, sporting a mop of unruly grey hair. 'You'll have to knock louder than that, ducky. I'm a bit Mutt and Jeff – deaf,' he translated in case she hadn't understood.

'I didn't like to,' she told him. 'I was afraid the door would fall apart.'

He tipped his head back and roared. 'Come in, come in.'

The room he ushered her into was absolute chaos. There were heaps of newspapers, books, boxes of clothes, and the table was littered with letters.

'Sit down.'

Dora glanced round. Every chair was piled high with something or other. 'Where?' she asked.

'What? Don't whisper.'

She raised her voice. 'Where shall I sit?'

'No need to shout, I ain't that deaf.' He looked quite offended as he swept one chair clear, letting everything fall on the floor. 'There.'

'Thank you.' She sat carefully. The chair didn't look too safe. 'Are you in charge?'

When he didn't answer she raised the volume a little. 'Are you in charge?'

'Me? Good Lord, no! I couldn't organize a . . . party in a brewery.'

From the look of the place, Dora would certainly agree with that! The room looked like a junk shop.

'The doc's the one in charge. Doctor Burridge, that is. Don't know if he's here, though. You want to see him?'

'If possible.' Dora was now positive she'd had a wasted journey.

'Come on then, ducky. Let's see if we can track him down.'

The chair gave an alarming crack when she stood up, but it stayed in one piece, much to her surprise. She almost had to run to keep up with him. He might be elderly, but he could certainly move at a pace, she thought, as she took two steps to his one.

He was darting a quick glance in each door along the corridor. Finally, he grunted in satisfaction. 'Ah, you're in luck. You'll have to wait until he's finished with one of the lads. He don't like being disturbed when he's working.'

'I understand.' Dora followed the man into the room, and they both stood just inside the door.

The doctor was middle-aged, Dora guessed, but it was hard to tell as the dark circles under his eyes and lines of fatigue probably made him look older than he was. It was a gentle face, though, she thought, as she watched him haul a young man upright.

'Bloody hell!' the man exclaimed. 'I'm never going to be able to walk with this!'

'You won't know until you try.' The doctor patted his shoulder, then helped him to stand, put a walking stick in his hand and stepped back. 'Have a go.'

Dora watched, hardly breathing. The concentration on the young man's face was intense, but he didn't move. She had her hands clasped tightly together, and everything inside her silently urged him to take that first step. When she saw his shoulders drop in defeat, she took an involuntary step forward.

'I can't do it! I can't!'

That was too much for Dora. Before she realized what she was doing, she was standing in front of the young man. 'My mother always told me that there's no such word in the English language.'

'What?' The patient scowled at her. 'What are you talking about?'

'There's no such word as *can't.*' Dora knew the doctor was watching her, wondering who she was, but she didn't care. This young man couldn't give up! 'If you don't persevere you'll be on crutches or in a wheelchair for the rest of your life. Is that what you want?'

He shook his head, near to tears, but he was standing straight again.

Dora took hold of his arm and smiled up at him, speaking gently this time. 'It isn't going to be easy, but given time I'm sure you'll master this.'

'Think so?'

'I *know* so! What's your name?'

'John.'

'Nice to meet you, John, I'm Dora. I'll hold you while you have another try, shall I?' She glanced at the doctor who was standing with his arms folded. He hadn't said a word, but she didn't doubt he would have a few to say when they were on their own. She didn't know what had come over her, but she hadn't been able to stand by. 'What does John have to do, doctor?'

'Lean on Dora, John, and try to throw the leg forward.'

After a lot of panting, John suddenly stepped forward.

'That's the idea, now one more,' the doctor urged.

In fact John managed two more steps.

'Well done!' The doctor placed a wheelchair behind John and made him sit down. 'That's enough for today. We'll try again tomorrow, but if you keep that up you'll soon be walking on your own.'

The young man took hold of Dora's hand, gratitude in his eyes. 'Thanks. Who's this beautiful girl, doc? She certainly brightens the place up.'

'I've no idea, John, but if you can look after yourself for a while, I'll find out.'

'I'm all right now.' John never took his eyes off Dora. 'Are you going to be around here much?'

'I was hoping to be.' She glanced at the doctor, but his expression was unreadable. 'I think I might just have ruined my chances, though.'

'Come with me.' The doctor glanced round at her when they reached the door. 'Miss . . . ?'

'Bentley.'

There was no sign of the man who had let her in when they walked along the corridor and into a small tidy room. The doctor indicated that she should sit.

'I'm not going to apologize,' she blurted out the moment he was also seated.

'Apologize for what?'

'For interfer—' Dora stopped suddenly when she looked into his eyes. He was laughing at her! 'Ah, I thought you'd be mad at me.'

'I'm always pushing these boys to try harder. I get sworn at quite regularly. But to have a stranger, and a pretty one at that, march up and tell him that he can walk, was just what John needed. For that I thank you. Now, will you tell me why you're here?'

'I met Alan Harrington in Regent's Park yesterday, and when I told him I was looking for work he gave me this address.'

'I know Alan well, and we can do with all the help we can get.'

'I can see that, sir, but I think Alan misunderstood. I need to earn a wage because I have a younger brother and sister to support. It's obvious that you need voluntary workers.' Dora shook her head and began to stand up. 'I'm so sorry. I would have liked to help here.'

'Sit down, please.'

She did as he asked, and sighed with disappointment. To be doing something so worthwhile, something she felt strongly about, would make her very happy. 'Would you tell me about the work you're doing here?'

'I set up this place in an effort to get some of the young men back on their feet, even if those feet are artificial. We rely on charity donations to help run this house, and I'm continually making friends and colleagues empty their pockets for me. And I don't apologize for that.' He looked up and the smile he gave Dora transformed him, wiping away the fatigue. 'I grew tired of seeing how little was being done for these men and decided to do something about it myself. This neglected house belongs to me, so I thought it was time to put it to good use. It's a place for the men to meet others who have also been injured, and I'm here as often as I can to give help and encouragement. Sometimes all they need is someone to talk to. They've come to regard this house as somewhere they can meet, relax and feel comfortable. I can only help a small number, but every man I see take a couple of faltering steps is worth all the hard work.'

Dora caught his enthusiasm, admiring his dedication. She leant forward eagerly. 'I could come in now and again, and perhaps bring my brother and sister with me.'

'That is kind of you, but wouldn't they find it distressing here?'

'No.' Dora dismissed the suggestion. 'Our neighbour was badly injured and has great difficulty walking, using crutches or a stick. He wouldn't let the doctors do what they wanted and he's still in a lot of pain. Tom and Lily are very fond of him, and when they met Alan, they treated him just like anyone else.'

'That's good.' He sat back and frowned. 'What's your neighbour's name?'

'Stan Crawford.'

'Ah, I met him on a train the other day. He seemed a fine young man, but he needs help. I asked him to come and see me at the hospital, but he hasn't turned up yet.'

'He never told us that. I'll let his sister know, and she'll try and persuade him to see you.'

'He'll probably ignore her.'

Dora's mouth turned up at the corners. 'No doubt.'

'Ah, I summed him up correctly then? He's a strong character.'

'And stubborn.'

'I'm glad to hear it. That means he'll keep on fighting. Now, if you work here four days a week I'll pay you four and sixpence. I know you can't live on that, but can I ask you to do it until you find a permanent job?'

'Yes!' Dora could hardly believe this, and accepted eagerly. It was better than nothing and would help. 'What days would you like me to come?'

'You can choose those yourself. Just let me know when we can expect you. When I'm here you can help me with the paperwork, the rest of the time I want you to talk to the boys and encourage them like you did with John. None of them stay here, they come in daily.' He sighed. 'I wish we could help more, but we haven't got the staff, and there are only twenty-four hours in the day.'

'I'm sure you squeeze in an extra one here and there.'

He gave a wry smile. 'I do try.'

Dora stood up. 'Thank you, sir, I'll be here tomorrow. Oh, and have you got any paint?'

Dr Burridge looked puzzled. 'What for?'

'I want to paint the front door. It's a disgrace.'

'Is it? I hadn't noticed.' He couldn't keep a straight face as he lied. 'What colour would you like?'

'Bright blue, please.'

He chuckled. 'That should get us noticed.'

'It's about time everyone knew what you're doing here. A sign on the gate wouldn't hurt, either. And we could put a donation box by the door.'

The doctor was openly laughing now. 'I must thank Alan for sending you here. I'll see you tomorrow, Dora.'

On the train home Dora's thoughts drifted back to her time with Dr Burridge, hardly being able to believe the way she had behaved. Only a short time ago she would never have dared to be so forward, always preferring to stay in the background. The change in her must have happened when their mother disappeared and she'd had to take responsibility for her brother and sister. She'd had to grow up quickly and become more self-assured.

She gazed out of the train window, and realized with satisfaction that she quite liked the new Dora Bentley.

Thirteen

'You didn't go to the station today.' Winnie was worried when she saw her brother staring moodily out of the front window.

'I'm only in the way, Win.'

'No you're not! Reg said you're a big help and they're always pleased to see you. What's the matter, Stan?' she asked gently. 'This isn't like you.'

He hunched his shoulders, still not looking at Winnie. 'I'm a bit down in the dumps today. It all seems so hopeless. It's as if that woman never existed.'

Winnie felt her insides churn. She had never heard him say that things were hopeless, and she had a strong feeling that he wasn't only referring to Mrs Bentley. Something was wrong, but she knew it would be impossible to get it out of him. If only he would talk to her and not keep everything bottled up inside.

'Have you seen Dora and the children?' she asked, in an effort to get him away from whatever gloomy thoughts were in his mind.

Stan sighed. 'Not for a couple of days. They all went out yesterday. Probably to a park, because Lily was carrying a little sailing boat.'

The tone of her brother's voice shook Winnie. He had wanted to go with them! At that moment she knew that although nothing on this earth would make him admit it, her dear brother was lonely. The future in front of him must appear bleak. Then another thought sneaked its way into her mind. Was he falling in love with Dora? She hoped not, because he'd said that he would never inflict himself on any woman. He had always been a very independent man, and he had a horror of being a burden to anyone. She knew that was why he insisted on living here on his own, so that no one could witness his daily struggle.

Thankful that he was still facing away from her, Winnie quickly wiped away a tear as it trickled down her face. He must never see her crying over him. He wouldn't tolerate pity from anyone.

She felt she had to keep talking. 'I expect Dora's out looking for work. I hope she finds something.'

'She will.'

Two simple words that showed his admiration for Dora. It was time to change the subject. 'Would you like a cup of tea, Stan? I've made you your favourite fruit cake.'

He turned then, his good-looking face etched with pain. 'Thanks, Win, that would go down a treat.'

Back home again, Winnie wandered aimlessly around the house, worried sick about her brother. It was a couple of hours before she had to collect June from school, and she couldn't settle to anything. It broke her heart to see him suffering so, and it frightened her to imagine what would happen if he decided that he'd had enough. He wouldn't be the first ex-serviceman to feel it was all too much.

'No!' she shouted to the empty house. He was a brave man and would face anything he had to. But please God, don't let him sink into apathy and despair. He had a right to a happy life!

At that moment there was a knock on the front door, and Winnie composed herself before seeing who was there.

'Dora, come in. I was just about to make a pot of tea.'

She followed Winnie to the kitchen and sat at the table.

The tea was soon made, and Winnie asked, 'What can I do for you?'

'Has Stan mentioned a Doctor Burridge to you?'

'No.'

It didn't take Dora long to tell Winnie about her visit to the Wandsworth house, her expression animated. 'This man's doing everything he can to help those injured in the war, and I got the impression he would really like to see Stan.'

Winnie felt the tears gathering again. 'If only he would go, but I know my brother, Dora, and he won't even consider it. The only glimmer of hope is the promise I forced him to make. I made him write down that he'll see a doctor when your mother's been found, but he only said that to stop me fussing.'

'That isn't much help, because I don't think she's ever going to be found.' Dora stifled a sigh, noting how distressed Winnie seemed. She would swear she had been crying. 'Is there something else worrying you?'

'I've just come back from Stan's. He's really down in the dumps, and I've never seen him this bad.' Winnie wiped moisture from her eyes. 'He said he hasn't seen you or the children for a couple of days. Would you call in on your way home, please?'

'Of course. But we haven't been to see him because we decided we were putting too much strain on him. He has enough problems without shouldering ours as well.'

'No, no, you mustn't think like that,' Winnie told her emphatically. 'He loves seeing you all, and he'll be anxious to know if you've managed to find a job. Knowing you have will cheer him up.'

'It's only four days a week and the pay isn't much, but it is something I'd really like to do.'

Winnie poured them both another cup of tea. 'You care about other people, don't you, Dora? You should have trained to be a nurse, not gone into service.'

'I wanted to.' Dora shrugged. 'But Mum didn't like the idea. I don't know why.'

'That's a shame. It isn't too late to do it now.'

'Yes it is. I've got Tom and Lily to look after and they come first. We're on our own now, and it's up to me to keep us together.'

'You really do believe your mother isn't coming back, don't you?'

Dora nodded.

The determination in Dora's eyes was clear, and Winnie's respect for this charming girl grew. 'You're not completely on your own. We're here for you if you need help.'

'That's kind of you, but we've got to make our own way in life. I don't know why Mum's disappeared, but obviously something's very wrong, and I'm beginning to believe it might be better if we never know what's happened. It's clear she kept things from us. She may have felt she had good reasons for doing so, but I'm beginning to feel we never really knew her.' Dora's expression was grim as she stood up. 'I'd better visit Stan and see if I can shake him out of his gloom.'

'You'll easily be able to do that.' Winnie kissed Dora on the cheek. 'Thank you, my dear.'

It was only five minutes' walk to Stan's, and Dora couldn't get there fast enough. Winnie was very worried about her brother, and after listening to her, so was Dora. She would tell him about her job, and the amusing things, like the paint falling off the door when she knocked and the man who was hard of hearing. Perhaps she'd be able to make him smile.

The front door was open, but she knocked first.

'Come in, Dora,' he called. 'Leave the door open.'

He was standing when she walked into the front room. 'I've come to report progress.'

His expression lightened. 'You've found a job?'

'It's only four days a week, but it should be interesting.'

'That's good news.' Stan smiled then. 'I'm not surprised you found something so soon. You look very smart.'

'Thank you.' She removed her hat, looking at it uncertainly before putting it on a chair. 'These are Mum's clothes. I suppose I shouldn't be wearing them, but I need to make a good impression when I'm applying for work. They fit me, and Tom said I should make use of them. We can't afford to spend money on clothes at the moment.'

'You don't have to make excuses to me, Dora,' Stan said gently. 'You're doing the right thing. Now, sit down and tell me about your job.'

She explained about her visit to the house, and the state it was in, making him laugh. She didn't mention the doctor, or what they did there. She didn't want to say anything to make him depressed again. She could only imagine what kind of horrific time he must have faced after being injured. It was very clear that he didn't want to go anywhere near a doctor again.

However, she knew she wasn't going to get away with that for long when the questions came.

'What are you going to do there?'

'I'm not too sure yet, but they need help with the paper-work, and anything else that needs doing.' She grinned. 'My first task will be to paint the front door. It's a disgrace.'

Stan looked disapproving. 'They've asked you to do that?'

'No, I volunteered. The place needs someone to care for it. The do— the man in charge is too busy.'

'I see. What exactly do they do there?'

Dora knew she couldn't avoid it any longer. 'It's a centre for injured ex-servicemen. The doctor's trying to get them used to artificial limbs so they can walk again.'

There was silence, and Dora was sure she saw Stan flinch. 'He's a very caring man, Stan.' She sat forward. 'It's appalling the way the servicemen have been abandoned since returning home. The doctor's angry with that, and he's trying to help as many as he can. They need encouragement, and to feel someone cares. If I didn't need to earn money I would work for him for nothing.'

'I know you would.' Stan nodded. 'How did you find out about it?'

'We met a man in Regent's Park yesterday and we shared our picnic with him. He was injured in the war, and he was on his own.'

'What was his name?'

'Alan Harrington.'

Stan gripped the arms of his chair, leant forward and demanded, 'What did he look like?'

'Nearly as tall as you, grey eyes, light brown hair, well educated—'

Stan surged to his feet with surprising speed, and Dora rushed to support him as he swayed alarmingly. 'Whatever is the matter?'

'You've just described Captain Alan Harrington. But he's dead! I dragged him back to the trenches. He was dead, I was sure.'

'Sit down.' Dora urged him back in the chair. 'It must be a different man. This Alan had lost part of his right leg, and his right hand.'

'Oh God!' Stan rested his head back and closed his eyes, breathing deeply.

Clasping his hand and holding on tightly, Dora knelt at the side of the chair and waited. She guessed he was reliving the horror of the war and needed time to recover.

After a couple of minutes he let out a ragged sigh, opening his eyes again. 'I suppose it's possible. I was injured soon after, and I was sure he was dead, so I didn't make any enquiries about him. I want to see if it's the same man. Is he at the house, Dora?'

'I didn't see him this morning.' Dora stayed where she was, gazing at him in concern. 'The men don't stay there, they come in each day. They treat it as a kind of a club, I suppose. I'm going tomorrow, so I'll ask about him.'

'Please.'

Dora gazed up at Stan. 'Why don't you come with me?'

Releasing his hand from hers, he gently ran his fingers down the side of her face. 'Crafty move, Dora, but you know the answer to that!'

She smiled engagingly, relieved to see him back to normal again. 'It was worth a try. Will you tell me what happened to you and Alan? Assuming it's the same man, of course.'

He merely shook his head and changed the subject. 'You haven't asked me if there's any news about your mother.'

Dora stood up. 'There won't be. She's gone!'

'You think she's run away and left you?' Stan asked.

'I don't know.' Dora's mouth set in a firm line. 'I expect one day we'll find out what's happened, but I've made myself accept that she won't be coming back to us. If I keep having sleepless nights fretting over where she might be, I'll go mad. My brother and sister are the important ones now and I've got to do my best for them. Does that sound hardhearted? I'm not unfeeling, but what will happen to Tom and Lily if I make myself ill by sinking into grief and confusion?'

Dora studied Stan's face, her eyes troubled. 'You do understand, don't you?'

'Yes,' he agreed. 'But don't be too hard on yourself. You're not alone. I'm here for all of you, no matter what happens.'

'I know, and Winnie's told me the same thing. It's the one glimmer of comfort we have in this terrible situation.'

'Dora!' Lily called. 'Are you in there?'

'She's here. Come in,' Stan said.

Lily and Tom tumbled into the room.

The depression that had plagued Stan all day had melted away after a visit from the Bentley children. The only trouble was that he was now worried about Dora. It seemed as if she was shutting out the disappearance of her mother in her concern for her brother and sister. He could understand what she was doing, but he didn't like it. By bottling everything inside her, she was in danger of eventually breaking.

Stan snorted in disgust. He was a fine one to talk! Wasn't he the expert at sidestepping the facts?

There was a sharp rap on the door and Reg strolled in. 'Missed you today, Stan. Not feeling too good?'

'I don't want to be always under your feet. You know where the whisky is.'

Reg poured two generous measures and sat down, raising his glass to his brother-in-law. 'Thanks, I need this.'

'Any progress?'

Stretching out his legs, Reg took a mouthful of the drink. He remained silent.

Stan eyed him carefully. 'You haven't answered my question.'

'What was that?'

'You know very well! What's going on, Reg?'

'This name Duval has cropped up again. But it can't have any connection to Mrs Bentley.'

His drink forgotten, Stan leant forward. 'Tell me.'

'Got a report from Bloomsbury station. A woman reported that she hasn't seen her neighbour, Mrs Duval, for over a week. The local police forced open the door of the flat but found nothing suspicious. In their opinion the woman's gone away on holiday or something like that. They only told us because we've put out a request for any information about the names of Duval and Bentley.'

'Bloomsbury, that's a nice area.' Stan looked doubtful. 'Most unlikely it's anything to do with our case.'

'I agree, but we must look into it. We've had bugger all to go on so far.' Reg downed his whisky and reached for the bottle. 'I haven't mentioned any of this to Dora because it'll probably turn out to be nothing. I've got permission to have a look at the flat and talk to the neighbour. I'm going tomorrow morning and I'd like you to come with me.'

'Of course.' Stan grinned, his depression a thing of the past. 'I've been on plenty of wild goose chases before.'

Fourteen

Early the next morning, Stan, Reg and a constable from Bloomsbury station were standing in front of an impressive Georgian house.

'It's been turned into self-contained flats,' the constable told them. 'Very expensive.'

Reg nodded. 'Have you had any news about the missing woman?'

'No, and there's nothing to indicate a crime of any kind. General opinion is the woman's gone away for a few days and forgot to mention she was going. Her neighbour, Mrs James, is worried, though. Says it isn't like her.'

'I think we're wasting our time,' Stan remarked as he studied the elegant façade. 'But we might as well have a look while we're here.'

'Second floor.' The constable held a key in his hand. 'We had to put a new lock on the door. Mrs Duval won't be too pleased when she sees what we've done to the door, but the neighbour was insistent there was something wrong.'

They walked into a spacious hall and up the stairs. The carpet was dark red, and so thick it absorbed any sound.

'Impressive,' Reg muttered.

'It is that.' The constable stopped by a door clearly showing the signs of a forced entry. 'Wait till you see the inside.'

Stan whistled softly when he saw the flat. You could have got the whole of his ground floor into the lounge area. The cream carpet, gold velvet curtains and sumptuously upholstered furniture wouldn't have looked out of place in a palace. Not that he'd ever been in one, but this was how he imagined it would look.

'My God!' Reg came out of another door. 'Have a look at the bedroom, Stan. There are real silk sheets on the four-poster bed!'

Stan went into the room and ran his fingers over the sheets, then turned and studied his surroundings thoroughly. The lounge had been tasteful and elegant, but this room was a different story. It was sensuous – there was no other word for it.

'This isn't anything to do with our missing woman, Stan.'

They went back into the lounge again just as a woman arrived.

'Have you any news?'

'I'm afraid not, madam,' the constable told her. 'These gentleman are looking for someone and wanted to see the flat.'

'Can you tell us who the landlord is?' Stan asked.

The woman looked down her nose at him, noting the crutches and then studying his face. 'There isn't a landlord, young man. These flats are all privately owned.'

Stan ignored her hostility and inclined his head. Just for a moment there her accent had slipped, and he had the feeling she wasn't quite what she seemed. But perhaps he was being oversensitive. 'And you are a friend of Mrs Duval?'

'We know each other quite well. She wouldn't have gone off without telling me.'

'Is there a Mr Duval?' Stan persisted, not prepared to give up yet.

'No, but her friend was here two or three times a week.'

'Do you know his name?'

The woman gave Stan an icy glare. 'I'm not in the habit of prying into other people's business, young man.'

Stan couldn't let that go. 'Business?'

The neighbour was looking exasperated at Stan's questions. 'She was a good hostess and entertained several times a week. I've already told the police all this!'

The photograph of Mrs Bentley was still in Stan's pocket, so he took it out and showed it to Mrs James. 'Is this Mrs Duval?'

She gave it a cursory glance and shook her head. 'Mrs Duval is older than that and always dresses in the height of fashion. No, she isn't that dowdy person.'

Another dead end, Stan thought as he put the photo back in his pocket. He turned to the constable. 'Can we search the place?'

'Already been done. My instructions are just to let you see the place and speak to Mrs James.' The constable consulted his watch. 'I've got to get back to the station now.'

After thanking the neighbour and the constable, Stan and Reg headed back to Kilburn station on the train. Reg was wearing his ordinary clothes for this trip. They had been told to attract as little attention as possible in such an elite area.

'You were right last night, Stan. This was a wild goose chase.'

'I agree, but I wish we could have searched the place.'

'Not our patch. We were lucky they even let us into the flat. Anyway, I'm convinced this has got nothing to do with our investigation.' Reg grinned. 'What a place! Makes you wonder what kind of *entertaining* went on here. And wasn't the neighbour offended when you asked who the landlord was!'

'These flats are all privately owned!' Stan mimicked.

They were both laughing as they walked back into the station.

'You staying for a while?' Reg asked as they grabbed themselves cups of tea.

'Might as well.'

'Good, you can write the report for me. You always were good with words.'

Stan accepted gladly. He was struggling with the desire to go to where Dora was working and see if he could track down Alan. Lord, that had been a shock. He had liked the captain, and he hoped he had survived. Dora had said she would find out where he lived, so he would leave it to her. Once he had an address, he'd go and see him.

'You haven't told me your name.' Dora paused, paintbrush in her hand.

'Eh?'

'Your name?'

'Dobbs.' He tipped his head to one side and studied the door. 'Bit bright, ain't it?'

Dora stepped back to get a better view. She had asked for blue, but the paint the doctor had left for her was more of a sea green. 'Maybe, but I think it's quite nice.'

'Hmph!' Dobbs clearly wasn't impressed. 'The doc won't

be here till this afternoon. He said you'd help me tidy my room.'

'I've nearly finished the painting. Give me ten minutes.'

'Eh?'

'I said, I'll be ten minutes.'

'Hard work, isn't he?'

'John! The doctor won't be here until later.'

'I know, I'm early. Nothing else to do. Let's go and see if Dobbs will make us a pot of tea, shall we?'

Dobbs was obviously used to this routine because the kettle was already boiling. Two more men had arrived, Charlie and Pete, and tossing everything into the corner of the room they cleared enough chairs to sit on.

Dora eyed it all with amusement. She couldn't imagine why Dobbs collected all this stuff. 'I think my next job will be to have a bonfire in the garden,' she remarked in her normal voice.

'No you won't!' Dobbs said indignantly, glancing round at the men crowding his room. 'We'll have to watch her. She'll have this place so tidy we won't be able to find a thing.'

'There wasn't anything wrong with your hearing that time, was there?' she remarked.

'Eh?'

'Don't you take any notice of him, Dora,' John smirked. 'Dobbs only hears what he wants to hear.'

The corners of Dobbs' mouth turned up, but he was serious when he spoke to Dora again. 'You leave these things alone, my girl. I can help quite a few people. These young blokes ain't the only ones who need help. Many around here don't have two farthings to rub together.'

Pete touched her arm and spoke softly. 'The old boy does a lot of good on the quiet.'

'I didn't know that. Thank you for telling me.' Dora smiled at Dobbs. Now she knew why she had seen him slipping out from time to time with parcels in his hand. 'I promise not to touch anything in your room.'

'Hmm,' was his only comment as he handed round the tea, and biscuits he kept in a tin.

Dora turned her attention back to the men. 'Perhaps one of you can help me. I'd like to know where I can find Alan Harrington. Do any of you know him?'

'The captain . . . he comes here. Decent bloke – for an officer. What do you want him for?' Charlie asked.

'A friend of mine would like to see him. He thinks he might be someone he knows.'

'And what's this friend's name?' The voice came from the doorway.

'Alan! I was hoping I'd see you. His name's Stan Crawford.'

Alan went absolutely still, then murmured, 'Crawford? Is he alive?'

Dora nodded. 'He's the man I told you about on Sunday.'

'Dear Lord! I thought Crawford was dead. I want to see him, Dora. I wouldn't be here now if it wasn't for his courage. I believe you said he was your neighbour?'

'Yes, that's right.'

'Would you give me his address? I must see him.'

'Of course, but if you've got the time you can come with me when I finish here. I told him about you and he wants to see you as well.'

'Thank you.'

'Doc's here!' Dobbs announced. It was the signal for them all to go and meet Dr Burridge.

The rest of the afternoon was hectic. Dora did her best to encourage the men as they struggled to master artificial limbs. They accepted her help without question, expressing their appreciation from time to time. She ran errands, prepared snacks to keep them all going, and loved every minute. Nothing she had ever done before had given her so much satisfaction. When the doctor remarked that she should have been a nurse, she knew he was right. She shouldn't have allowed her mother to talk her out of taking up the profession. They could surely have made arrangements for Tom and Lily when she wasn't around. But it was no use regretting it now.

During a brief lull, Dora decided that she wanted to stay here for as long as she was needed. It would be a struggle to manage, but there was always the pawnshop. She would have to talk it over with Tom first, though.

'The front door looks . . . er . . . bright.' Dr Burridge had finally stopped working, and this was the first time he'd mentioned Dora's handiwork with a paintbrush.

'Don't look so amused, sir. It's the colour you left for me.'

He grinned, looking almost boyish. 'So it is. The man in the hardware shop down the road donated it. I suspect he couldn't sell it.'

'Most likely,' Dora said thoughtfully. 'Do you think he's got more he can't sell? The shiny front door has made the rest of the place look shabby.'

'I'll ask. Now, go home, my dear, and thank you for today. You're a real asset to have around the place.'

'I've enjoyed every minute,' she told him truthfully. 'Good night, sir. I'll be here tomorrow.'

'Good night, Dora.'

She watched him walk down the path and out of the gate, heading, no doubt, for the hospital. She couldn't help wondering if he ever stopped working.

'All finished for the day?' Alan stood beside her.

'Yes, Dobbs told me he always locks up for the night.'

Alan hesitated. 'Perhaps you'd better give me Crawford's address, and I'll make my own way there.'

'Are you feeling too tired to go now?'

'I'm fine, but I'll slow you down, and you might be in a hurry.'

'Tom brings Lily home from school and looks after her until I get back. It won't matter if I'm a bit late.'

It suddenly dawned on her what he was doing, and she was offended. 'You think I'll be ashamed to be seen with you! Do you really think I'm that kind of a person?'

'I'm sure you're not, and I apologize if I've insulted you.' Alan tipped his head to one side, studying her intently. 'But a lot of people can't seem to deal with the injuries so many of us have received.'

'Well, I'm not one of them!' She placed her hand on his arm. 'Let's have no more of this nonsense, Captain. I'm taking you to see Stan.'

'Yes, nurse.'

They talked about all manner of things on the journey, but the subject of the war was never mentioned. When they arrived in Kilburn, Alan insisted on buying a bottle of whisky for Stan so they could have a drink together.

The front door was open. Dora knocked and called, 'Stan, it's me, Dora.'

'Come in. I'm in the kitchen,' he answered.

'I've brought someone to see you.'

Stan was already standing, having heard the sound of crutches on the tiled floor of the passage.

The two men stared at each other, and Dora saw a mixture of relief, pain and pleasure in their eyes as they examined each other.

Suddenly, Stan smiled widely. 'Captain! My God, I was sure you were dead. It's wonderful to see you again.'

'I thought the same about you. I owe you a drink.'

Dora could see that they needed to be alone so they could talk freely. 'Before you start on the bottle Alan has in his pocket, you needn't bother about food. I'll bring you something when it's ready.'

'Thanks Dora, we'd appreciate that.' Stan placed his hand on Alan's shoulder. 'Come into the front room, Captain. We'll get comfortable and start on that whisky.'

'That's a splendid idea – and the name's Alan.'

Dora didn't wait to hear any more and left at once, not wanting to be in the way of their reunion.

Tom and Lily were already home when she arrived, and they bombarded her with questions about her day.

'Sounds good.' Tom nodded with satisfaction.

Lily was giggling about the front door, and Dora was overcome with a feeling of wonder that they were all managing to carry on so normally. But deep in her mind was the fear that this wouldn't last. Their mother was missing, and the terrible mess was bound to blow up in their faces. When that happened, she was going to have to be even stronger . . .

'Did you see Alan?' Tom's voice broke through her troubled thoughts.

Dora smiled and told them that Alan was with Stan. 'Isn't it wonderful! They do know each other.'

'Can we go and see them?' Lily was already heading for the door.

'Not yet, sweetie.' Dora called her back. 'They've got a lot to talk about, but we'll cook a meal and take it round to them. You can see them long enough to say hello, and then we must leave.'

'All right.' Lily came and sat down again, her little face serious. 'I liked Alan. He's almost as nice as Stan.'

'They're both brave men,' Tom declared. 'And I'm glad the

doctor's trying to help some of the men. You must stay there if you want to, Dora. We'll manage somehow.'

'I would like to keep working at the house, but we'll have to see how things go, Tom. Now, have we got enough food to feed two extra?'

'Should be able to manage it if we put the meat in a pie. You're good at pastry, Dora.'

They all set to work on the meal. When it was ready they popped theirs into the oven to keep warm, and hurried to Stan's.

Dora went straight to the kitchen and laid the table, listening to Lily's excited chatter and Tom's deeper tones. It seemed as if his voice was beginning to break already. He was certainly growing up fast, and he was such a tremendous support. Dora didn't know what she would do without him. Their lives had been thrown into confusion, but Tom was proving to be steady and dependable.

'Food's on the table,' she announced, walking into the front room. 'Don't let it get cold. Now, we must get back to ours or it will be baked to a crisp in the oven. Don't worry about the plates, Stan. I'll collect them in the morning.'

Dora ushered her reluctant brother and sister out and said over her shoulder, 'If either of you need anything, you know where we are.'

Fifteen

'Shall I collect the plates from Stan?' Tom asked.

'No, that's all right. I'll do it or you'll be late for school.' Dora chewed her lip anxiously as she looked at Lily's unhappy face. 'What is it, sweetie?'

Lily shook her head, refusing to speak. They hadn't had a word out of her since she'd woken up.

'Talk to us, sweetie.' Dora stooped down beside Lily's chair. 'We can't help if we don't know what's wrong, can we?'

Tom leant against the sink, arms folded and a deep frown on his young face. 'Talk to Dora,' he said gruffly.

'I dreamt of Mum last night.' Her eyes were swimming with tears. 'She was laughing and happy – so were we. I want it to be like that again.'

'We all do.' As Dora said those words it felt as if something snapped inside her. She could try to pretend all she liked that this wasn't happening – but it was! Their mother was missing, probably dead, but until they knew for certain, their lives were in confusion. They tried to deal with each day as best they could, but it was hard to make decisions. They didn't know which way to turn. And she worried so about her brother and sister . . .

The carefully erected dam burst. Gathering Lily into her arms, she gave way and the tears came in torrents, heartbroken sobs racking her body. She collapsed on the floor.

Tom was horrified and very frightened. This couldn't be happening! Their big sister was strong, someone they could rely on. But it was too much for her. They had put too much on her.

Feeling completely helpless, Tom did the only thing he could think of. He ran to Stan's, banging on the front door frantically.

When it was wrenched open, he literally fell into the hall,

nearly knocking Stan off his feet. 'Please help!' he gasped. 'It's Dora – please help!'

Without a word, Stan grabbed his stick and shoved Tom out the door, hurrying as fast as he could. They heard Lily screaming before they reached the house.

Stan *ran*.

Tom had never moved so fast in his life. He burst into the kitchen and swept Lily off the floor, where she had been leaning over Dora and hitting her to try and make her wake up. Her screams were deafening. 'Stop that!' he demanded.

Stan was there then, and examining the unconscious girl. He pulled her up, sat her on a chair and pushed her head on to her knees. When she groaned, he sat her upright again. 'Tom, get me a glass of water.'

There was no way Tom could put Lily down because she was holding on with all her might, absolutely terrified. He managed to get the water using only one hand and gave it to Stan.

Dora had her eyes open now, but they were unfocused, unaware of what was going on around her.

Lily began fighting Tom, trying to get to her sister, screaming again, 'Dora!' over and over.

'Stop it!' Tom shouted at his little sister. It was something they had never done, and the shock silenced Lily. He kissed her cheek by way of saying sorry and said softly, 'Stan's looking after her. He knows what to do.'

'Drink this.' Stan held the glass to Dora's lips. When she took a sip, he urged, 'Again.'

She obeyed by taking two large gulps, then Stan put the glass on the table and began to rub some life back into her hands. 'Come on, Dora, take deep breaths. Come back to us.'

'Do we need a doctor?' Tom could feel his heart crashing against his ribs. Nothing must happen to Dora! They loved her. She was holding them together. They'd never manage without her. They'd be put in a home! 'Stan, do we need to get a doctor?'

'No, Tom.' It was Dora who spoke. 'I'm sorry. Just give me a minute or two. I'll be all right soon.'

'On your feet.' Stan pulled her out of the chair and led her to the front room. Then he eased her on to the settee, sat beside her and supported her in his arms.

She rested her head on his shoulder. 'I'm so tired of pretending I'm all right.'

'I know.' Stan stroked her hair away from her eyes. 'It gets too much at times, doesn't it?'

She nodded. 'And you know all about that, don't you?'

'Only too well.'

Suddenly Dora tried to sit up, alarmed. 'Lily, is she all right?'

'Shush, she's with Tom. I think they're making a pot of tea.' Stan made her relax again. 'Stop worrying about other people for a moment. Think of yourself for a change. I suspect that's something you seldom do, and that's why this has been building up. You can't protect Tom and Lily from this. They've got to face up to it in their own way. You can't do it for them, Dora, as much as I know you want to.'

Tom came in with a tray of tea, Lily beside him, drained of all colour. As soon as she saw Dora, she ran and climbed on the settee wrapping her arms around her. Tom knelt in front and grasped one of his big sister's hands. 'Hell, Dora, you frightened us.'

They remained like that, giving Dora time to recover. After a couple of minutes, she said, 'I could do with that tea now, Tom.'

'Of course.' He scrambled to his feet.

Dora sat up straight and bowed her head. 'I'm so ashamed. I'm sorry.'

'You haven't got anything to be sorry about.' Tom gave her a cup of tea. 'You're struggling to see we live like we used to. That isn't right. We've been selfish by telling you we want to stay in this house when we know it isn't going to be possible. We can't go on leaving it all to Dora, Lily. She's trying to support the three of us and the strain's too much. We've got to help more.'

Lily nodded, looking thoroughly confused.

'I'll get a job after school.' Tom finished pouring tea for the rest of them. 'And we'll move to a cheaper place if we have to. All right, Lily?'

'Yes,' she whispered, too upset to protest.

'I don't want you working, Tom.' Dora had recovered enough to make decisions, but she still held tightly to Stan's hand, grateful for his calm support.

'Maybe so, but we don't have a choice.' Tom lifted his head in determination. 'We're getting through our money at a fast rate. I'm not daft, I know what a mess we're in.'

Dora nodded miserably. What Tom said was correct. 'I'll start looking for a permanent job immediately.'

'No, you won't!' Tom had had enough of this. It was time someone thought about Dora. She'd worked as a housemaid because their mum hadn't let her do the thing she wanted to. Then in the evenings she had looked after him and Lily, never complaining. What kind of a life had she had? 'I saw how happy you were when you told us about the doctor, and I know you really want to work at that house. So you stay!'

'We'll see how it goes, Tom.'

Lily had snuggled close to her sister and was gazing up at her. 'Are you all right now, Dora?'

She bent her head and kissed Lily's cheek. 'Much better now, Lily. I'm sorry I frightened you.'

'Stan took care of you. I was glad Tom fetched him.'

'Yes, that was kind of him.' Dora turned to Stan who had remained with his arm supporting her. 'Thank you very much. I'm sorry we've been such a nuisance to you, but we're grateful for your help.'

'Don't keep apologizing.' Stan removed his arm and moved away from her slightly. 'I'm here if you need me for anything.'

'Thanks, Stan.' Tom was relaxing now he could see his big sister was all right again. That had scared him, and made him realize that he must shoulder more responsibility from now on. After all, he would be thirteen in two months' time, and a lot of boys were out working by then. Their mother had always insisted that schooling was the most important thing. But she damned well wasn't here now!

Lily scrambled off the settee, went to Stan and pulled his hand until he leant forward. Then she planted a smacking kiss on his cheek. 'Thank you for helping Dora. We'll look after her better, won't we, Tom?'

'We will. Now, do you feel well enough to go to school, or do you want to stay at home with Dora?'

'I'm not staying home,' Dora protested. The colour was coming back to her face. 'You must both go to school.'

When Dora began to stand up, Stan stopped her. 'You ought to stay at home today and rest.'

'No, I need to be busy, and I'm fine now, really.'

'All right, but promise me you'll come home if you feel ill again.'

'I promise, but it won't happen again. It was just a moment of weakness.'

When Stan nodded and stood up, Tom was there with the stick Stan had dropped in the kitchen, and walked with him to the front door.

'Find her, Stan.' Tom was furious. 'Find our mother, and if it turns out that she's abandoned us, I'll kill her, I swear!'

Stan rested his hand on the boy's shoulder, the youngster now seeming so grown up. 'I understand. But after what I've seen this morning, I'll bloody well do the job for you!'

It took Stan at least an hour before he could even consider going to see Reg at the station. He was physically weakened by his efforts to get Dora off the floor. Seeing her like that had shaken him, which was surprising when he recalled the terrible things he had witnessed in the war.

But this was different. He was in love with Dora!

Resting his head in his hands he swore with ferocity. Didn't he have enough problems without adding a hopeless cause to the list? Of all the stupid things to do . . .

'Stan!' Winnie had arrived. 'I've never heard you use such language. Are you all right?'

'No, I'm not,' he growled. He told her what had happened.

'And you say she's gone to work? She shouldn't have done that. Why didn't you stop her?'

'I can't give her orders. But those three are suffering and I feel so damned helpless. I've got to do something!' Stan's first two attempts to stand up failed. 'Get the crutches for me, Win.'

With those, and his sister's help, he eventually got to his feet. 'Do one more thing for me. Get my bike out of the shed, please.'

Winnie studied him with concern. 'You don't look in a fit state to even go out, let alone ride a bike! But there's no point me asking you to stay here, is there?'

'None at all.' Stan dredged up a grim smile. 'I'll be all right once I get moving.'

It was then Winnie spotted the nearly empty bottle on the floor by the fireplace. 'Have you got a hangover? Is that what's wrong with you?'

'Stop worrying, I didn't drink all that on my own.' He told her about Alan.

She smiled. 'Oh that's wonderful, Stan. You must have been so pleased to see each other.'

'It was good. We did our best to drink the bottle dry, and we didn't stop talking for three hours. Dora made sure we had some food.'

'Sensible girl.'

'Alan was still sober enough to make it home. At least, that's what he said.'

'You should have asked him to stay.'

'I did, but he refused.' Stan took a couple of tentative steps, grunted with satisfaction and changed the crutches for the stick. 'You going to get my bike for me, Win?'

She pulled a face. 'Men! No sense at all.'

The station was quiet when Stan arrived, but Reg had just returned from pounding his beat.

'Stan, you look awful. What have you been up to?'

'Working my way through a bottle of whisky with a bloke I thought was dead. But I'll tell you about that later. Is there any glimmer of hope in the search for Mrs Bentley?'

'Not a damned thing!'

Stan ran a hand over his eyes, weary beyond belief. 'Dora collapsed this morning.'

'Oh Lord, I'm sorry. Is she all right now?'

'Says she is, and she's gone to work.' Stan let out a ragged sigh. 'Why can't we find this blasted woman, Reg? Do you think she's in the Thames?'

'It's possible, but I'm beginning to doubt she's dead.' Reg perched on the edge of the desk, his expression thoughtful. 'I think she's done a runner. Do you think Dora and Tom would mind if we went public with this?'

'The newspapers?' When Reg nodded, Stan said, 'I don't think they'd mind what we do any more. They're really suffering, but let me clear it with Dora first. I'll go and see her right away.'

Sixteen

Feeling stronger now, but ashamed of herself for falling to pieces like that, Dora walked into the Wandsworth house. The bright front door seemed to welcome her, and when Dobbs waved cheerily, she felt better. Things were all right. Not normal – they couldn't be – but it was as if a pressure inside her had been released. It had obviously been building, and Lily's unhappiness had brought it to the surface. The little girl was understandably confused. They worried and protected their sister. She had been a delicate baby, often sick, and they spoilt her. That had been easy to do because she was a bright child, and so easy to love. But they couldn't protect her from every heartbreak in life, as much as they wanted to.

Dora made her way to the large room at the back of the house. It had been turned into a place where the young men could meet. There was a dartboard, table tennis, easy chairs, and tables where they could play cards. Any ex-serviceman was welcome, and she had discovered that many came to pass the time. The injured couldn't find jobs, and they gave up in discouragement after a while. At least they were welcome here.

She opened the door and smiled brightly. 'Good morning. Who would like tea?'

Six men were already there. They nodded, returning her smile.

'Coming right up.'

'Hey, Dora,' Pete called, as she turned to leave the room. 'Any chance of sandwiches?'

'I'll see what I can do.' She hurried to the kitchen, glad to be busy. She had never fainted before in her life, and it wasn't something she would want to repeat. Everyone had been frightened – including herself.

Dobbs followed her to the kitchen carrying a bag. 'Here lass, you'll need this. I expect those boys are hungry as usual.'

The bag contained bread, milk, cheese, butter, tomatoes and even slices of ham. 'Wow!' Dora exclaimed. 'Where did you get all this?'

'Donations.' He smirked. 'I can't hear when people say no.'

She laughed. 'They give up trying to refuse and just hand the things over, do they?'

'Eh?' Dobbs' expression remained serious, but there was amusement in his pale grey eyes. 'I'll have a couple of cheese sandwiches when you've made them. Keep a bit of ham for the doc. He said he's going to pop in this morning.'

'I'll do that.'

'Right, now I'll be in with the boys. I'm gonna thrash them at ping pong!'

Dora soon had two large plates piled high with sandwiches, and had turned to put the kettle on to boil for the tea when she saw the doctor standing in the doorway, studying her intently.

'Oh, hello, sir, I didn't hear you come in.'

He walked towards her, placed one hand on her forehead, and with the other held her wrist. 'How do you feel?'

'All right.'

'Liar. You look drained. What's happened, Dora?'

There was an air of quiet authority about him, and much to her shame, her eyes filled with tears. 'I fainted this morning.'

He led her to a chair and made her sit down. 'Tell me about it. I'm a good listener.'

Dora began hesitantly at first, but it was such a relief to talk freely. The story tumbled out, and when she had finished she looked at him, anguish in her eyes. 'It's terrible,' she admitted.

'I'm so sorry, my dear. I suppose the burden of keeping your little family together has fallen on your shoulders.'

'Like a ton of bricks.' She grimaced. 'That isn't strictly true. My brother Tom is supporting me all the way, and we've got the help of our neighbour, Stan Crawford, and his family. They're very good to us.'

'Hmm.' Dr Burridge gazed into space as he held her wrist. Then he patted her hand. 'You tell me if you feel faint again.'

She nodded and watched him walk away, intent on the day's work. He was such a kind man, she thought, and easy to talk to. She went back to preparing the tea and sandwiches.

With everything loaded on trays, Dora picked up the first one.

'Here, let me help you with those.'

Recognizing Alan's voice, Dora turned to say that she could manage. The words died as she saw him. 'Oh, you've got your leg!'

'And a hand.' He held it up for her to see.

'That's wonderful! Please, show me how you can walk.'

He walked across the room and back again. Dora couldn't stop smiling. 'I'm so happy for you. You walk well!'

'Not bad, huh?' He grinned and bowed. 'Would you dance with me, miss?'

'I'd love to, sir.' Dora joined in his pleasure and curtsied gracefully. They waltzed around the kitchen, Alan singing softly.

The burst of applause from the doorway stopped them. Dobbs was actually smiling. 'Well done, sir.'

'Thank you, Dobbs. I had them fitted this morning at Roehampton. The first leg they gave me was terrible, but this one feels fine.'

'You must come and show the doc.' Dobbs picked up the heavy teapot. 'Let's get this lot to the boys and we can have a celebration. Always good to see another young man back on his feet – so to speak.'

Dora and Alan picked up a tray each and followed Dobbs in procession along the passage.

'Look at the captain, doc!' Dobbs was shouting as soon as they entered the room. 'He can even dance. Bloody wonderful I call that!'

The doctor came straight over to Alan. 'Ah, good, you've got them at last. Let me see what you can do.'

Alan obliged, receiving smiles of approval from the other men in the room.

'Good, good.' Dr Burridge took a close look at the limbs. 'Well done, Alan. Now, don't overdo it for a few days, but you should be all right now.'

'Thanks for all your help, doc. I don't know what we'd do without you.'

The doctor waved away the compliment. 'All I do is give you advice, encouragement and a place to meet.'

'That's just what we need,' Charlie told him. 'Some of us

would have given up without your support. When I came out
of Queen Mary's, Roehampton, I felt as if my life was over.
Then I found this place. It's the best thing that could have
happened to me.'

John was nodding. 'Knowing we can come here and meet
others makes it worth getting up in the morning.'

There were murmurs of agreement.

'Tea's poured out,' Dobbs announced, and they all crowded
round for the refreshments, talking and smiling. Seeing Alan's
success had given them all the hope that they would soon be
able to do the same. Many had more severe injuries and
wouldn't be able to walk as well as Alan, but the proof that
it was possible was lifting their spirits.

The food was demolished amid lively talk. Collecting the
empty trays, Dora left them to it and returned to the kitchen.
The doctor would call her when he needed help with something, but there was plenty here to keep her busy. She couldn't
get over how fine Alan had looked, so tall and straight. He
was obviously a good dancer, as well.

Dora was giving the kitchen sink a good clean when Dobbs
looked in. 'Bloke's just arrived. Said he's got to see you. Never
been here before, but he's another poor sod who can hardly
walk.'

Dora dried her hands, hoping the man hadn't heard Dobbs'
comments. Being hard of hearing he was included to speak
rather loudly. When she looked up she was astonished to see
the figure who stood in the doorway. 'Stan!'

'You know him?' When she nodded, Dobbs went back to
whatever he had been doing.

'Have you come to see Alan? He's got his new leg, and he
walks ever so well. Come and meet everyone. They're all in
the other room . . .'

Stan held up his hand to stop her. 'I've really come to see
you. I need your permission for something.'

Now she was curious. 'What's that?'

'It's an idea Reg has.' Stan sat on a chair by the table.
'We're getting nowhere with the search, and he's suggested
that we put an appeal in the newspapers. Someone somewhere
must know something. But we won't do it if you object.'

Dora sat beside him, considered the idea for only a few
moments, took a deep breath and said, 'Go ahead. We need

an end to this – whatever that end might be. If there's the smallest chance it will help, then do it. I know Tom will agree.'

Stan nodded, looking at her with respect, knowing it hadn't been an easy decision to make. 'You understand this might mean unwelcome publicity and you could be pestered by reporters?'

She nodded, not liking the idea, but they had to do something. The longer this went on, the more strain it was putting on all of them. 'It's got to be done, hasn't it? If it finds Mum, then it'll be worth it.'

'We want to hit the evening papers if we can.'

'I understand. I'll tell Tom and Lily this evening.' With that settled, she stood up. 'Now, while you're here you must meet everyone.'

'I can't stop.' Stan gripped the table to help him stand. 'I've got to get back and let Reg know he can go ahead.'

'There's a telephone at the police station, isn't there?' Dora wanted to keep Stan here if she could. For one thing the journey had exhausted him, and as hard as he tried to hide it, the strain showed. And it would be a good chance for him to meet the doctor again. 'Come on, there's a phone in the office.'

She swept out, leaving him no choice but to follow. She waited while he spoke to Reg, then said, 'You must meet everyone while you're here. And if you're lucky there might be a couple of sandwiches left.'

Without a word of protest, Stan walked beside her. Seeing he was in considerable difficulty, she placed a hand through his arm. 'You ought to be using your crutches.'

'I know, but I went to the station on my bike. I didn't know I was coming here as well.'

She stopped suddenly. 'You didn't ride your bike here, surely?'

'No, came on the train. Reg will take my bike home for me if I don't go back to the station today.'

'Here we are.' As soon as she opened the door, Alan saw Stan and walked over.

'Stan! How's the hangover?'

'I've had worse.' He looked the captain up and down. 'You're walking well on that thing.'

'I'll be even better when I get used to it.'

'Crawford, isn't it?' Dr Burridge was beside them and holding out his hand. 'We met on the train.'

Stan shook hands with him. 'Did you get that poor devil to the hospital all right?'

'Yes, and he's being taken care of now.' The doctor studied Stan's face. 'You're not any better, are you? I hope this visit means you'll let me examine you?'

'I'm not coming to hospital.' Stan was adamant.

'I have an examination room set up here. I'll tell you exactly how things are. No lies, no pressure.'

Dora was longing to plead with Stan to allow this, but knew it wasn't her place to interfere.

'Go on, Stan,' Alan urged. 'Won't take long, and the doc's good. Not remotely like the treatment we received on the front line.'

Dora decided it would be best if she left the men to it, so she went over to talk to John. Although he was still finding it difficult to walk, she could see an improvement on yesterday, and told him so.

'Thanks. Doc says I've just got to persevere.'

She had been talking to John for a few minutes when Alan joined them. Casting a quick glance back she couldn't see Stan or Dr Burridge.

Alan noticed her anxious glance. 'Stan's agreed to let the doc have a look at him. But don't raise your hopes too much. He's been told there's nothing they can do for him, and the doc might agree.'

Dora nodded. 'I know, but it would help if he could be made more comfortable.'

'You really care for him, don't you?'

'I care about everyone who's still suffering because of that terrible war. This house is a little oasis in the middle of indifference. But don't start me on that subject, Alan, or I'll rant on for hours!' Dora picked up two cups from under a chair. 'I must get back to work, but I'll see you later.'

Dobbs had collected most of the crockery, but hadn't attempted to wash up, so Dora set about the task. She hoped Stan would come and see her before he left.

It was nearly an hour before anyone came into the kitchen, and she had started to wash down the walls, with the idea of giving the kitchen a fresh coat of paint. She might even be able to persuade some of the more able-bodied men to help. Dora had seen enough to know that some of them felt useless, but that wasn't true, there would be some jobs they could do.

'Leave that, Dora.' Dr Burridge looked in. 'I could use your help in my office. What's your handwriting like?'

'Very neat, so I'm told.'

'Excellent. Come with me.'

'Where's Stan?' she asked as soon as they were in his office.

'Having a game of cards with Alan and some of the others.'

'Oh, that's good. He'll enjoy that.' Dora hesitated. She had no right to ask, but just couldn't stop herself. 'He let you examine him then?'

'Hmm.' The doctor handed her a pile of letters. 'I've scribbled my decisions at the bottom of these. Answer them for me. And I can't discuss my patients, Dora.'

'No, of course not.' She looked him straight in the eyes. 'Is Stan your patient, then?'

'You'll have to ask him that.' He added another letter to the pile. 'I'd like to post those this evening, that's if you think you can get them ready by then?'

'They'll be finished and waiting for you.' Knowing she wasn't going to get anything out of him, she set to work. The doctor's notes at the bottom of each letter were brief, leaving her to compose a proper reply in her own words. She had always been good at this kind of thing, and found it very enjoyable.

Dr Burridge disappeared for the next hour, obviously pleased to leave this task with her. By the time he returned, she had the replies in a neat pile awaiting his approval and signature.

He read each one, signing as he went along. Dora was expecting him to pass some back to her to be redone, but he never did.

'We'll post these on the way home.' He looked thoughtful and shuffled through the letters again.

Dora held her breath. When he said nothing, she asked, 'Are they all right?'

'They're excellent. Where did you learn to write like this?'

'Mum used to give us lessons at weekends. Her writing was beautiful.' Mentioning her mother made the pain return – not that it was ever far away.

'Stan told me they're doing everything they can to find out what's happened, my dear,' he said, gently.

'I know, but it's distressing not knowing.' She pulled the letters towards her, not wanting to talk about it any more. 'I'll do the envelopes, shall I?'

'Please, and then come and find me. I'll drive you home.'

'Oh, that's very kind of you, but there's no need. I'm fine now.'

'I'm taking Stan home, so you might as well come with us.' The doctor headed for the door, then looked back. 'Don't argue, Dora.'

'No, sir,' she replied smartly, noting the brief smile on his face as he disappeared.

Seventeen

This was a luxury, Dora thought as she sat in the back of the car. Stan was in the front with the doctor, and she was relieved he didn't have to struggle with the trains. He looked terribly tired. She knew him well enough now to know that whatever had passed between him and Dr Burridge would not be mentioned. She would have to curb her curiosity and wait to see what happened.

When they arrived at Stan's house, Tom and Lily came rushing out to look at the car, a rare sight on their road. On the way home they had stopped to post the letters and buy an evening paper. The article was brief, appealing for people to come forward if they had any information about the whereabouts of a Mrs Bentley from Kilburn. There was a description of their mother and the photograph. Dora kept the newspaper out of sight as they greeted her brother and sister.

Dr Burridge got out of the car as well. 'Ah, you must be Tom and Lily.'

Dora introduced him. Lily couldn't take her eyes off the distinguished man, but Tom was more interested in the car.

'She's a beauty, sir,' he remarked, after inspecting it in detail.

'Thank you. I find it useful.'

'Stan,' Dora laid a hand on his arm. 'Will you come in and have dinner with us tonight?'

When he nodded, she motioned her brother over. 'Take Stan in, Tom. I'll be there in a moment.'

'You're welcome to eat with us as well, doctor.'

'Can you?' Lily asked eagerly. 'Dora's a good cook.'

'That's very kind of you, but I already have a dinner engagement.' He smiled down at Lily. 'But I wouldn't say no to a nice cup of tea.'

'I'll go and put the kettle on!' Lily tore off as fast as her legs would carry her.

'Your brother and sister are delightful, Dora.'

'Yes, I love them very much.' She took the doctor into the front room. Stan was already sitting in one of the armchairs.

Lily was very excited about having visitors. This was something their mother had never encouraged, and it was quite a novelty for the little girl. She handed round the biscuits, smiling politely. When everyone had been served, she sidled up to Dr Burridge, leaning forward to whisper in his ear. 'Our Dora fainted this morning. I was very frightened. She's never done that before.'

'She's better now,' he whispered back. 'I examined her and there's nothing wrong. She was overtired, I expect.'

Lily drew in a deep breath as she nodded, turned away, and then spun back. 'She worries about us, you know?'

The doctor nodded.

The little girl obviously hadn't finished because she stayed where she was, still holding the plate, and casting a furtive glance around the room. When she saw that they were all busy talking and not taking any notice of her, she moved even closer. 'Would you like another biscuit?'

'No thank you, Lily.'

'Erm . . . are you a proper doctor?'

'Very proper.'

'Hmm. Well, we *all* worry about Stan. Can you make him better?'

'I can't do anything unless he asks me to.' The doctor spoke seriously to Lily. 'And even then there might not be anything I can do for him. He was badly injured in the war. Do you understand?'

She nodded. 'That nasty war killed my dad.'

'I'm sorry to hear that.'

'Hmm. I don't remember him.'

'Lily!' Dora came over, smiling apologetically at Dr Burridge. 'You've taken up quite enough of the doctor's time. Help me collect the cups and plates.'

'We've been talking.'

'So I noticed. What about?'

'Oh, just things.' Lily gave the doctor a hesitant smile. 'I've got to help Dora now. We've got to look after her better. Will you come again?'

'I would like that. Thank you.' He stood up. 'It's been a pleasure to meet your family, Dora, but I must be on my way.'

When Stan made a move to stand, the doctor placed a hand on his shoulder to keep him in the chair, smiling down at him. 'No need to get up, my boy. You'll always be welcome at the house if you feel like company.'

'Thank you, sir.'

The three Bentley children saw the doctor to his car, Tom holding the door open for him. They watched until the car was out of sight, and then returned to the house.

Dora immediately set about preparing the meal while her brother and sister kept Stan company. She had slipped the newspaper in one of the kitchen drawers. They would eat before discussing that. It was a relief to have Stan here because he would be able to explain about this far better than she could.

Once the meal was over and the dishes piled in the sink, Dora retrieved the newspaper. 'Leave the washing-up and come into the other room. We've got something to tell you.'

Tom and Lily followed her.

'Is it news of Mum?' Tom wanted to know, eyeing the paper in Dora's hand.

'No, that's the problem. There isn't any news, so we've done something that might help.' Dora told them about putting it in the newspaper. 'I hope you don't mind, but Reg wanted to catch the evening editions.'

'It's all right by me,' Tom said without hesitation. 'Can we see the paper?'

Lily nodded as well, not really understanding, but she scrambled over to her brother so she could have a look. 'Oh, that's Mum's picture!'

'Yes, sweetie. We're hoping someone will see it and be able to tell us where she is.'

Stan leant forward and spoke for the first time. It didn't take him long to explain why they had done this. 'Someone out there must know something,' he told them, 'but if reporters pester you, you're to say nothing and send them to Reg or me. We'll deal with them.'

'Thanks.' Tom folded the paper up again. 'We've got to do everything we can, haven't we?'

'Yes,' Stan agreed. 'I'm sorry this was necessary, but every way we've turned has led us up a blind alley.'

'It's almost as if she never existed, but she did. She was our mother, and we love her.' Dora was bewildered.

'This whole business is unbelievable,' Tom said, shaking his head. 'The longer it goes on, the more I'm convinced she's taken off for some reason. You haven't been able to find any trace of her, so that makes me think she doesn't want to be found.'

'We can't rule out anything.' Stan got to his feet. 'There's nothing more we can do tonight, so let's all try and get some sleep. See what tomorrow brings.'

There was too much on Stan's mind for sleep to be possible, but it was a relief to stretch out in bed and rest. The Bentley children had shown courage by agreeing so readily to the newspaper appeal. He wished he'd taken more notice of the mother, spoken to her, then perhaps he would have a better understanding about her character. As it was, she was just a shadowy figure, without substance. It was like searching for a ghost. She had hidden things from her children, and if she'd gone away and left them, then she had covered her tracks well.

Stan shifted to get more comfortable, his mind racing, going over and over the day's events. It had surprised him to see how at home Dora had been at the Wandsworth house. She was in her element, giving encouragement and looking after everyone who came to the house. And from what he'd seen, the place was well used. She cared, and that appeared to be an innate part of her nature. It was much appreciated, as many men were struggling to survive and hang on to their dignity. He thanked God for people like Dr Burridge, who were at least trying to help. Alan and the others he'd met today had high praise for him. If there were delays in getting limbs, or anything else was troubling them, they went to the doc and he sorted it out for them. Stan couldn't understand how he found the time. The hours he worked at the hospital must be long and demanding. He devoted every waking hour to men in need, and for that he deserved a medal.

That thought now brought Stan to the question uppermost in his mind; the one he'd been avoiding. The doc had said he would be honest, and by God he had been. He needed to have Stan at the hospital so he could carry out a detailed examination. When Stan had flatly refused, he'd told him that there was a risk that he would be dead within the year.

Stan hauled himself up to a sitting position, resting his head against the headboard. That had shaken him, and he had demanded to know how he could tell that.

'Because, young man,' the doctor had declared, standing over him, 'you've still got pieces of shrapnel in your body. If only one piece is near your heart and it moves, that will be that. There are a couple of pieces quite near the surface, and they can easily be removed, but we need to see how many more there are. And while we're at it, I can do something about that leg. It needs resetting, and more extensive repair work carried out. You'll always limp, but you should be pain free and able to walk reasonably well.'

'How sure of all this are you?' Stan had wanted to know.

'No guarantees. I may be entirely wrong in my assumption about the shrapnel. After all, this has only been a cursory examination. But my professional opinion is that we can do something for you.' Dr Burridge had been blunt when he'd said, 'If you want any kind of a future, then you would be wise to consider having the operation.'

He had told Stan to think it over and then come to see him. But he advised him not to wait too long.

Well, he was thinking. A short time ago he wouldn't have cared too much, but things had changed. He now cared *very* much. If there was the slightest chance of him living a normal life, then he had to take it. He had accepted the medics' verdict that there was nothing more they could do for him; now there might be hope. The doc was right, he'd be a fool to refuse.

Sliding down in the bed again, he tried to relax. He would go to the hospital tomorrow, after checking in at the station to see if there was any response to the appeal.

For the first time since his return from the war, he began to think ahead. If things went well he would be able to take Dora out, and hope she fell in love with him. That's if Alan didn't get there first. He hadn't missed the way the captain looked at her. But if he could walk properly again, then Alan would have a fight on his hands. And then there was also the chance that he'd be accepted back in to the force again.

With his decisions made, Stan drifted off to sleep, the glimmer of hope for the future helping him relax.

*　　*　　*

It was ten o'clock before Stan arrived at the station. Reg was busy writing, frowning over a report he was trying to compose.

He glanced up and smiled when Stan sat beside him. 'Ah, the very man. Any chance you could help me with this?'

Stan laughed, feeling better than he had done for a long time. 'Thanks for returning my bike. And you're just as capable as I am, you crafty devil. Anything to get out of a job you don't like doing.'

Pushing back his chair, Reg grinned. 'You know me too well. You're looking better today, Stan.'

'Sorted a few things out and made a couple of decisions.'

'You going to tell me what they are?'

'Not yet. Have you had any response from the newspaper appeal?'

'A couple of time-wasters, that's all so far. One old man tottered in and said he'd killed her.' Reg shrugged. 'You know how it is. We gave him a cup of tea and a bun and then sent him on his way. He was happy enough.'

Stan nodded. Some people would confess to anything just to get some attention. 'I can't stay, but I'll pop in later.'

'Where you off to?' Reg was surprised. When Stan was at the station he usually settled in for a while, enjoying seeing the men coming and going, the lively atmosphere.

'I need to set in motion one of those decisions I made.' Stan settled himself on his crutches.

Reg eyed him with curiosity. 'This decision means doing a bit of travelling, does it?'

'You know I can't handle trains using a stick. And I might have a lot of walking to do.'

'I see.' Reg frowned. He knew his brother-in-law didn't like them to fuss, but he was pushing himself too hard, and it showed on his face. 'You take care, Stan.'

'For the first time since I came home I am taking care.' He turned and walked out of the station. He just hoped the doc was at the Royal London Hospital in Whitechapel this morning, and able to see him.

The hospital was very busy when he arrived, and the nurse he spoke to wasn't sure if he could be seen without an appointment.

'Dr Burridge said I was to come any time and he would see me,' Stan told her. 'Look, will you tell him Stan Crawford's here? If he's too busy I'll come another time.' This wasn't what Stan wanted to do, because now he had decided to go ahead with this, he wanted to get on with it.

The nurse was writing down his name when Stan heard a call. Turning, he saw the doctor walking towards him, smiling broadly.

'Glad to see you, my boy.' Dr Burridge nodded to the nurse. 'It's all right. I was expecting Mr Crawford.'

As the nurse hurried back to her duties, Stan gave the doctor a quizzical look. 'You were expecting me?'

'Of course, come with me. I'll get my team to give you a thorough examination and then we'll find you a bed.'

'What?' Stan stopped suddenly. 'You want me to come in at once?'

'No, within the next couple of days will do.' Dr Burridge's expression was compassionate. 'I'm sorry, my boy, but I don't want to delay your treatment.'

'You've frightened the hell out of me, do you know that?' Stan began walking again.

'Good,' was the doctor's only comment.

Eighteen

After a busy day Dora was clearing up the back room before making her way home, when Reg walked in. 'Is there news?' she asked eagerly.

'Nothing yet.' Reg glanced around. 'Have you seen Stan?'

'No, he hasn't been here today. Why, have you lost him?'

Reg pulled a face. 'You could say that. I know we worry about him too much. He's a grown man and doesn't have to account to us for everything he does . . .'

'But that still doesn't stop you worrying.' Dora nodded, understanding. 'I know exactly how you feel. He's lucky to have family who care so much. Many aren't so fortunate.' She studied the man in front of her. She didn't know much about him. 'Were you in the war, Reg?'

'Navy. This is an interesting place,' he said, quickly changing the subject. 'Will you show me round?'

'Of course.' All the men had left, but Dora introduced him to Dobbs, and explained what Dr Burridge was doing here.

'So, it's like a club where they can meet?' Reg asked.

'More than that, mate,' Dobbs told him. 'The doc comes in several times a week and gives advice, medical and personal. Good bloke, the doc.'

'He must be.' Reg looked at Dora. 'I've got a police car outside. If you're ready to leave I'll take you home.'

'Thank you. I'll just get my purse.' Dora was grateful because it would save her fare. They weren't going to be able to manage much longer without pawning something. Each expense was now carefully considered, but there was one thing she wouldn't cut back on and that was decent food. They must all eat properly or become ill, and that would be foolish.

When they arrived home there were three men standing by Dora's gate, and she could see Lily peering out of the window. She waved in relief when she saw Dora.

Tom came out immediately. 'Reporters,' he told Reg, as they began to crowd around firing off questions. 'They won't go away.'

'Leave this to me. Go in the house both of you.'

The reporters let them go, drawn to the policeman. They watched from the window as Reg spoke with the men. After a while they all walked away.

Tom opened the door for Reg to come in.

'They won't bother you again. I've promised them news if they come into the station.'

'Thank you very much.' Dora had been holding her breath; now she breathed out in relief.

'There's the doctor's car again!' Tom was already halfway out of the door. 'And Stan's with him,' he called back.

'Doctor?' Reg spun round to Dora. 'Is Stan seeing a doctor?'

'It's Doctor Burridge from the Wandsworth house. Stan met him when he came to ask me about the newspaper appeal. They'd met once before on a train, evidently.'

'He never mentioned this to us! Is that who he's been with all day?'

'Reg,' Dora caught hold of his arm to calm him down. 'Stan let the doctor have a look at him, but neither of them would say what the result was.'

'Stan told me this morning he'd come to a decision.' Reg ran a hand through his hair, agitated. 'We've tried so hard to persuade him to get another opinion, but he's flatly refused each time. Is this man good?'

'I believe so.'

'Look who's here!' Lily came in holding the doctor's hand, smiling up at him. 'I'll put the kettle on.'

'Have you had trouble with reporters?' Stan demanded the minute he walked in.

'I've dealt with it, Stan. And what the hell's going on?' Reg asked under his breath.

'Get Winnie and I'll tell you about it.' Stan sat down and grimaced. 'I hurt everywhere, doc!'

'Sorry about that, my boy, but it couldn't be helped.'

Reg was already heading for the door when he stopped. 'I'll have to bring June as well. Do you mind, Dora?'

'Not at all. She can keep Lily company. Tom, we'd better make sandwiches, and there's a cake in the larder I made last night.'

'I'll help.' Lily raced for the kitchen.

Dora watched her, then said, 'She does love to have visitors. Can you stay and meet Stan's sister, doctor?'

'Of course. It's kind of you to let us invade your home like this, Dora, but Stan wants you all to hear what he has to say.'

'It's only right,' Stan told her. 'You came to me for help and I won't be able to do that now. But Reg will take good care of you.'

Dora's hopes kept rising and falling. She couldn't decide if this was going to be good news or bad. 'I know he will.'

Winnie arrived out of breath, with Reg following behind, carrying June in an effort to keep up with his wife. She burst into the room. 'Stan, are you all right?'

He raised his eyebrows.

'I know. Don't fuss!' Winnie turned to the one person in the room she hadn't met before. 'You must be the doctor Reg told me was here.'

He gave a slight nod of his head, waited for everyone to be seated, then glanced at Stan. 'Do you want to explain, or shall I?'

'Go ahead, doc.'

'Right, I'll be brief. Stan has had a thorough examination by my medical team. He'll be coming into hospital for treatment in two days' time.'

'You can help him?' Winnie asked.

'We believe so. There are no guarantees, but if we're successful he should be able to lead a normal life.'

'And if not?' Reg spoke gruffly.

'Stan?' The doctor gave him an enquiring glance.

'Tell them.'

'Then his future is uncertain.'

Dora felt a chill creep through her, and at that moment she knew her feelings for this courageous man had grown to more than friendship. In the midst of such distress she had fallen in love. And it wasn't pity for him, or her need to have support, it went deeper than that – much deeper. One thing she knew for sure was that she must not let him know. It would embarrass him.

'Meaning?' Winnie demanded.

'The doc means just that, Win,' Stan told her, the tone of his voice warning her to leave it there. He smiled. 'It's going to be all right. I'll be in good hands, and whatever happens I'll be no worse off than I am now.'

Listening to this exchange and studying the faces of Stan and the doctor, Dora saw beneath the casual attitude. What they were planning was risky, but then any medical procedure had risks. They would not have decided to operate unless the chance of success was reasonably high.

While everyone was digesting this news, Dora stood up, went over to Stan and grasped his hand. It seemed a perfectly normal thing to do because he was more like family now to all of them. 'When you're well again you'll be able to play football with Tom.'

Stan held tightly to her hand and laughed. 'You'd better get in some practice, Tom, I was pretty good.'

Laughter eased the tension, and Stan gave Dora a grateful wink. 'Did you say something about sandwiches? I'm starving.'

Lily and June scrambled to their feet and ran to the kitchen, yelling, 'We'll get it ready!'

The doctor only had a cup of tea, then left. The others stayed for another hour until Reg stood up. 'I've got to take the car back to the station, but I'll drop you and June off first, Win.'

'Don't worry, we can walk.' Win helped her brother out of the chair. 'Have an early night, Stan. You must rest.'

He yawned, not protesting, clearly very weary. 'Thanks for the sandwiches and tea.'

'Any time,' Tom said, rushing to open the door. 'Everything's going to be all right, I just know it.'

'Of course it is. For all of us.'

Later that evening Alan arrived. 'I've come to see how you are, Stan.'

'Tired. Come in, Alan. I've been pushed and prodded. My God! The doc was thorough.'

'You'll be in good hands. This man is considered the best, and he's ahead of his time with some of the procedures he's carrying out. If anyone can help you, it's Doctor Burridge.'

'If I had any doubts about that I wouldn't let him near me.'

They talked for a while, and then Alan consulted his pocket watch. 'It's eight thirty. Do you think Dora would mind if I called on her at this hour?'

'I really don't know, but she'll be too polite to tell you if it is.'

Alan smiled. 'She's a nice girl, isn't she? Do you know they shared their picnic with me in the park? They all treated me so normally. It was like a breath of fresh air, I can tell you.'

Stan eyed Alan through narrowed eyes. 'They're special people. Don't do anything to hurt them because they've got enough problems at the moment.'

'I wouldn't dream of hurting them!' Alan remarked rather sharply. 'And what do you mean about them having problems?'

'You don't know?'

'They told me they'd lost their father in the war, but apart from that they never talked about themselves.'

Stan reached out for the newspaper and handed it to Alan. 'Page two.'

He read in silence, then looked up. 'This is awful! What's being done?'

'Everything possible, but we've had no luck so far.' Stan gave a worried sigh. 'We might never find her, and they could spend the rest of their lives wondering what happened to their mother.'

'Let's hope you find her soon.' Alan looked thoughtful. 'Perhaps Dora would like to go out one evening?'

'Perhaps.' Stan knew he had no right to object considering the state he was in. 'I'll have Tom and Lily here if she wants to.'

'That's good of you, Stan.' Alan stood up. 'I'll go and ask her now.'

'One thing you should know before you go, Captain. If the doc puts me back together again properly, then you'll have competition.'

'Ah, like that, is it?' Alan grinned. 'I outrank you, Sergeant.'

'Not out of the army, you don't!'

'True. In that case, may the best man win.'

They shook hands.

Lily was ready for bed when there was a knock on the door. Tom went to see who it was and returned with Alan.

'Oh!' Lily couldn't take her eyes off him. 'You're walking!'

'Dora told us.' Tom was just as pleased. 'You look good!'

'Thanks.' Smiling, Alan turned his attention to Dora. 'I hope you don't mind me calling so late, but I was with Stan and thought I'd pop in while I was here.'

'That's quite all right. You're just in time to say good night to Lily.'

'Dora!' the little girl protested.

Alan bent down and scooped her up, making her scream in delight. 'Show me where she goes, Tom.'

Dora listened to the laughter as they made their way upstairs. It was such a normal sound, but a rarity since their mother had disappeared. They had begun to refer to her in the past tense – even Lily. And really it was the only way they could cope with this terrible thing. If by some chance she was still alive and returned one day, Dora wondered if she would be able to forgive her for putting them through this horror. Their mother would have to have a very good reason before she did.

Alan was soon back, leaving Tom to settle Lily down for the night. He was serious now. 'I'm so sorry to hear about your mother. I only saw the newspaper this evening. If there's anything I can do for you, please do ask.'

'That's kind of you, but we're all right. Stan and his family are keeping an eye on us.'

'That's good, but I'll be around if you need me.' He smiled. 'I was wondering if you would come out with me one evening. We could have a meal and then go dancing. I'd really like to try out this leg,' he joked.

'That sounds lovely, but I don't think I could. It wouldn't seem right considering what's happened, and I couldn't leave my brother and sister on their own.'

'Stan said they could go in with him.' Alan wasn't about to give up.

'Did he?' Dora didn't know why, but that didn't please her. 'But he'll be going into hospital soon.'

'We could go out tomorrow.'

Dora shook her head, smiling to soften the refusal. 'Not at the moment, but you could ask me again when Stan's had his operation. I might feel more like going out then.'

'All right, I'll do that. And I won't take no for an answer.'

Nineteen

Two days later Stan went into hospital, ready for his operation on Monday. Nothing helpful had come from the newspaper appeal, and the rain was coming down in torrents on this Saturday morning, only adding to the Bentleys' gloom and worry.

'Is it ever going to stop raining?' Tom complained. 'What can we do in weather like this?'

Dora watched the water running down the windows. 'We can't go out, but tell you what, let's have a look and see what we can pawn. Then if it eases we can go and see how much money we can raise.'

'Are we broke?' Lily asked.

'Not quite, sweetie, but our money's going faster than I thought it would. Once Stan's had his operation we can go and visit him, so we're going to have fares to pay.'

'Yes.' She nodded eagerly. 'What are we going to sell? You can have my doll. I don't play with it now, I'm too big.'

She was touched by her sister's unselfish offer. She was small for a six-year-old and didn't look her age, and there was no way she would take her doll from her. It was always on the chair beside her bed, and even though she said she didn't play with it any more, Dora knew it was precious to her. It was the last gift their father had bought her – a father she didn't remember much about. 'Thank you, sweetie, but we have lots to sell before we need to consider your doll. We'll get rid of some of Mum's things first.'

'She isn't coming back, is she?' Lily's expression clouded.

Stooping down, Dora rested her hands on her sister's shoulders. 'I don't think she is. I could be wrong, but too much time has passed without word of her. We've got to think about ourselves now. Do you understand?'

Lily nodded, throwing her arms around Dora to give her a

quick hug, then she smiled. 'There's pretty things on her dressing table. We could sell them.'

'Good idea.' Dora stood up, relieved. It looked as if her sister was accepting the situation at last. Her biggest worry in all this was the little girl. She was missing her mother dreadfully and clinging to Tom and herself, but was trying so hard to be brave. Dora loved her all the more for it, and longed with all her heart that she could protect her from this distress. But, of course, she couldn't.

After an hour they had collected together several items, and as the rain had eased off, decided to go to the pawnbroker at once.

He was only a short walk away in the High Street, and by the time they reached the shop the rain had stopped completely. There was even a tiny patch of blue to be seen.

'Ah, hello.' The shopkeeper eyed them with pleasure. 'What have you brought me?'

They put the dressing table set and two glass dishes on the table. 'These are very pretty,' Lily told him, standing on tiptoe so she could see over the top of the counter.

He gazed down at her serious little face and even smiled. 'So I see. And what do you think I should give you for them?'

'Lots!'

'Well, I don't know about that.' He was all business again now and picked up each item to examine it carefully.

Lily couldn't stand the silence. 'We need lots because our friend is in hospital and we want to go and see him. The bus costs money,' she told him, almost accusingly.

Dora and Tom stood there saying nothing and fighting to remain serious. The pawnbroker obviously had a soft spot for children, especially Lily. They were quite happy to let her work her magic on him.

'I see.' He pursed his lips. 'In that case I'll give you three and sixpence for the lot.'

'That's no good, is it, Dora?' She turned to her big sister. 'They're worth more than that, aren't they?'

'Definitely!' Dora began to collect up the items. 'I think we'll find another pawnbroker, don't you Tom?'

'There's plenty of them around,' he agreed.

'Just a minute.' He wasn't one to let trade walk out the door. 'I'll make it five bob, and that's my final offer.'

She laid the items back on the counter. 'We'll take it.'

He shook his head ruefully. 'You youngsters, I'll be broke if I'm this generous with every customer. Too soft, that's what I am.'

Lily scooped up the money and handed it to Tom. All three of them left quickly, well pleased with the deal.

On the way home they called in to see Winnie and June. The two little girls disappeared out in the garden immediately, playing ball and chatting away quite happily.

'Hope you don't mind us calling, Winnie,' Dora said. 'But Lily wanted to see June. This weather has been terrible and we haven't been able to get out until now.'

'You're always welcome here.' Winnie ushered them into the kitchen. 'And you must stay for lunch. I've made a big saucepan of mutton stew, so there's plenty to go around.'

It smelt wonderful, but Dora was doubtful. 'There's three of us, Winnie. You can't afford to feed us all.'

'Of course I can. I've just bought a fresh loaf to have with it and soak up the gravy.'

Tom almost groaned with pleasure, and Dora smiled, readily agreeing to stay and share the mutton stew.

The following evening was nine o'clock before Reg finally arrived home. 'Where have you been? It's too late to go and see Stan now. It's a good job Dora's gone tonight. They're going to operate tomorrow.'

'Sorry, love, but I just couldn't get away.'

Winnie clenched her hands, unable to hide the concern she felt for her brother. 'I'm going to the hospital in the morning and I'll stay there until I know he's all right. Dora and Tom have agreed to look after June for me.'

'He'll be all right.' Reg placed an arm around her. 'He's a tough devil.'

She smiled up at her husband. 'Yes, he is, and wouldn't it be wonderful to see him free of pain? I know he's never said much, but the strain shows on his face.'

'This doctor's a good bloke, so if anyone can help Stan, it's him.' Reg looked preoccupied.

Winnie handed him a cup of tea and made him sit down. 'Have you found out anything yet?'

'We keep coming across another name, but you know I can't

discuss it with you, love. And we don't want a hint of this to reach those youngsters. We could be completely wrong and we don't want to cause them any more distress than necessary.'

'I can tell from your face you don't believe you are wrong.'

Reg shrugged. 'Too many coincidences, and that makes me suspicious.'

'Hmm.' Win pressed for more information. 'Do you think this is more than an ordinary woman running out on her children?'

'We don't know what to think at this point.' He smiled at his wife. 'How about getting me something to eat?'

'Sorry love, you must be starving. It won't take me long to heat up your dinner.' Winnie busied herself with the meal, knowing he wouldn't say any more about the case, but she didn't like his reference to another name cropping up. She had a nasty feeling about Mrs Bentley, and it was growing with every snippet of information she heard.

By the time she put his dinner on the table, her husband had a faraway expression on his face. He finished his meal in silence.

She chatted away, telling him about them coming round today. 'They're decent youngsters, aren't they? Whatever secrets their mother's been hiding, she's made a good job of bringing them up.'

When Reg merely nodded, Winnie couldn't help asking softly, 'Are they in for unpleasant news, love?'

He sighed, lit a cigarette and said nothing.

Twenty

S tan fought his way back to consciousness, vivid flashes like shells exploding around him – then awareness. He wasn't in the trenches again, but in a clean, comfortable bed.

'He's coming round,' he heard someone say. 'Tell the nurse, Win.'

Win? That was his sister. He moved his head from side to side in an effort to clear the muddle as panic swept through him. What had they done to him? He must have been crazy to agree to this.

'Take it easy, my boy. It's all over.'

Dragging his eyes open, he peered at the man bending over him. Dr Burridge. He lifted his head from the pillow so he could look down the bed . . .

'You're still in one piece.' The doctor held his wrist to check his pulse. 'Everything went well, and we expect you to make a good recovery.'

'Am I going to walk properly again?' He managed to croak out the words.

'That should be possible.' The doctor smiled. 'And I believe we've been able to safely remove the pieces of shrapnel from your body. But we'll be keeping an eye on you for a while just to make sure.'

'Thanks, doc.' Stan relaxed and screwed his eyes up tight, tears of relief threatening to spill over. Was he going to have a future after all?

'You may stay for another ten minutes,' the doctor said to Winnie and Reg. 'Then you must leave him to rest.'

Stan was already drifting off into a natural sleep.

'We must collect June and tell them that Stan's come through all right.' Winnie slipped her hand through her husband's arm as they headed for the bus stop. 'They'll be anxious for news.'

They were right. The door of the Bentleys' house was flung open before they had a chance to knock. Tom pulled them inside.

'How is he?' They all spoke at once.

Winnie told them what the doctor had said and watched their faces light up. The three youngsters had obviously become very attached to her brother.

'Oh goody!' Lily was hopping about in delight. 'When can we go and see him?'

'Tomorrow evening should be all right,' Winnie told them.

'We could go as soon as you get home, couldn't we, Dora?' Lily was gazing expectantly at her big sister. 'Did you get enough money for our fares? We could sell some more things if you didn't.'

'We've got enough. Don't you worry about that, sweetie.' She gave their visitors an embarrassed smile as Lily beamed.

After listening to that exchange, Winnie frowned. 'How short of money are you?'

'We can manage.' Dora smiled confidently.

Winnie wasn't convinced. 'You'll come to us if you're struggling, won't you?'

'We're doing all right,' Tom said, relieving Dora of the need to answer.

Reg stood up. 'We must go. Thank you for looking after June for us.'

'We'd be happy to do that any time.' Dora saw them to the door. 'And thank you for telling us about Stan. It's such a relief to know he's all right.'

Once they were away from the house and June was dancing along several steps ahead of them, Winnie's mouth set in a grim line. 'They're selling things. That job of Dora's can't pay much. She's beginning to struggle to keep her family together. How can she continue to pay the rent and keep those children in school? She'll need a better job. Why isn't she looking for one?'

'Win!' Reg stopped his wife. 'We can't force them to take help from us. They've got their pride, you know, and at the moment they must feel that's all they've got. They're sensible and they'll manage for a while. But I realize it's urgent for us to find their mother – dead or alive. Then the children will be all right. I promise.'

'I wish I knew what was going on because I can't see how you can make a promise like that.'

'I'll tell you as soon as we know we're not following a false trail. Now stop fretting, love. We'll keep an eye on them, and Stan will see they don't starve.'

'You're right, of course. I've always been a worrier, haven't I?'

'And I love you just the way you are.'

Winnie relaxed then, and smiled. 'You can be a real charmer at times, darling.'

He smirked. 'That's why you married me, isn't it?'

'When can I get out of this bed, nurse?'

'Not yet, Mr Crawford.' She gave him a stern look. 'Don't be impatient. You don't want to undo all the doctor's good work, do you?'

'Can I at least sit up?'

'Is he giving you trouble, nurse?' Dr Burridge appeared suddenly.

'Mr Crawford wants to sit up, sir.'

'I see. Well, let me have a look at him first.' The doctor took his time, and then stood back. 'I can give you something for the pain if it's too bad.'

Stan shook his head. 'It isn't as bad as it was before you operated.'

'That's a good sign.' He turned to the nurse who was patiently awaiting his instructions. 'Mr Crawford is well enough to sit up. I'll help you because we don't want to disturb his leg.'

It was good to see something other than the ceiling. He rested back on the pillows and sighed. 'That's better, thank you.'

Dr Burridge nodded. 'Now you behave yourself, my boy, and we'll soon have you back on your feet.'

The nurse straightened his blankets as the doctor left the ward. 'How about a nice cup of tea?'

'Thanks. Ah, can you make that two?' Reg was striding towards his bed.

'It isn't visiting time, Mr Crawford, but seeing he's a policeman I'll allow it this time.' The nurse hurried away to get the tea.

'You look a lot better today.' Reg pulled up a chair and sat beside the bed, pleased to see the improvement in his brother-in-law.

'I feel it. Something must have happened to bring you here in the morning. Have they found her?'

'Ah, I see your mind's in good working order again. I went to the station before coming here, but there's no trace of her. They are taking it seriously now, and they've agreed there might be a connection between Bentley and Duval. I've asked for permission to do a thorough search of the flat. They're going to let me know when it's agreed.'

'Damn!' Stan closed his eyes for a moment, then opened them again. 'And I'm stuck in this bed for who knows how long. I hope to goodness you find something to connect them soon, because we haven't got anything else to work on.'

'I'm convinced it's the same woman. The name's coming up too many times for it to be otherwise, Stan.'

'I know. How are they?'

Reg told him what Lily had said about the Bentleys selling things. 'They're coming to see you this evening, but don't say I've told you about this. Dora will be embarrassed.'

'I won't say a word. Poor little devils!' Stan became agitated. 'Don't let them move out of that house. I'll deal with this as soon as I can. And you can tell them at the station I'm coming back to work!'

'I'll be pleased to do that.' Reg stood up. 'And don't tell Win I've been here making you think. She'll never forgive me!'

Both men gave amused grins, then Stan waved him away. 'Get going. You've got investigating to do.'

As soon as his brother-in-law had gone Stan rested his head back and closed his eyes, but the case was running through his head, denying him rest.

An hour later the nurse found him scribbling away, listing everything they had found out about the case so far in an effort to clear his mind. There must be something – some small detail they had missed. The longer this went on, the harder it was on Mrs Bentley's children.

'Mr Crawford!' the nurse scolded. 'You're supposed to be resting.'

'I've been resting all day, nurse. And I'm only using my mind,' he joked. 'This is important.'

'It may well be, but visitors will be arriving in fifteen minutes.'

'Ah, sorry.' Stan quickly tucked his notes under the pillows, then rested back while his bed was straightened. He had an idea, and he hoped Reg would come back this evening.

His first visitors were the Bentleys, and he was so pleased to see them. The more he got to know them, the more he liked them – all of them, not just Dora. When their faces lit up with smiles as they walked towards him, he was determined to make a full recovery so he could look after them.

Lily was the first to reach him. She whispered, 'The nurse said I could come in if I behave myself.'

'And do you think you can?' he teased.

She giggled, holding on to his hand while her brother and sister greeted him. She prodded Tom until he pulled an apple out of his pocket and handed it to her. 'This is for you. I've polished it.'

Stan accepted the shiny piece of fruit, looking suitably impressed by its magnificence. 'Why thank you, Lily. I'll enjoy that very much.'

Looking pleased, the little girl now turned her attention to his leg, swathed in bandages and being held immobile in a cradle. She gave him a shy smile but said nothing.

'Find some chairs, Tom,' he said, 'and you can tell me what you've been doing.'

They spent the next half hour telling him about school and the Wandsworth house. Stan listened intently, watching their expressions. They never mentioned their mother, but he was uneasy. The strain was showing in their eyes, especially Dora's. He wanted to take her in his arms and tell her everything was going to be all right. But it wasn't. And that hurt him.

The nurse appeared. 'You have more visitors, Mr Crawford, and you aren't allowed more than two at a time.'

Dora was immediately on her feet. 'We're just leaving, nurse.'

After making them promise to come and see him again, Stan watched them leave the ward. Alan came in, walking confidently. Stan prayed that he himself would soon be able to do the same.

'You look good, Alan.'

'I feel it. And you don't look too bad yourself, considering.

I saw the doctor as I came in and he said they had high hopes for you.'

'It's going to take time though, and patience has never been one of my virtues.'

'Or caution, and I thank you for that. If you'd hesitated I wouldn't be here now.'

'You'd have done the same.' Stan changed the subject. 'How are you getting on?'

'Fine, I've even found myself a job.'

'That's good news.' Stan was pleased for him. Alan had never expected his men to do anything he wasn't prepared to tackle himself, and that had earned him respect among the ranks. Stan liked him as a man as well. Although he obviously came from the middle classes, he treated everyone with the same easy attitude. 'What are you going to do?'

'I was studying law before the war, and I'm going to work for a firm of solicitors. I'll take up my studies again and try to qualify.'

Stan gripped Alan's left hand. 'Congratulations!'

'Thanks, we might find ourselves working together some-time if you go back into the police force.'

'Or against each other.' Stan grinned at the thought.

'That too.' Alan glanced at his watch. 'Your sister and brother-in-law are waiting outside, so I'll make room for them. I've asked Dora and her siblings to wait for me. I've bought a car, so I'll be able to take them home. I'll come again.'

'Bring a bottle with you next time!'

Alan winked in agreement, then left.

Stan rested his head back, beginning to feel drained.

'Are you all right, Stan?'

At the sound of his sister's concerned voice he opened his eyes and smiled. When he saw Reg was with her he was immediately awake. 'I'm doing fine – so they tell me. How's June?'

'Waiting outside the ward. One of the nurses is letting her help make tea.'

'You can bring her in. Lily's just been in to see me.'

'Nurse said she'd let her in to see you about ten minutes before the end of visiting. She's quite happy, Stan.'

He nodded and looked at Reg. Both men were bursting to discuss the case, but thought it unwise while Win was there.

'Who was that man with you?' Winnie asked.

'That was Alan. I knew him in the army.'

'Hmm.' Winnie pursed her lips. 'Nice-looking man. Dora's waiting for him. Is he a friend of hers?'

'He was one of the doc's patients.' A slight smile touched Stan's lips, guessing just what his sister was thinking. 'He won't hurt Dora, because he knows if he does, he'll have me to deal with.'

That made his sister shake her head in disbelief. 'You couldn't deal with a kitten at the moment.'

'No, but give me a couple of months. Now, why don't you go and see if June's all right. I want to talk to Reg.'

She sighed and raised her hands in resignation. 'I might have known it. You've been working, haven't you?'

He merely looked innocent, and chuckled when his sister left them. He turned to Reg. 'I think you ought to see Roger Grant again. It's only a hunch, but I've got a strong feeling he's implicated in some way or another.'

'I trust your hunches. I'll be at that factory as soon as the gates open in the morning. And if I can find any proof that the man had a relationship with her, I'll have him down the station at once.'

'A night in the cells might jog his memory.' Stan rested his head on the pillows, drained.

'You'd better rest now.' Reg stood up and looked down at his brother-in-law. 'Try not to worry too much, Stan, we'll find the truth in the end, no matter how long it takes.'

'Whatever that is!' Stan pulled a face, aware that the truth could turn out to be unpleasant.

There was no further chance to talk as June came running into the ward, with her mother right behind her.

'Get back on your feet, Stan,' Reg murmured. 'We all need you.'

Twenty-One

True to his word, Reg was through the factory gates as soon as they were opened.

'Can I help you, Constable?' The gatekeeper stopped Reg, eyeing him in his uniform.

'I'd like a word with Mr Roger Grant, please.'

'Don't know if he's around, but I'll take you to the boss. He'll probably know where his son is.'

'Thanks.' Reg fell into step beside the man.

'One of your blokes was here not long ago. You still looking for that missing woman?' When Reg nodded, the man shook his head. 'If you ain't found her yet, then she's dead. Here we are.' The gatekeeper knocked on a door and opened it for Reg to enter the room.

Mr Grant senior stood up and shook hands with Reg.

'They're still looking for that woman,' the gatekeeper informed his boss, then left immediately.

'I don't know how I can help you. I told your colleague everything we know.'

'Just routine enquiries, sir. Your son worked on the night shift. I wondered if I could have a word with him?'

'Roger? I'm not sure if he's here. I'll send someone to look for him.' Mr Grant left the office, but was soon back. 'Might take a while, this is a big place. I've ordered tea for us while we wait.'

They had drained the teapot before the door opened. A man of around thirty walked in, and Reg studied him carefully. He was of average height with dark brown hair and eyes, very much like his father. And the policeman in Reg didn't trust him.

'This officer wants a word with you, Roger. You can use my office.' With a nod of his head he walked out.

As Roger sat in his father's chair, Reg thought it strange that his father hadn't stayed. It would have been a natural reaction to a policeman wanting to interview his son about something concerning the factory. Perhaps he knew his son too well?

'What can I do for you?' Roger asked. He was clearly nervous, but trying hard not to show it.

Removing his notebook from his top pocket, Reg pretended to read from it, taking his time before speaking. When he looked up there was a hint of perspiration on Roger's face. The man was anxious, and he wanted to keep him that way. 'When was the last time you saw Mrs Duval?'

'Who?'

'Duval.' Reg smiled. 'I believe you knew her.'

'Never heard of her.'

'Perhaps you knew her as Bentley?' Reg shrugged as if confused. 'Not sure what name she's using, but it was definitely Duval when she worked here on your night shift.'

'Duval.' Roger gazed into space as if trying to remember. 'Now I come to think about it, there was a woman by that name, but I didn't know her very well. Kept herself to herself. Why are you asking about her?'

Reg felt a tingle of excitement. Roger's voice had risen slightly, showing he was lying. 'She's missing. Hasn't anyone told you?'

'Oh, that one. Jim did mention it to me, but as I didn't know her very well I didn't take much notice.'

'So, when was the last time you saw her?'

'How the hell am I supposed to remember? She must have left when we closed down the night shift!'

Good, now the man was getting angry. 'She left about six months before that.'

Roger tried to look uninterested. 'That was the last time I saw her then.'

'You didn't meet her outside of work?' Reg persisted.

'No, I bloody well didn't!' Roger stood up suddenly. 'I've got work to do and I'm not answering any more of your questions.'

After writing in his notebook, Reg tucked it back in his pocket and stood up, holding out his hand. 'Thank you for your time, Mr Grant.'

When they shook hands, Roger's was wet with perspiration, and Reg left the factory feeling as if they had something to go on at last. He would be seeing Roger Grant again, that was for sure!

He'd pop into the hospital and see Stan. He'd want to know about this.

It had been a busy day at the house and Dora loved being here, but she couldn't help feeling guilty that she wasn't out looking for a job with better pay. Dr Burridge was relying on her more and more. She had taken over his office work, and he called on her quite often to help with the men. Sometimes they just needed someone to pour out their troubles to. There were often tears of despair from these shattered men, and it gave her immense satisfaction to see a smile appear on their faces again.

Word about the house was spreading and a constant flow of young men now came daily. This was where she wanted to be, and the thought of leaving upset her. She was now working a full week, some of it without pay. Tom was adamant that she should stay, assuring her that they would manage. He had wanted to get a job after school, but that was impossible as he had Lily to look after until Dora arrived home. She didn't dare look too far into the future. The prospects were frightening.

'Ready to go, Dora?'

At the sound of Alan's voice she turned and smiled. 'You mustn't keep doing this,' she scolded. 'I can get the train.'

'Why, when I've got my car outside? And this is the last time I'll be able to drive you home. I'm starting work tomorrow.'

'Oh, that's wonderful.' She knew how much these men wanted to work; to regain a little of their dignity.

He gave his usual easy grin. His features were perfectly sculptured, and his grey eyes seemed to show his every emotion. The only time they became veiled was when the war was mentioned. This was a kind man, and she knew Stan had great respect for him.

'And you said you'd come dancing with me when you knew Stan was all right.'

'I don't know that I can, Alan. What about Tom and Lily?'

'We could ask Stan's sister to have them for the evening. I'm sure they'd be pleased to do that for you.'

He was hard to resist, and she realized that she would like to go out with him. Just to have an evening where she could put all the worry behind her – and have fun. It made her feel selfish to be even considering it, but she had never been asked out before . . . The thought of doing something so normal was tempting.

Alan bent slightly so he could look into her eyes. 'Does this hesitation mean you'll come?'

'I'll have to see Winnie first.'

'We'll go there now, and then I can take them to visit Stan.'

They were both soon in the car and heading for Winnie's.

Reg was also at home when they called and Alan didn't hesitate. 'We've come to ask a favour. I want to take Dora out dancing, but she's concerned about leaving Tom and Lily alone for the evening. Would you be kind enough to look after them?'

Dora was uncomfortable, and she spoke quickly. 'We'll understand if you can't do it.'

'Of course we can.' Winnie smiled at Alan. 'When would you like to go?'

'Tonight? I'll drive you to see Stan, and we'll collect the children around eleven.'

'Oh, that's far too late for Lily!' Dora protested.

'Why not let Lily sleep here?' Reg suggested, glancing at his daughter who was beaming from ear to ear at the prospect. 'I'm sure June would be happy to share her bed.'

'Excellent idea! That's very kind of you.'

Dora could only stand there feeling helpless as Alan arranged everything. 'I can see you're used to giving orders, Captain!'

He broke into a lazy smile, and Dora could see that Stan's family were just as captivated with him. June had remained quiet, never taking her eyes off the tall man.

'We'll be back in an hour,' Alan announced as he guided Dora out of the house.

He was chuckling quietly to himself as they got back in the car. 'There, that wasn't any bother, was it?'

Dora blew out a pent-up breath. 'Oh, no trouble at all. You never gave them a chance to refuse.'

'Are you saying I'm bossy?'

'Yes!' Dora glanced at him and they burst out laughing.

When they reached the house, Alan organized Tom and Lily with the same authority. Cramming seven in his car was impossible, so he drove Winnie and all the children to the hospital first and then came back for Reg and herself. They dropped Reg off at the hospital and Alan whisked Dora away, wasting no time.

'I thought we were going in to see Stan for a couple of minutes?'

'Take too long, and you can see him tomorrow.'

He drove to a private officers' club in Piccadilly. It was only when they walked in that Dora realized Alan was not middle class, as she'd assumed, but a step up from that. After her hat and coat had been taken from her, she tipped her head to one side and studied him thoughtfully.

'What?' he asked.

'I was just wondering if you have a title.'

'No.' He slipped her hand through his arm as they walked into the dimly lit room. There was a small dance floor surrounded by tables. He led her over to one near the band and held the chair for her. Then he sat down and raised his eyebrows to the waiter.

'Yes, sir?'

'Champagne, please.'

'Certainly, sir.'

Dora gazed around with interest. This was a very different world from the one she lived in, but she had no fears that she would disgrace herself. Their mother had taught them how to behave, no matter what class of society they found themselves in. Dora had never given it much thought before but now she wondered, how had her mother known so much about etiquette?

'Hey.' Alan touched her hand. 'I'm being ignored here!'

'Sorry, that's rude of me.' Dora picked up her glass and took a sip. 'Are you a member here?'

'No, too stuffy for my liking. I prefer the Wandsworth house. They let me in because my father's a member.'

'Is he an army officer as well?'

'Not now, he's retired.' Alan stood up and bowed elegantly. 'Will you dance with me, Miss Bentley?'

'Thank you, sir. I'd love to.'

The time seemed to fly by, and for a short while Dora

relaxed enough to push away the horror of her mother's disappearance. Alan was good company, charming and attentive.
He had a dry wit, making her laugh often.

They were about to leave when a distinguished couple came
in and walked straight up to Alan. He introduced Dora to
Brigadier Stanton and his wife.

After the introduction, the brigadier turned his attention
back to Alan. 'How's the General?'

'He's fine, sir.'

'Good, good. Tell him I'll be in touch.'

'I'll do that. He'll be pleased to see you.' Alan took Dora's
arm and led her out.

She stopped when they were on the pavement and stared
at him. 'General?'

'Hmm, retired.'

'And what does the *General* do now he's retired?'

'He's a barrister.'

'Alan!' Dora was shaking her head in astonishment. 'What
on earth are you doing taking me out? I'm nothing more than
a housemaid!'

'Don't you ever put yourself down like that!' He spoke
sharply. 'You're a lovely caring girl, and obviously well
educated. You're as good as anyone else – and don't you
forget it!'

'No, sir!' The laughter faded from her eyes when she said,
'You sounded just like my mother then. She always told us
that.'

'And she was right,' Alan said softly. 'The war has changed
a lot of the old ways, Dora. The class barriers aren't so important now. We all fought and died together. Things will never
return to the way they were, and that's a good thing.'

'Yes, I agree.'

Twenty-Two

Two weeks later Stan had had enough. Reg hadn't been able to make any progress with the investigation. Bloomsbury police had given him access to their findings in the hunt for Mrs Duval – which were next to nothing – but had not considered the connection with Mrs Bentley strong enough to give him permission to do a thorough search of the flat. Both men were frustrated about this, but there was nothing they could do until they had some proof that the missing Mrs Duval was indeed Mrs Bentley. And another thing fretting Stan was the fact that Alan was seeing far too much of Dora.

'Damn it, doc!' Stan swore when Dr Burridge appeared at his bedside. 'How much longer are you going to keep me tied to this bed?'

'Is he always this bad tempered, nurse?' he asked mildly.

'I'm afraid so, sir. If he could get hold of a pair of crutches he'd be out of here as soon as my back was turned.'

Stan calmed down and grinned. 'She's hidden them.'

'Hmm, very wise. I'll have a look at your back first. How does it feel?'

'Better than ever. There's no pain there at all now.'

'It's healed well.' The doctor examined Stan's leg, nodded in satisfaction and sat on the edge of the bed. 'It will be at least another two weeks before you can put any weight on your leg, but it's looking good. Your back's now strong enough for you to use crutches. Nurse will find a pair for you, if she can remember where she's hidden them.'

'Can I go home?' Stan asked eagerly.

'In a day or two. I want to see how you manage first. You're going to be rather weak when you start to move around, but you're a tough man and it shouldn't take you too long to get back to normal.'

The nurse appeared with the crutches. She was accompanied by a young man.

'Ah, good, you've brought help. Let's get Mr Crawford on his feet before his language gets any worse, shall we?' The doctor stood up and moved away from the bed.

Stan's head swam alarmingly when he stood up.

'Take deep breaths,' the nurse ordered, seeing his difficulty.

As his head cleared he straightened up. 'I'm all right now.' The walk to the other side of the ward and back was hard, but he made it and was satisfied.

'Use the next couple of days to get your strength back,' the doctor said, giving him a stern look. 'And remember, *don't* put your foot on the ground until I say you can.'

'I'll be careful,' Stan promised, grateful he was moving around again at last. 'Thanks for everything you've done for me.'

'Glad we could help.' The doctor's eyes glowed with amusement. 'One of the first things you've got to do when you get out of here is to stop Dora going out with Alan. He isn't the man for her.'

Stan's mouth opened in astonishment. 'I agree with you, but what makes you think I can do that?'

'I've got eyes in my head, and I have every faith in your powers of persuasion.' The doctor began to turn away, then faced Stan again, his expression serious now. 'And you must find out what's happened to her mother. That poor family aren't going to be able to get on with their lives until this mystery is resolved.'

Stan nodded. 'I'm convinced she's dead.'

'Then find the body and let them bury her. It's important, Stan. Dora's putting a brave face on things, but she has the added responsibility of her brother and sister. That weighs heavily on her. She needs an end to this nightmare.'

'I won't let her down, doc.'

Dr Burridge nodded, then left the ward.

'Look at you!' Reg strode in. 'You're out of bed.'

'And I'll be home in a day or two.' Stan was pleased to see his brother-in-law. Reg never bothered with official visiting times, he just came in whenever he felt like it and no one stopped him.

'You must come and stay with us until you're completely recovered.'

'Thanks, but I'd rather be in my own home. I can manage well enough.' To prove this he did the walk again, smiling all the time. 'See. I've got to use the crutches until my leg's healed, then the doc's sure I'll be able to walk again.'

Reg smiled with relief. 'I've told them at the station that you'll be coming back on the force. Now, sit down and I'll bring you up to date with things.'

Stan settled, hoping there was some progress.

'I've finally convinced the Bloomsbury police that there could be a connection between the two women, and they've agreed to let us search the flat. But I want to wait until you can come with me. You've got a sharp eye and might see something I'd miss.'

'We'll go as soon as I'm out of here,' Stan said eagerly. 'Anything else?'

'Nothing solid.' Reg sat back and sighed deeply. 'One minute I'm convinced Duval is Dora's mother, the next I'm sure she can't possibly be.'

'I know the feeling, but it's all we've got to go on, Reg. Have you spoken to Roger Grant again?'

'Yes, but he's still denying he knew her. I'm sure he knows more than he's telling though. He's uneasy and evasive, and he couldn't get away from me fast enough.'

'Leave him to stew for a while. We'll get back to him later. All we've got are suspicions that he's hiding something from us, and that isn't enough.'

Reg's expression was grim. 'I wish we could find her. We're worried about those youngsters. Lily won't talk about her mother any more. It's as if she's closed her mind because it hurts too much. Tom's masking his worry with anger, he's convinced that their mother has just abandoned them. And then there's Dora . . .'

'How is she, Reg? I haven't seen much of her lately because Alan's been taking her out, I believe.'

'They've been out a few times, but it's hard to tell how she's feeling. We do know they're struggling and are pawning things to survive. Every time we offer to help she just smiles brightly and tells us they're quite all right.' Reg slapped the bed hard in frustration. 'If that woman's dead there must be a body somewhere. Why the hell haven't we found any trace of her?'

'London's a huge city and an easy place for people to disappear in.' Stan held his brother-in-law's gaze. 'She might be in the Thames.'

Reg was shaking his head. 'The river gives up her dead

eventually. She'd have surfaced by now. But our immediate concern must be for the children. Dora's too proud to ask for help. We need to do something!'

'That's all we bloody well keep saying!' Stan muttered irritably. 'When the Bentleys came to me for help I never dreamt this would become such a tangled web.'

Dora was thrilled when Winnie told her that Stan was coming home the next day. 'Is he staying with you until he's fully recovered?'

'No, he's insisting on going back to his own house. I've talked myself dry trying to persuade him to live with us for a while.' Winnie gave a helpless shrug. 'But he's determined to manage on his own, and you know how stubborn he can be.'

'I do,' Dora agreed. 'But don't worry. I'll keep an eye on him to make sure he's all right.'

'Thanks, that does ease my concern. Alan's going to collect him tomorrow evening and bring him home in his car.'

'That's good.'

'You look tired,' Winnie said gently. 'Is there anything I can do?'

An expression of anguish suddenly appeared on Dora's face, so intense that it nearly made Winnie cry. 'Oh, my dear . . .'

'Why haven't they found her?' Dora's self-control wavered. 'It's nearly six weeks. We've got to know. We can't go on like this! I'll soon have to find us somewhere cheaper to live.' She spun in a circle as if lost. 'But where? Lily and Tom like it here, they love their schools. I can't ask them to leave. It'll break their hearts. Tom's doing so well. He's a clever boy. I've been trying to find another job, but even if I do I'll never earn enough for us to stay here. I don't know how Mum did it after Dad was killed. Where did the money come from? Where is she? What's going on, Win?'

'Dora!' Winnie stopped the distressed girl. 'I know you've got a thousand questions running through your head, it's only natural. And things do look hopeless at the moment. But you have friends. Stan is coming home and he's going to be well again. We'll all help because we care about you.'

Taking a deep breath, Dora stepped back. 'I won't take money from any of you. You can't afford to help in that way.

Your own family must come first. I've got to sort this out myself or we'll end up in the workhouse.'

'No!' Winnie was horrified that things were this bad. They'd been so concerned about Stan that none of them had noticed Dora's struggle. And knowing the girl as she now did, she was certain Dora had not told her brother and sister about this. 'That will never happen!'

Dora was standing, head bowed and arms hanging limply by her sides, a picture of dejection. Then her head came up, mouth once again set in a determined line. 'No, of course not. Please forgive my outburst, but it's so hard.'

'You don't have to ask forgiveness, my dear. I doubt there are many people who'd cope as well as you. Be proud of the way you're managing this terrible tragedy. Now, I'll walk you home.'

'That isn't necessary.' Dora spoke with conviction. 'I'm quite all right, I just have to let it all out sometimes or I'll burst! I only wish Stan and Reg would tell us what they've found out. I believe it's something they don't want us to know, because they've stopped talking to us. I haven't said anything while Stan's been in hospital, but we need to know, no matter how bad. Will you tell them that, Win?'

'Of course.' She watched Dora leave the house and walk up the road. Her head was held high, but Winnie now recognized the terrible strain Dora was under. She cried for all three of Mrs Bentley's children, but mostly for the eldest who was giving all her love and support to others when she was the one most in need.

An hour later Reg arrived home, soon after June had finished school for the day. 'You're early.' Winnie kissed her husband. 'We can all go and see Stan tonight.'

'Hmm.' Reg studied his wife's face. 'You're upset. Is there something wrong? Stan's all right, isn't he?'

'He's fine. But you're right, something has happened. I'll tell you about it later. Stan needs to hear this as well.' She was now very cross. Stan and Reg had no right to keep anything from the youngsters, and she was going to make sure they damned well knew it! But she wasn't going to discuss this in front of June in case she said something to Lily and upset her.

'Can't you tell me now?'

'No, I need the two of you together.'

The corners of Reg's mouth twitched. 'Ah, I know that tone of voice. I think we're in trouble. What have we done?'

'It's what you haven't done that's the trouble. Now, sit down and have your tea, then we can go to the hospital.'

'Is Dora coming with the children this evening?'

'No, I don't think they can afford the fare. Not that Dora would admit to that.'

Reg frowned. 'Alan brings them sometimes.'

'He's busy.'

Her husband noted the sharp tone and was wise enough to let the subject drop.

They were waiting outside the ward before visiting hours. June was already being amused by one of the junior nurses, and Winnie couldn't wait to see Stan.

As soon as it was time, she marched into the ward, but Reg beat her to Stan's bedside.

'Oh-oh! I know that look. What have we done, Reg?'

Winnie waded straight in. 'You can wipe those smirks off your faces. I don't know what you've found out about Mrs Bentley, but whatever it is you've got to tell her children. This can't go on! I've just found out Dora's situation is getting desperate. She might do something stupid like marry Alan to give Tom and Lily a secure future.'

The amusement drained from Stan's face. 'Tell us what the hell you mean by that!'

Winnie sat on the edge of the bed and told them what had happened when she'd seen Dora this afternoon. By the time she'd finished her eyes were clouded with tears, and both men were silent.

Stan leant back against the pillows, his mouth set in a straight line. 'Thank God I'm getting out of here tomorrow. We thought we were protecting them, but all we seem to have done is made things harder for Dora.'

'You see you put this right as soon as you can. I got the impression that Dora would rather have any news than nothing at all, even if it is bad.'

Reg took hold of Winnie's hand. 'Don't upset yourself so, darling. We'll tell them everything we know – though it isn't much. Won't we, Stan?'

'As soon as I'm home.'

Twenty-Three

'They're here!' Lily was thrilled about Stan coming home, rushing to the front door as soon as Alan's car turned into the street.

Tom caught hold of his little sister at the gate, and Dora joined them so they could wave and let him know how pleased they were to see him home again. They waited while Reg helped Stan out of the car.

'Oh, he's still on crutches,' Lily said, disappointed.

'It'll only be for a little while.' Tom ruffled his sister's hair and smiled down at her. 'Then he'll be able to walk without them.'

Stan looked across and smiled at them, then called, 'I could do with one of your special cups of tea, Lily.'

'I'll put the kettle on.' Lily was fighting to open the gate, but was still being restrained by her brother.

Winnie walked over to them. 'Stan wants you all to come in.'

'Are you sure?' Dora was hesitant. 'He probably needs peace and quiet on his first evening out of hospital.'

'Not a bit of it.' Winnie's smile was one of pure joy. 'I haven't seen him this lively since he was hurt. He's free of pain, Dora!'

'That's wonderful. And we'd love to come in . . . if you're sure it's all right?'

'Positive!'

Tom was just as eager to see Stan again. Keeping a firm grip on his sister he opened the gate and made straight for the car.

'Come on, Dora,' Winnie urged. 'He wants to see you.'

'He'll need something to eat.' Dora walked beside Winnie.

'We've already thought about that, and I'll see to it. He's got plenty of food because I've stocked his larder today.'

When Dora walked into the front room, Stan was already

in his favourite armchair, his leg resting on a stool. He looked up and smiled, making emotion well up inside her. What a difference! The deep lines of strain that had marred his strong features were already smoothing out. Lily was standing beside him, holding his hand.

Alan came up to Dora and spoke softly. 'It does your heart good to see the improvement, doesn't it? I owe him a debt I'll never be able to repay.'

'Right!' Winnie called for attention. 'Reg is going to the chippy. Who wants fish and who wants pie?'

The orders were called out and Reg wrote them down, but Alan shook his head. 'Not for me, Reg. As much as I'd like to, I can't stay.'

'Thanks for bringing me home, Alan.'

'My pleasure. You look after yourself, Sergeant, and soon we'll both be able to take Dora dancing.'

'That's a date, Captain.' Both men grinned at each other, the mutual respect obvious. They came from different backgrounds, but their experiences in the trenches had made them equal.

'I'll drive you to the chippy, Reg.' Alan waved to everyone and left, promising to come back the next evening.

'I'll put the plates in the oven to warm.' Winnie went to the kitchen and Dora followed.

'You can't pay for all this food, there are three of us. I'll go home and get my purse.'

'Stan's insisted on paying by way of celebration. He'll be offended if you don't accept.'

'Oh, I didn't realize that. It's kind of him.'

'He's a kind man.' Winnie smiled indulgently as she thought about her brother. 'He can be a bit sharp at times but he's a strong man, and I thank God for that. I don't think he would have survived if he hadn't been.'

'I know. Tom and Lily adore him. I don't know what we'd have done without him.'

Winnie gave Dora a sideways glance. 'And what about you? Do you adore him as well?'

Dora busied herself finding the salt and vinegar, speaking quietly. 'I like him very much.'

'As much as you like Alan?' Winnie persisted.

'Alan's good company and he's pleased because we treat him like a human being and not a damaged casualty of war, but his world is different from ours.' Dora looked up, a slight smile on her face. 'His father was a general and since he retired he's become a barrister. Can you imagine what his family would say if he brought home a housemaid?'

'You're not serious about him then?'

'Good gracious, no! He insists the class barriers are crumbling, and between himself and Stan that's true. But for the rest of us they still exist. It would never do for us to be more than friends.'

Reg arrived back with his arms full of packets wrapped in newspaper. It was a scramble to get it all dished out on the hot plates. And rather than disturb Stan, they decided to eat in the front room like a picnic.

This was greatly enjoyed, especially by Lily. As soon as they'd finished, Winnie took the plates into the kitchen, made tea and ordered Dora to sit down.

'We want to tell you what's been happening in the investigation to find your mother,' Reg told them. 'We haven't said much because it's all supposition and coincidence, but you should know what little we've found out.'

Stan told them how the name Duval kept turning up, and everything they'd done in the last weeks. He left nothing out.

Tom was shaking his head. 'But you've no proof Mum was using that name. And why would she? It doesn't make sense.'

'I agree it's confusing.' Stan leant forward. 'Didn't your mother ever talk about her past, what part of London she came from or anything like that? Do you know where she met your father?'

'She came from where all the big ships are,' Lily piped up. 'Dad was on one of them.'

Dora and Tom looked at their sister in astonishment. 'How do you know that?'

'She told me once when I was sick and not at school. Long time ago, but I remember.'

'Was your dad unloading the boats?'

Lily gazed at Stan, screwing up her face in concentration. 'Don't think so. She said he sailed on them.'

'Oh, that's right.' Tom slapped his head. 'Dad told me once that he'd been in the merchant navy but had given it up when they'd moved to London.'

Reg was now pacing the floor. 'Why didn't you tell us this before?'

Tom shrugged. 'Can't see what it's got to do with Mum disappearing.'

'Probably nothing, but we need every scrap of information.' Stan looked questioningly at his brother-in-law before turning his attention back to Tom. 'Do you know what port he sailed from?'

'No idea. Why, do you think Mum's gone back there?'

'It's something we'll have to look into. What do you think, Reg – Southampton or Portsmouth?'

'We'll have to make enquiries at both, but first we must search the flat. There might be something there.'

Stan agreed. 'We'll go in the morning.'

'We'll come with you.'

Both men looked sharply at Tom, and Reg shook his head. 'I don't think so.'

'It's no good you saying no to us!' Dora was on her feet now. 'You seem to think this Duval woman is our mother. I don't for one moment believe that's true, so let's clear this up once and for all. If there's anything in that flat belonging to Mum, then we'll know.'

Tom was standing shoulder to shoulder with his big sister, feet slightly apart, an expression on his face that left no doubt about his determination. He wasn't going to back down on this point. 'We're grateful you're looking for Mum, but you seem to have wasted a lot of time chasing after some other woman.'

'Now look here, young man,' Reg bristled at the youngster's tone, 'the name Duval has cropped up too many times for us to ignore it!'

'Have you considered she might be a friend of Mum's?' Dora was also very sceptical. She didn't want to argue too much with these men who were trying to help them – Stan's family had been very kind to them and the last thing she wanted to do was seem ungrateful – but like her brother she'd had enough. They had stayed in the background while the investigation went on, but things had been kept from them. They would not allow that to happen again.

Stan studied the two rather angry youngsters. 'We've considered every angle, Dora,' he said gently. 'There's no denying that the name has a strong connection to your mother. They're both missing – if it is two women – and finding one might lead to the other.'

Alarmed by the heated discussion, Lily looked from one person to another, then ran to Winnie who was sitting quietly with her daughter. 'Why they shouting at each other, Auntie Winnie?'

'They're not shouting, dear. They don't agree with each other, that's all.'

Lily was shaking her head vigorously. 'Oh no, Tom's mad, and so's Dora.' She left Winnie and ran to her brother and sister. 'Stop it! Stan's just come out of hospital. You're upsetting him!' She stamped her foot. 'I won't let you do that. He's got to be looked after or he won't get well.'

There was a stunned silence as all eyes turned on the little girl who was now standing protectively beside Stan. Her bottom lip jutted out, daring them to raise their voices again.

'Who would have believed it?' Reg ran a hand over his face, trying to control his amusement. 'The three Bentley children have thorns.'

Dora winked at Lily, making her giggle, then she turned to Reg. 'What time shall we be ready in the morning?'

'We? Tom and Lily have to go to school.'

'They'll be having the day off. All three of us will be coming to have a look at the flat.'

'I don't think Lily should come—'

'I'm coming!' Lily stopped Reg in mid-sentence. 'I don't know where we're going, but I'm coming. Aren't I, Dora?'

'You most certainly are. We're all in this together.'

Lily nodded proudly. 'And I've got to come because I've got to look after Stan.'

'My God, Stan, you've made a conquest there!' Reg could hardly contain his laughter.

Stan grinned. 'Might as well give in, Reg. And they're right, if there's anything in the flat belonging to their mother, they'll spot it.'

'True.' Reg nodded in resignation, then turned to Dora. 'I'll call for you at ten tomorrow morning.'

'Thank you, we'll be ready.' Dora then held out her hand to Lily. 'Come on, sweetie, time we left Stan in peace.'

When the Bentleys had left, Reg sighed. 'I need a stiff whisky. What about you, Stan?'

'A double will go down well. You know where I keep it, Reg.'

Winnie and June were busy in the kitchen as the men settled down to enjoy their drinks. Reg looked intently at his brother-in-law. 'You look worried, Stan. I think there's something else on your mind.'

Taking a gulp of whisky, Stan grimaced. 'It was Tom's remark that we've been wasting our time.'

Meaning?'

'Well, we've been concentrating on London. But what if she wasn't a Londoner? Why is the woman such a mystery, Reg? Somehow we've got to find out more about her.'

'Hmm, you're right, of course, but no one seems to know a damned thing about her! Perhaps we'd better start looking into the father. He was a merchant seaman and only moved back to London after he'd married her. We need to find out what port he sailed from.'

Stan downed his drink. 'This is such a tangled web, and I'm beginning to imagine all sorts of unpleasant things.'

'We'll get to the bottom of it eventually, Stan. Try not to worry. You've got to get well again. Another drink?'

'Thanks.'

'We won that argument,' Tom said as soon as they were back in their own house, obviously very satisfied with the outcome.

'I never had any intention of losing. They're wrong about that other woman and the flat. You were right to say they've been wasting their time.' Dora headed for the stairs to put Lily to bed, and Tom followed. 'They have been wasting their time!'

'Reg didn't like us telling him that, did he?'

'We can't worry about hurting his feelings, Tom. And anyway, once Lily waded in, that was the end of the objections.'

'I stopped you all, didn't I?' Lily told them proudly, and then gave them a stern look. 'You mustn't upset Stan. He's got to get better and then he can take care of us.'

Dora was stunned. 'We can't expect that of him, sweetie. He's agreed to help us find Mum, but we can't expect more than that of him.'

'He told me he would.' Her bottom lip trembled. 'What we going to do without Mum?'

'Hey, what's all this?' Tom sat on the edge of Lily's bed. 'You've got us to care for you. Isn't that good enough?'

'Oh, yes, but you're not very old, and you need someone to love you as well.' Lily gave Dora a hesitant glance from under lowered lashes. 'Now Stan's going to get better you could marry him, and then we'd have a big family. I'd like that.'

'I expect you would!' Dora dug her brother in the ribs to stop his spluttering laugh. Their sister had obviously been turning this over and over in her mind, and the idea had to be squashed at once. 'Lily, things don't work out like that. People have to fall in love before they marry. I like Stan very much, but he told me that he'll never marry.'

'Oh. He'd make a lovely dad.' Lily thought this over for a few moments and then smiled again. 'Alan's nice too.'

'Lily!' Dora was laughing now. 'Alan comes from a posh family. He'd never want to marry me. Anyway, I like him as a friend, that's all.'

'You'll soon find someone. You're very pretty, Dora.'

'Thank you very much.' Dora kissed her sister. 'Now, I think it's time you stopped making all these plans for me and went to sleep.'

'Hmm . . .' The little girl snuggled down under the blankets and then popped her nose out again, a saucy grin on her face. 'I did stop you all arguing though, didn't I?'

'You certainly did. We're very proud of you.'

Tom ruffled her hair. 'Next time I get in a fight I'll expect you to come and rescue me.'

She reached out to catch hold of Dora's hand. 'Will Stan be all right on his own tonight?'

'Of course he will. He has his family looking after him.'

'We're his family as well. And I'll look after him tomorrow.' She yawned and fell asleep immediately.

Downstairs again Tom opened the cocoa tin and looked inside. 'We've just got enough for two cups. Do you want one, Dora?'

'Please.' She sat down and stared thoughtfully into space. 'It looks as if our sister has adopted Stan and is trying to get me married off. She's looking for a father figure in her life, isn't she? Someone to make her feel secure.'

'That's because she's frightened.' Tom put two cups of steaming cocoa on the table and sat down. 'And let's be honest, Dora, we're all frightened.'

'Of course we are. The worst part is not knowing. What do you make of this nonsense about Mum using a different name? Why on earth would she do such a thing?'

'Goodness knows.' Tom cradled his drink in his hands. 'Like you, I believe they're wrong, but one thing I have found out is that it's not cheap living here. Mum was getting money from somewhere and we know it wasn't from the factory. So she was doing something she didn't want us to know about. It's a bloody mystery.'

'Watch your language,' Dora scolded.

'Sorry, but it's enough to make anyone swear. And talking about money, we need to pawn something again.'

At the mention of money, worry gripped Dora. 'We can't go on like this. In another couple of weeks we'll really have to talk about moving.'

'I know.' Tom sighed deeply. 'But where can we go?'

'I'll find somewhere, but in the meantime we need to raise some money. What can we pawn this time?'

'There's the necklace. It might be worth something.'

'We promised that to Lily. I don't want to sell it unless we're desperate.'

Tom grimaced. 'We're getting that way, aren't we?'

'I still don't want to sell the necklace, and it's probably not worth much. I was looking at it yesterday and it shines very nicely in the light, so I think it's more than glass – some fake stones probably . . .'

Tom snorted. 'Of course it is. If they were real diamonds it would be worth a fortune. We could take it somewhere and have it looked at.'

Dora rubbed her hand over her eyes, too tired to even think clearly. 'I'm getting more confused by the day. And I don't think I want to know if it's valuable.'

'What you need is a good night's sleep.' Tom stood up and pulled her to her feet. 'Come on, we've got a busy day tomorrow.'

Twenty-Four

The building was impressive, making Tom draw in a sharp breath.

'I know,' Dora said, reading his mind. 'This is ridiculous. Mum could never afford to live in a place like this.'

'Be careful now!'

Lily's voice made Dora turn. Stan had somehow managed to borrow a car for the day. Reg had driven them here and was now helping his brother-in-law out, with Lily watching anxiously. Once he was safely on his crutches they went inside.

'Oh, lots of wide stairs,' the little girl gasped as she reached up to touch Stan's hand. 'You can stay down here. There's a nice chair in the corner.' She sounded so grown up as she worried about the man she had become very fond of.

He smiled down at her. 'I can make it, and there are even nicer chairs in the flat. You go on up and I'll be there in a minute.'

Reg handed Dora the key. 'It's the first door on the right at the top of this first flight of stairs.'

Tom stayed behind as well. Seeing that Stan had plenty of help and probably didn't want them to see his struggle to climb the stairs, she took Lily by the hand. 'Come on, let's see what this posh flat is like, shall we?'

The key turned easily, and as Dora walked into the lounge she had the most peculiar sensation. She almost expected to see her mother sitting there with a book in her hands. She was a great reader. But her imagination had run away with her again. This place was nothing to do with their mother. It couldn't be!

Lily was gazing round the room, eyes wide in wonder. She trotted across the carpet and stopped at an exquisite gold satin settee, running her hands over the soft furnishing. 'Can I sit on this?' she whispered.

'Of course you can.' Stan came in, swung himself over to

Lily and sat down, patting the seat beside him. When the little girl clambered up beside him, he said, 'There, told you there were more comfortable chairs here, didn't I?'

Her smile couldn't get any wider. 'Is this like the house you worked in, Dora?'

'Not really.' She didn't quite know what to say. Everything here was clearly expensive, but it lacked the elegance of the Barrington house. This was too bright . . .

Tom had been darting from room to room. Finished with his first inspection, he stood beside his sister. 'Strange place,' he muttered under his breath. 'Wait till you see the rest of it.'

'I'm not sure I want to.' She felt uneasy and it wouldn't have taken much to make her walk out. But she had better stop being silly and get on with what they had come here for. 'What do you want us to do, Reg?'

'Go through every cupboard and drawer. We're looking for papers, letters, photographs – anything that might have been missed in the first search. There must be something to tell us who this woman was.'

'Right.' Tom was immediately opening a desk in the corner of the room.

An hour later they had nothing. Every piece of correspondence was in the name of Duval, and there was very little of that. One thing that struck all of them was that there wasn't a photo in the place.

'Knew it was a waste of time,' Tom declared. 'This woman is nothing to do with our mum.'

'These are Mum's. She was wearing these when she left for work.'

They all spun round to face Lily. She had a pair of shoes in her hand.

Dora rushed over and took them from her sister, willing her hands to stop shaking. She wasn't going to show weakness again. A couple of times she had crumbled – and she wasn't going to allow that to happen again. It was too worrying for Tom and Lily. Willing her racing heart to slow down, she examined the shoes. Their mother did have a pair like these and they weren't in the wardrobe at home, but . . .

'Are they?' Stan was beside her now.

'They are her size, but it's a common shoe sold in all the shops. Where did you find them, Lily?'

'There's a cupboard by the front door.'

Tom was soon on his hands and knees searching through the jumble of things packed in the small space. Eventually, he sat back on his heels. 'There's nothing else here that could possibly belong to Mum.'

'That's a relief,' Dora said under her breath. 'I don't want Mum to have anything to do with this place. I don't like it.'

'Why?' Lily looked puzzled. 'It's pretty.'

'I don't know why, sweetie.' Dora shrugged. 'Put the shoes back. I expect the lady used them for walking when the weather was bad.'

''Spect so.' Lily handed them to Tom and watched him close the cupboard door.

Tom stood up. 'Dora's right. Loads of women have shoes like those.'

'Well, there's nothing more we can do here.' When Reg opened the front door he was confronted with the neighbour.

'Oh, it's you again. Have you found her?' she demanded.

'No, madam.'

She pushed past him, staring at the Bentleys. Her eyes narrowed as she studied Dora. 'Who are you? What's your name?'

'Dora Bentley, madam.'

Lily slid behind Dora, peering out at the imposing woman.

Before the neighbour could ask more questions, Stan moved forward, smiling politely. 'If you'll excuse us, madam, we must be going.'

He was taking up so much room with his crutches that the woman had no choice but to step back on to the landing. Reg locked the front door and urged them down the stairs, staying behind to help Stan.

'Who was that?' Dora asked as soon as they were in the car and on their way. 'I wouldn't like to get on the wrong side of her!'

Reg chuckled. 'She's a concerned neighbour. The local station say she's haunting them, demanding to know what they're doing.'

Dora said nothing. After seeing the flat she had expected to be able to dismiss this other woman from her mind, but that hadn't happened. She was ill at ease, and during the morning she had come to a decision. It was time their mother's past was uncovered, because there had clearly been lies and secrets. To her mind that meant there was something her parents had kept hidden. And now she wanted to know . . . *had* to know. How were they ever going to put their lives back together again with unanswered questions hanging over them? And it was no good continually pawning things so they could pay the rent. They would have to move, and soon. The waiting to see if their mother returned was over! There were tough decisions to make about their future.

'We're home.' Tom touched her arm, bringing her sharply out of deep thought. He was frowning, looking as troubled as her. 'We've got to talk, Dora.'

She gave a nod. Her brother was a bright boy and she knew that, like her, he'd had enough of waiting for the police to turn up any clues. Lily was still bubbling with energy after their morning, and Dora was pleased to see Winnie waiting by Stan's gate. The little girl ran to her, the words tumbling out in her excitement to tell about the flat.

'You look tired,' Winnie said to Dora when she reached her. 'Did you find anything this morning?'

'Nothing.'

'Lily could spend the rest of the day with me if you like.'

'Would you like that, sweetie?' she asked her sister.

'Yes please!'

'Good.' Winnie smiled. 'You can have tea with June, and Dora can collect you after that.'

While they had been talking, Stan had gone into the house. After helping him, Tom came out again. 'Stan'll sleep this afternoon,' he told them. 'This morning's trip has tired him out. He shouldn't have come really. I don't think he's strong enough yet.'

Winnie pulled a face. 'You can't stop my brother doing anything he wants to. I've never met such a determined man.'

'So we've noticed.' Tom took Dora's arm. 'Come on, we'll leave him in peace for a while.'

'I'm going with Auntie Winnie,' Lily told her brother.

'Ah, in that case you behave yourself, urchin.'

She gave him an offended look. 'I *always* behave myself!'

'Funny, I hadn't noticed.' He gave her a distracted pat on the head and urged Dora towards their own house. Once inside he wasted no time. 'We can't go on like this. They're still keeping secrets from us. We've got to do something!'

'What do you mean? And stop pacing, Tom!' Dora grabbed his arm to make him stand still. 'What secrets?'

'Reg was looking through a drawer when he handed Stan a letter or something. After looking at it, Stan slid it into his pocket. They didn't know I'd seen them.'

This news hurt Dora more than she would have believed, the hurt quickly turning to anger. 'How could they? Well, that settles it. I honestly believe there's something unpleasant hidden in our mother's background, and we need to know what it is!'

'Ah, that's my big sister talking.' Tom nodded in approval and then, surprisingly for him, he gave her a hug.

Her mouth set in a determined line. 'We'll give Stan time to rest and then we'll demand to know what he took from the flat. And it's strange that we haven't found a marriage certificate, or anything relating to our mum and dad's past. Why aren't the police looking into this? They were ordinary decent hard-working people and I can't imagine what they were hiding. But it was something they obviously didn't want us to know.'

Tom was shaking his head in disbelief. 'I can't believe any of this is happening. We'll never be able to rest until we know what the hell's been going on!'

'I agree, and there's a very urgent matter we must discuss.' Dora's practical mind was trying to sort out the mess they were in. There was one thing she had been avoiding, but now it would have to be faced. 'You understand we've got to find somewhere cheaper to live, don't you?'

'I know, Dora. I'm not daft.'

'I've never thought you were. I'm not looking forward to telling Lily, and we'll wait until I've found another place for us.'

'She's not going to be happy about moving away from Stan, but when we explain I'm sure she'll accept it.'

'I do hope so. But she's also become very fond of Reg and Winnie. Have you noticed the way she calls them Auntie and Uncle now? I think she's reaching out to other people for comfort and a sense of stability.'

Tom shrugged. 'Well, if it makes her feel better, then there's no harm in it, is there?'

'No, I suppose not. They don't seem to mind, and they're

kind people.' They had been sitting round the table talking for nearly two hours when Dora stood up. The time had passed without them noticing. 'Stan's had time to rest and now we must talk to him.'

Reg let them in and Dora said, 'Ah, I'm glad you're still here. We want to know what you found in the flat this morning, please.'

Reg darted a quick glance at his brother-in-law. 'What do you mean?'

'I saw you hand something to Stan, and he put it in his pocket,' Tom told him.

'Tell us what it was, please.' Dora couldn't hide the hurt in her voice. 'Why do you keep things from us? I'm sick and tired of secrets! Do you think we're so silly that we wouldn't understand, or so weak that we can't face anything unpleasant?'

'Of course we don't! But this is a police investigation and we can't—'

'And this is our mother we're trying to find!' Tom rounded on Reg angrily. 'Surely we have a right to know about anything you find, or even suspect?'

Stan was now on his feet. 'We intended to tell you when it's been looked into. There's no point raising your hopes for nothing.'

'The uncertainty's tearing us apart, Stan.' Dora didn't believe these men, however kind, had the faintest idea what they were going through. 'We're desperate for news, even if it leads to nothing. And we need to find out what our mother was hiding, so please tell us what you're keeping from us – again!'

Stan spoke firmly. 'I know I've been out of action and will be for a while yet, but the police are doing all they can—'

'But it isn't enough!' Tom lifted his hands in an apologetic gesture. 'Sorry, but it's taking too long. We can't stand much more. Can't you understand that?'

'We do know how you feel, and we're just as frustrated, but you must remember that this isn't the only case the police have on their hands.' Stan looked imploringly at Dora. 'I know it's a hard thing to ask, but you must try to have patience and trust the police. This is a complicated case and there's no telling what may come to light.'

'We do know that the chances of our mother still being alive are slim.' Dora's tone of voice showed the deep sadness she felt. 'But you must stop trying to protect us ... And I know that's what you're doing. Now, we'd still like to know what you found.'

'It's nothing of importance.' Reg was still reluctant.

'Then there's no harm in letting us know, is there?'

Reluctantly, Stan pulled the letter out of his pocket and handed it to Dora. 'It's only the name and address of a firm of solicitors. Reg is going to see them in the morning. It needs to be someone in uniform. They won't talk about a client otherwise.'

'I doubt if they'll say anything even when they're faced with the police,' Reg told them. 'But I'll do my best to persuade them.'

Tom scribbled down the address on a dog-eared piece of paper from his pocket and Dora handed the letter back.

Stan was grim faced. 'Don't go there yourselves. You'll only be interfering with the work of the police.'

'If we agree to that then you've got to promise to tell us exactly what they say.'

'You have my word, Dora.' Stan nodded in agreement.

'Thank you. Now we must go and collect Lily. Tom?'

'Dora!' Stan caught her by the door. 'We've only been trying to save you from unnecessary distress.'

'We realize that, but you can't protect us from what's happening. It's something we can't escape. We have to face it, and not knowing what's going on is making things worse, not better.' The expression on his face tugged at her heart. He obviously cared very much. Forcing her mouth into something like a smile, she reached up and kissed his cheek. 'Stop worrying about us and get some rest. You've got to take care of yourself or Doctor Burridge will have you back in hospital.'

He ran the back of his hand gently down her cheek. 'I'll take care. And trust me, Dora.'

Flustered by his gentleness, she merely nodded and hurried to catch up with her brother.

Twenty-Five

There was a new air of purpose and determination about Dora as she made her way to Wandsworth the next morning. Her discussion with Tom yesterday had cleared her mind. They were on their own now and had to move on with their lives. As frightening as that was, they had each other, and that was a great comfort. The main priority was to find a cheaper place to live. Once that was done they prayed that the police would be able to find out what had happened to their mother. They missed her dreadfully, and knew that it wasn't going to be easy to recover from the distress her disappearance had caused. The fact that the police were having so little success only added to their agony. She would give them a couple of days to talk to the solicitors, and if they didn't find out anything she would visit them herself. Not that it would do much good, but at least she would feel as if she was doing something. And the need to find somewhere else to live was now urgent. Their little sister was going to be upset. They all were, but the move was unavoidable.

Dora was pleased to see the doctor's car already parked outside the house, and she headed straight for his office.

'Ah.' He looked up and smiled when she walked in. 'Good morning, Dora. You're nice and early this morning.'

'Yes, sir. Would it be all right if I left at two o'clock today?'

'Of course you can.' His eyes narrowed as he studied the strain showing on her face. 'Sit down, my dear. You're tired. Is there anything I can do for you? Is there news of your mother?'

'No, there's no trace of her, and we can't afford to stay where we are. I need the time off to find somewhere else for us to live.'

'Finding it hard, are you?'

'Impossible is the word I'd use.' Dora had always found it

easy to talk to him. 'I had no idea how expensive it was to live in that nice house. Even if I still had my other job I would have found it too expensive. I don't know how Mum managed.'

'Is the move urgent?'

'I'd say so. We can't leave it much longer. We're pawning things every week now in order to pay the rent, but it's silly to keep doing that. We must assume Mum isn't coming back, and we've got to learn to take care of ourselves.'

Dr Burridge looked thoughtful for a few moments, and then he stood up. 'Come with me.'

Dora followed him up the stairs to the top of the house, a place she had never been before. He stopped by a door and unlocked it, then led her along a wide passage with a series of rooms either side.

'This used to be my grandmother's private flat when my family lived here. There's a kitchen, bathroom, sitting room and three other rooms that could be used as bedrooms. The place needs a good clean, of course, it hasn't been used for years.'

'Erm . . . it's very nice.' Dora was almost afraid to ask, but she did anyway. 'Why are you showing me this?'

'I've come to rely upon you, Dora. You're efficient – in fact the best help I've ever had – and you're good with the men who come here. You see past their injuries and they appreciate you being so natural with them. You make them smile, and some of the poor devils have little to be cheerful about.'

'I enjoy helping them.'

'That's obvious, and I'd be a fool to let you go. So, I'll make a deal with you. Work for me full time, here and at the hospital, and you and your family can live here rent free. I shall, of course, increase your wages, but they'll still be rather low. However, if you don't have to find rent each week, then you should be able to manage better. What do you say?'

Say? Dora just stared at him as the full import of what he was offering her struck home. She had come to work this morning feeling that their lives were in ruins, dust at their feet, and this wonderful man had wiped out their desperate need. Not only was he offering them a home – and a very nice one at that – but he was offering her full employment.

He was waiting patiently for her answer, and she grasped his hand and shook it. 'Oh, thank you, sir. Thank you. You won't regret this. I'll work very hard for you.'

'I know that.' He smiled and glanced around the room. 'And it will be good to have a family living in the old house again. Now, let's go and see who's arrived. John is still having difficulty walking and needs lots of encouragement.'

There were already six men in the main room, including John, who appeared very dispirited this morning. Nevertheless, he brightened up when they walked in.

'Good morning, gentlemen.' The doctor's gaze swept over every face in turn, missing nothing.

'Morning, doc. Morning, Dora.'

'I'm here for most of the day,' he announced, 'so if you have any problems come and see me. And I have some news. Dora and her brother and sister are moving into the rooms upstairs, but they are in a state of neglect. If any of you feel able to help Dora make the place habitable, she would be most grateful.'

The men were immediately standing and smiling, even John. 'What do you want us to do, Dora?' he asked eagerly.

'Well . . .' She glanced at the doctor, not sure this was right. When he gave her a sly wink, she realized what he was doing. He was showing the men that they were needed. She winked back and said, 'The place needs a good clean, and some paint to brighten up the rooms.'

John grabbed his sticks and began moving with more ease than she had seen before. 'Let's get the place cleaned up, and then Dora can tell us what paint she wants. How old is your sister?'

'Six.'

'Ah, that would be pink for her room, then?'

'I don't think Lily would argue with that.' Dora laughed, suddenly more light-hearted than she had been since their mother's disappearance.

John gave a boyish grin and began to organize the men, allotting them different tasks.

'Better show them where to start, Dora.' The doctor was looking at the activity with satisfaction. 'Then come down and leave them to it. I need you this morning.'

There was much banging and crashing going on upstairs as Dora worked, and the sounds were accompanied by the men's laughter and whistling. During the morning others arrived, disappearing upstairs to join in the fun. At one point she stopped to gaze up at the ceiling, picturing the men working upstairs. 'I wish the government would do more to help these men find proper jobs. It would give them a purpose in life again.'

The doctor nodded, his eyes reflecting his inner sadness. 'They need to feel useful, and so many of them have lost their self-respect because they can't provide for their families. Alan is one of the lucky ones. He has family connections to ease his way back into normal life.'

'He is,' Dora agreed. 'He's studying hard and looking forward to following his father as a lawyer eventually.'

'He'll do well. Are you still going out with him?'

'We only went out a couple of times when he needed to find his feet, so to speak. He appreciated support from someone who understood. Now he's making a new life for himself. No doubt he'll soon find a suitable wife.'

'And he'll have plenty of choice. So many young men were killed in that madness, and that means many girls will have little or no chance of marrying.'

Dora sighed. 'The women outnumber the men and many will remain spinsters.'

'And what about you, Dora? Would you like a family of your own one day?'

'I would like to marry one day, of course, but if I don't it wouldn't be too bad for me.' She smiled. 'I already have a family to take care of. They're going to need me for quite a while. And another thing, I can't imagine a man wanting to take on a ready-made family.'

'Oh, I'm sure there must be a man out there who would be delighted to have such lovely youngsters to care for.'

She pulled a face. 'You're an optimist, doctor.'

'If I wasn't I would never get up in the mornings.' He glanced at his watch, fished in his jacket and handed Dora some money. 'Those men are going to be hungry, so go and buy some food. Then prepare a hearty meal for all of us. I'll eat here today as well.'

Dora ran all the way to the shops at the top of the street, where she spent every penny Dr Burridge had given her. Then she ran back, holding the parcels tightly to make sure she didn't drop anything. As she tumbled through the door, Dobbs began relieving her of the food.

'Oh good,' she gasped. 'You're here. I need your help.'

'What?'

'Come with me,' she yelled, and then rushed into the kitchen, leaving him to follow her.

'What's going on?'

'We're going to cook a meal for everyone here today. I'm moving in upstairs and they're cleaning the place up for me.'

'Ah, that's what all the racket is.'

She stopped pulling pans and dishes out of the cupboard, giving Dobbs an incredulous glance. 'I thought you were deaf?'

'Eh?'

'I thought you were Mutt and Jeff,' she teased, raising her voice.

He smirked. "'Ow many up there?'

'No idea. We started with six but more have arrived, so will you go and check for me?' Dora stared pointedly at him, daring him to say 'What?'

This time he just chuckled and headed for the stairs.

Three pans were soon full of sizzling sausages, and Dora was peeling potatoes as if her life depended upon it.

'There's twelve of them.' Dobbs had returned, highly amused. 'They're making a right mess. There's water everywhere. They're right fond of you, girl. Now, what do you want me to do?'

'Help me peel these potatoes. Hope I bought enough. With the doc and us, that makes fifteen to feed.'

Dobbs got stuck in. 'Who paid for all this grub?'

'The doctor. Have we got enough plates?'

'There's some more under the sink.'

Dora found them and tossed them in the sink to give them a good wash.

They worked together well with Dora giving the orders, and they soon had a long table laid out. She had even found a couple of tablecloths – not as clean as she would have liked, but they would do.

'Go and call them,' she told Dobbs, as she dished out the hasty meal of sausages, onions and mash, with large chunks of bread and butter to help it down.

Once they were all seated she served them, and it was one of the liveliest times this fine house had seen for some years. The simple meal was demolished with obvious enjoyment.

As the men settled to enjoy a cup of tea and a cigarette, John raised his cup. 'My compliments to the cooks.'

'What's this? A party?' Alan arrived, swung another chair to the table and sat down.

'You're too late, mate,' Dobbs told him. 'We've eaten it all. But you're welcome to a cup of tea.'

'Thanks.' Alan handed round a packet of cigarettes, smiling at Dora. 'Going to tell me what this is all about?'

'Our Dora and her family are moving in upstairs.' John tossed the empty packet back to Alan. 'We're helping to get the place ready for them.'

The amusement left Alan's eyes, but he didn't question Dora in front of the others. Instead he stood up. 'Show me, Dora.'

Once upstairs, Alan surveyed the chaotic mess of steps and buckets everywhere. 'This must have been a fine house at one time.'

Feeling that Alan disapproved, Dora explained. 'The doctor's kindly going to let us live here rent free, and I'm going to work for him all the time.'

'The job's good, but couldn't you stay in your own house?'

'I'm afraid not. It's too expensive. We're broke, Alan.' She saw little point in denying it.

'I can help you out—'

'No.' She stopped him before he could finish. 'That's very kind of you, but we've got to deal with it ourselves. This isn't a temporary difficulty, Alan, it's permanent, and we must make adjustments, however painful.'

'But what are Tom and Lily going to say?'

'Tom's in agreement, though he doesn't know about this place yet. And we haven't told Lily about moving. She's going to be upset, but we don't have a choice.' She looked up into his face, her eyes troubled. 'This is something we've tried to avoid. But we never realized how expensive it was to live where we do. I have no idea how Mum managed to afford it.'

'Oh, hell! I'm so sorry, Dora. Does Stan know yet?'

'No, we'll tell him tonight.'

'He isn't going to be happy.'

Dora was well aware what Stan was going to think. He would probably explode when he knew, but this was their life and they had to live it as best they could. It was up to them – nobody else! She changed the subject. 'How are you getting on? We haven't seen much of you lately.'

'I'm working and studying hard, but I love what I'm doing. When I got back from the war I thought my life was over, but it isn't. Things are beginning to work out well for me.' He fell silent, staring at nothing in particular. 'I've met someone, Dora. She's a friend of the family and doesn't seem to mind the injuries . . .'

'Oh, I'm so pleased for you, Alan. Are you going to marry her? What's her name?'

His laugh was one of relief at her obvious pleasure. 'I haven't got that far yet, and her name is Sybil.'

'But it's serious?'

He nodded, studying her smiling face. 'I wasn't sure how you'd take this. We went out a few times . . .'

'As friends when you needed support to get back to normal. And I hope we can remain friends.'

'Always.' He bent and kissed her cheek. 'You're a remarkable young woman. You take pleasure in other people's happiness, feel their sorrow, and yet you have terrible problems of your own. It hurts me to see you suffering so much – and no matter how brave a face you show to the world, I know you are suffering. I wish I could wipe away all your unhappiness.'

'Only finding our mother alive and well would do that. But you mustn't worry about us, Alan, there are good, kind people looking out for us.' She touched his arm in an affectionate gesture. 'You have a happy life from now on.'

Twenty-Six

D ora was home early and waited impatiently to tell Tom and Lily about the flat. Now the decision had been made, she wanted to get away from this house with all its memories. It would be a fresh start, and that was just what they needed. They had to let go of the past by carving out a new life for themselves. And what better place to start than Dr Burridge's house? She had explored the area and it was close to schools and everything else they could need.

'You're home early.' Lily ran to hug her.

'Yes.' She nodded to Tom as he walked into the room. 'I've got some good news. Sit down and I'll tell you all about it.'

As Lily scrambled on to a chair, Dora whispered to her brother, 'I've found somewhere for us to live.'

He said nothing, but pulled his chair close to his little sister.

'First, Doctor Burridge has offered me a full-time job with him. I'll be working at the hospital some of the time and spending the rest at the Wandsworth house.'

'That's wonderful.' Tom smiled as Lily clapped.

'The pay isn't quite as much as I was getting in my other job, so that means we'll still find it hard to manage.' She sounded this note of caution before explaining about the move. 'You know the house in Wandsworth is big. Well, it belongs to the doctor, and he said we could have the whole of the top floor to live in – rent free! Isn't that wonderful?'

'It certainly is!' Tom was clearly pleased. 'What do you think about that, urchin?'

The little girl's face crumpled with distress at the news. 'But we can't leave here! What about Stan, and school, and . . .'

'There's a nice school in the next road, and one only twenty minutes away for Tom. And we'll still be able to see our friends. They won't be far away.'

Lily's eyes filled with tears. 'Can't we stay here, Dora? What if Mum comes back? She won't know where we are.'

'Sweetie, we've got to accept that she isn't coming back. We haven't got enough money to pay the rent on this house any longer.'

'We're broke,' Tom explained. 'It isn't fair to put all this worry on Dora. She's had a struggle trying to keep us in the life we've been used to, but she can't do it any longer. There are three of us to feed. Can you understand that?'

'You could sell my dolly. We've still got that,' she sniffed, a tear trickling down her cheek.

Dora reached across the table and took hold of her sister's hand. 'That's so generous of you, sweetie, but it wouldn't be enough. Why don't you both have the day off from school tomorrow and come with me. Lots of men are helping to get it ready for us. Alan came as well.'

'Does Stan come?' Lily swiped a hand across her eyes.

'Of course he does. Once he's well again I'm sure he'll come lots to see you. And as soon as we get it looking nice we'll have June and Winnie over for tea, shall we?'

Lily drew in a ragged breath. 'Is it a very big house?'

'Enormous!' Relief raced through Dora. Her sister was coming round to the idea much faster than she'd dared hope. 'This house would fit in it at least three times.'

After thinking about this for a few moments, Lily said, 'We'll see it tomorrow. Can I go and tell Stan now?'

'Yes, we must do that.' Dora glanced at her brother, receiving a nod of approval.

Stan's smile of pleasure faded as soon as he saw the expressions on their faces. 'What's happened?'

Gulping back tears as they threatened to spill over again, Lily said, 'I won't be able to look after you any more, because we've got to move.'

His face turned to thunder and he rounded on Dora. 'What the hell is she talking about? I told you not to move! I said we would work something out if it came to this!'

'Don't you shout at my sister!' Tom glowered at Stan. 'She's only doing what she thinks is best for us.'

'Best for you?' He was furious. 'Where are you going? Back to the slums?'

'Do you think I'd do that to my family?' Dora was hurt and

angry at Stan's accusation. And why was he carrying on so? This was their business, not his! As much as she loved the man, she wasn't going to put up with this. Turning sharply she walked out of the house.

Once back in her own home she leant against the closed front door, shutting her eyes tightly. *She loved him.* He was stubborn, infuriating, kind and strong at the same time – and she had fallen in love with him. What a stupid thing to do. Didn't she have enough problems without adding to them?

'Now look what you've done!' Tom stared at the door his big sister had just closed firmly on her way out. 'Do you think this is easy for her? I hear her walking up and down during the night as she worries about finding enough money to feed us and keep us together. And worse than that is to hear her crying quietly – she's worried sick. Oh, she tries to fool everyone that she's all right, but I know different. She's trying to protect us from the worst of this disaster and she's taken the whole bloody mess on her shoulders. We're trying to help and support her in any way we can, but she's the eldest and she has all the responsibility. Isn't that right, Lily?'

The little girl nodded, her face drained of all colour.

Stan was stunned. Lily slipped her hand in his, looking up at him, pleading for understanding. 'We've got to go. We're broke. The doctor's giving us a place in the big house. Don't be angry with us, please.'

If he could take back those harsh words Stan would have given everything he owned, but the damage was done and he'd hurt the people he cared about. 'I'm sorry, sweetheart, I'm not angry with you – I'm angry with myself.' He reached out and squeezed Tom's tense shoulders. 'I apologize, son. My sharp tongue – it's always been a problem. But I never meant to hurt you. Stay here with Lily while I go and beg Dora to forgive me.'

'She might not,' he muttered, still upset. 'I've never seen her walk out on anyone before.'

Stan didn't waste time getting to Dora's house. The front door was shut when he arrived. After receiving no reply to his repeated knocking he really thought Tom was right and she wasn't going to give him a chance to put things right between them. 'Let me in, Dora, please!'

He breathed a sigh of relief when the door opened. 'May I come in?'

She stepped back, and without a word turned and walked to the kitchen. Stan followed.

Dora was looking out of the window and didn't face him. 'I'm sorry. You don't deserve to be spoken to like that.'

'No, I don't!'

'You must do what you feel is right, and I've got no right to question your decisions.'

'No, you haven't.'

'You're not making this easy for me.'

'Should I?'

'I suppose not. Win always said my bad temper would get me into trouble.' When she didn't speak this time, he propped the crutches against the wall, and being careful to put all his weight on his good leg, he reached out and drew her towards him. 'Forgive me, please?'

When she still said nothing, he couldn't take any more. 'Turn and face me, Dora!'

'Temper,' she murmured, as she turned in his arms.

He lifted her chin so he could look into her face, shaking his head in disbelief. 'Are you laughing at me?'

'Of course not, but you do apologize nicely – when you're able to hold your temper in check.'

He shook his head in disgust. 'And that isn't for long, is it? Saying I'm sorry isn't something I've been used to doing, until I met you,' he joked, relieved she was talking to him again.

'And I hope you're not standing on that leg,' she said severely.

'No, I'm using you to prop myself up. Now, if I promise not to shout at you, will you tell me about the new home you're planning?'

'Sit down then.' After helping him to a chair, she explained about her arrangement with Dr Burridge.

They had been talking for a while when Lily's anxious face appeared round the kitchen door. 'Are you friends again?' she whispered. 'Can we come in now?'

'Of course you can.' Dora held out her hand and Lily rushed towards her, smiling.

Tom followed and sat at the table. 'Has Dora told you?'

Stan nodded. 'It sounds like a good arrangement, the doc's

a fine man, but I'd still be happier if you stayed here. I'd help you.'

'We know you would, but you can't help us for the rest of our lives,' Tom explained.

'We've got to make our own way, Stan.' Dora spoke with determination. 'We've been very lucky to have been offered such a nice place to live.'

'Nice?' Stan was astounded. 'That house is a mess!'

'It won't be when we've finished, and we've got plenty of help. I only wish we could pay the men for the work they're doing.' Dora sighed deeply and changed the subject. No matter what they said, Stan would not be happy about them moving. 'Did Reg see the solicitors today?'

'Yes, but as expected, they wouldn't say anything about Mrs Duval unless there was proof she was dead. They insisted she might just have gone away on holiday.'

'It would be a long holiday!' Tom gave a snort of disgust and stood up to make some tea. 'And anyway, I still don't believe this mysterious woman is anything to do with our mum.'

'I don't know how you can sound so sure,' Stan said. 'The name's in the front of the notebook you found.'

'Along with a lot of others,' Tom pointed out. 'Are you looking for all of those as well?'

'Don't be sarcastic, young man. Think! There was a Duval at the factory too.'

'Coincidence.' Tom didn't apologize for being sceptical. He slipped the cosy over the freshly made pot of tea. 'And what about that notebook? Have you any idea what it's all about yet?'

'No, it doesn't make sense,' Stan admitted.

He was right about that, Dora thought. Nothing had made sense from the time of their mother's disappearance, and all these other things just made it downright confusing. It should have been a case of searching for a missing person, but the investigation appeared to be going in all directions except the right one. She could understand her brother's frustration. In many ways he was much like Stan, not known for his patience. The uncertainty was driving them mad. 'We haven't found Mum and Dad's marriage licence. How would we go about getting a copy?'

'The police will do that, Dora. They'll let us know as soon as they have one.'

She glanced at Tom. 'We'll leave that with them for the time being, shall we? We're going to have enough to do with moving.'

'All right. We'll concentrate on the new flat first.'

Stan went back to his own house still unhappy that they were moving, but perhaps the move wasn't such a bad thing. The investigation was going along lines that were disturbing, and at least this would keep them occupied for a while.

Reg was waiting for Stan when he arrived back.

'Where the hell have you been? You're supposed to be resting.'

'Don't you start on me, I'm in the mood for a fight! I've been at Dora's.' He sat down and leant back his head, closing his eyes. 'They're moving. I didn't want them to do that. I would have helped them, but they won't let me.'

'Of course they won't, Stan. They've got to plan for a future without their mother. Dora's got a lot of pride in her quiet way, and she'll do whatever she can for her brother and sister. Maybe you could have helped for a short time, but you can't support the three of them for years to come.'

'That's what they said.' Stan opened his eyes. 'And I know you're right. But I hate to see them struggling like this.'

'Dora and Tom aren't stupid, and they know what they've got to do to survive.' Reg poured Stan a whisky and handed it to him. 'They've got more intelligence than you're crediting them with. Don't treat them like children, Stan. Only one of them is still a child and that's Lily. The other two have grown up quickly – they've had to. We'll still keep an eye on them. Where are they going?'

Stan told his brother-in-law about the arrangement they had made with Dr Burridge.

'Well, what are you worrying about? That sounds ideal for them.'

'It could have been worse.' Stan sipped his drink. 'We ought to get hold of a marriage certificate. Have you got one yet?'

Reg took a swig of his drink. 'We've only just started on that line of enquiry. At first, what happened that long ago didn't seem relevant to tracking a missing person, but knowing her maiden name might help. So far we've found nothing. I don't think they were married, Stan.'

'Oh God!'

Twenty-Seven

The next morning Dora arrived at Wandsworth with her brother and sister. Dobbs beamed when he saw Lily. 'My goodness! What a pretty girl you are. I suppose you've come to have a look around your new home?'

She nodded shyly, spinning round as other men came through the door.

'Ah, you must be Lily.' John leant against the wall so he had a hand free to shake hands with Tom. 'And you're Tom. Are you free today? We could do with the help of an able-bodied man.'

Tom stood up proudly at being called a man. 'I can stay.'

The men all crowded round, except one who was keeping in the background. John pulled him forward and introduced him as Ray.

'We're pleased to meet you, Ray.' Dora's gaze was direct, smiling up into his face. He had a patch over his left eye, his face was badly scarred and his left arm was missing. He was clearly nervous about being with strangers. 'This is my brother Tom and my sister Lily.'

'Nice to meet you, sir,' Tom said, shaking his hand.

Lily tipped back her head to look up at him. 'You're very tall. Have you come to help us? We're going to live here.'

'So John told me. He said they're going to paint your room pink.' Ray spoke in a soft, musical voice, looking to have been put more at ease by the acceptance he was receiving.

She giggled. 'I haven't seen upstairs yet, but I like pink.'

'I told you it would be all right,' John whispered in Ray's ear. 'These are good youngsters. They're not going to run away screaming when they see the mess we're in.'

'Tea and sandwiches are ready!' Dobbs bellowed.

Lily put her fingers in her ears and pulled a face at Ray. 'Dora said he's deaf – sometimes.'

Ray laughed at the little girl's antics, and Dora guessed it was some time since he'd done that. While they all made a stampede for the refreshments, Dora took Tom and Lily upstairs.

The place was thoroughly explored and, much to Dora's relief, appeared to meet with approval. Her sister had even chosen her room.

'Come and look at the size of this garden!' Tom was leaning out of the window. 'Will we be able to use it?'

'Of course you can.'

At the sound of the doctor's voice, Tom shot up, banging his head on the window. 'Sorry sir, I didn't know you were here. I've always wanted to have a go at growing things. Would that be all right?'

'Go ahead, Tom, I'll be pleased to see it being used again. It's become rather overgrown, I'm afraid.'

'I'll soon see to that.' Tom was enthusiastic. 'Thank you, sir. Our garden at home is too small and mostly concrete.'

There was the sound of clattering on the stairs, and when John and Ray appeared Lily pounced on them. 'I've picked my room. I'll show you.'

They followed her obediently. Dr Burridge watched them leave and then turned to Dora. 'She's accepted the move?'

'It looks like it. She was upset when we told her but now she seems quite happy. I think seeing a lot of people around has helped. She does like company.'

'Good. I spoke to Ray before coming up here. He's quite overcome by the way none of you have shied away from his injuries. We've been trying to get him here for some time but he was afraid to go out much. John and Alan have been talking to him about the house, explaining that he need have no worries as he'll be among people who understand. His disfigurement won't be commented on and he'll be treated like everyone else.'

A look of disgust crossed Tom's face. 'I don't understand how people can be so cruel!'

'No, it's sad, but it makes some people uncomfortable, and they don't know what to do or say. We mustn't judge them too harshly, Tom. Now, I must get on with my work. Come down when you're ready, Dora, but don't rush.'

Just as the doctor left, Lily erupted back into the room.

'Pink! I'm going to have bright pink.' She skidded to a halt. 'Ray draws pictures and he's going to paint me one on the wall! He's an artist,' she announced with awe.

Dora smiled at Ray. 'Thank you. That's very kind of you.'

He inclined his head. 'It will be my pleasure, and your delightful sister has already thanked me. Do you think you'll like living here?'

'It should be all right. There's a big garden and the doctor says Tom can grow things if he wants to.'

'Oh.' John turned to Tom, immediately interested. 'Would you like to do that?'

'I always wanted to. I don't know the first thing about it, though, only what I've read in books.'

'I was a gardener before the war. I'd be glad to give you a few tips.'

'Would you?' Tom was fairly bouncing with excitement. 'Where did you work?'

'At Kew Gardens.'

'Gosh, you must be good. Will you go back there now you're walking again?'

'I doubt they'd have me back. I wouldn't be able to climb trees to do the pruning, or any of the heavy work.'

'There would be plenty of other things you could do,' Tom insisted.

'Maybe.' John's smile was wistful. 'But let's get this place into shape first. The soil's good, just right for growing vegetables.'

Dora watched as Ray joined in the conversation, and the familiar anger raced through her. Sometimes she wished these shattered lives didn't touch her so much, but she couldn't help it. It was the way she was. They were all young, with their lives ahead of them. Some, like Alan and hopefully Stan, would be able to lead normal useful lives again, but what about others? What did the future hold for them? There was a wealth of talent amongst these men and it was being wasted. It wasn't right after the sacrifices they had made!

Lily bounced over to Dora. 'John's a gardener and he's going to help Tom grow things.' Her smile was animated. 'And they're going to let me help.'

'That will be lovely.' Dora stooped down in front of her sister. 'We'll be all right here, Lily, won't we?'

The little girl nodded. 'I was upset when you said we had to move, but I like it here. And Stan can come and see us lots, can't he?'

'Of course, sweetie. And with the big room you're going to have, June will be able to stay overnight sometimes. We can easily put two beds in there.'

'Why isn't anyone working?'

'Alan!' Lily was on her way over to him, but stopped suddenly when she spotted the imposing man beside him.

'Who's that?' Tom whispered. 'Do you think it's Alan's father? They look alike.'

'Father, this is Dora, Tom and Lily.'

'Good to meet you. Alan's told me a lot about you.'

The man was so overpowering that Dora had a struggle to stop herself from curtseying. 'Good morning, sir.'

Alan's eyes gleamed with amusement when he saw Lily trying to hide behind Dora's skirt, and Tom dip his head in a parody of a bow.

'Come here, girl,' Alan's father demanded, holding out his hand to Lily. 'Let me have a look at you. Don't be afraid of me. I don't bite.'

Alan stifled a laugh.

His father shot him an offended glance, and then looked back at Lily. He was actually smiling. 'Not often, anyway. My son told me that you were very kind to him when you met in the park. You shared your picnic with him.'

Lily nodded, edging forward a step. 'We had plenty.'

'He said you didn't seem to mind that he was injured.'

'Er . . .' Her expression was puzzled as she looked at Dora, not understanding what he meant.

Tom spoke for his sister. 'Dora's always told us that the injuries don't make them any the less of a person, and they should be treated just like anyone else. And she's right. We like Alan.'

His steely eyes fastened on Dora. 'Your sister has a wise and understanding heart.'

'We think so too, sir,' Tom said proudly. 'We'd be in a terrible mess now if it wasn't for her.'

Alan's father stood up, took a card out of his pocket and handed it to Dora. 'I was sorry to hear about your mother's disappearance. If you ever need any legal help then contact me.'

Dora examined the gold-embossed card. It bore the name 'General Arthur Harrington' followed by a string of letters, and then the address of his chambers. His services were obviously very expensive. 'This is kind of you, sir, but I'm sure we could never afford you.'

'Don't worry about that.' He smiled again. 'It would be my pleasure to return the kindness you've shown to my son.'

Alan winked at her.

'Now introduce me to Doctor Burridge, Alan, and the rest of the men.'

Letting out a pent-up breath as they walked away, Dora said to her brother and sister, 'Do you think Alan will be like his father when he's older?'

'I expect so.' Tom's shoulders were shaking in amusement. 'You can already see they're alike.'

'Dora.' The doctor came over to her. 'General Harrington wishes to discuss something with me, and I'd like you present to take notes. You know how easily I forget things if they're not written down.'

'That's only because your days are so full. It's easy to forget things.' She had done this for him on many occasions now and, much to her surprise, found that she was good at it. She had an orderly mind, and that was just what the doctor needed with his busy schedule. 'Will you and Lily be all right, Tom?'

He nodded. 'We'll make ourselves useful up here.'

Alan stayed as well. His jacket was already off and his sleeves rolled up, ready to wield a paintbrush.

Once in the doctor's office, Dora sat discreetly in the corner of the room, pen in hand, ready to make notes. She was curious about the visit from Alan's father.

The general wasted no time. 'My son has told me what you're doing for the men. It's admirable, but the need is great and there's more that could be done. From what I've seen, you have plenty of room here to expand your activities. You could open your doors to all injured and unemployed ex-servicemen, including their wives and children, if they have any. People are going hungry out there, doctor. Get that kitchen sorted out and you could provide a lunch for those in need, free of charge, of course. You'll need a regular cook. I know just the woman for the job.'

Dora had been writing quickly, not wanting to miss a word

of what was being said. She glanced up when the general stopped talking. The doctor was resting his arms on the desk and studying the man opposite him, but he said nothing.

'I know what you're thinking. Where the devil is the money coming from?'

The doctor inclined his head.

'How much do you want?'

'How much have you got?'

Dora nearly spluttered with laughter, thoroughly enjoying this exchange between the two men, but managed to turn it into a cough. They were both strong, but in very different ways. The general was used to giving orders and being obeyed; the doctor was quieter, preferring to lead people, but equally determined.

'I'm good at getting money out of people, and you shall have every penny you need. You have my word on that, so there's no need to worry about the expense. You send all the bills to me and I'll see they're paid. What do you say? Can we do it?'

'We can have a damned good try!'

The general surged to his feet, wreathed in smiles. 'I'll send builders round to start on the kitchen. And from what I've seen, you need a new roof.'

'I've longed to be able to do something like this. Thank you, General.'

'A pleasure.' He flipped open his pocket watch, frowned, then snapped it shut again. 'Must leave at once. Court appearance in half an hour. Tell my son I've had to leave. Good to have met you all.'

They watched him sweep out of the office. The doctor, looking rather stunned, sat down again. 'A new roof as well? Did I just dream that, Dora?'

She made a show of studying her notes. 'No, it's right here – new roof, new kitchen and all the money you need. Oh, and not forgetting a cook.'

'Then it must be true! This is Alan's doing. I must thank him.'

'And I must see about preparing a meal. Do you mind if my brother and sister stay for the rest of the day? They won't be any trouble.'

'Of course they can stay. This is going to be their home, and I'm sure Lily will want to make sure they get the colour right for her room.'

Dora grinned. 'Dobbs has managed to get several pots of

paint, so she'll have to take whatever colour he's managed to scrounge.'

The doctor was halfway out of the room when he turned. 'Where did he get it from?'

'He has contacts, he said.'

'I'll bet he has. Dobbs is absolutely invaluable. I don't think I could have kept this place open without him. Come with me, Dora, and let's tell him the good news.'

They found Dobbs in the kitchen peeling potatoes. ''Ow many we feeding today?'

Dora couldn't believe her eyes. There were bags of carrots, onions, potatoes, and stewing steak piled on a plate. 'Where did all this come from?'

'I sold some things from my room.'

'Oh, you shouldn't have done that. I brought some money with me today to help out.' In truth they had made a quick call at the pawnbroker's on their way here. The men were working to get their flat ready, and she felt that feeding them was the least she could do.

'They was things given to me for the house.' He shook his head when he looked at her. 'You ain't got enough money to feed this lot, girl. You leave it to me. I thought you could make a nice pie to stretch the meat.'

'Thanks, Dobbs.' She smiled at him. 'Have you ever been told that you're a good man?'

'What?'

She laughed, already pulling pie dishes out of the cupboard next to the larder. 'Doctor Burridge has something to tell you.'

'What?'

It was funny, but Dobbs never missed a word when he was told about the general's offer.

'That's bloody marvellous! Begging your pardon for the language, miss. What a turn-up. Now we'll be able to help more men.'

'We will indeed. I must tell the others the good news.' The doctor headed for the door, humming quietly to himself.

'Would you ask Tom and Lily to come down?' Dora called after him. 'They can help us with the food.'

Twenty-Eight

It had been a busy, exciting day and they were all tired when they arrived home, but Dora was pleased. Lily was now happy about the move, and Tom was already planning what he was going to do in the garden with John's help.

They made a pot of tea and sat down to enjoy it in the first quiet moment they'd had that day.

'Phew!' Tom gulped his tea. 'What a day!'

Lily just yawned.

'I think we all need an early night.' Dora stifled a yawn of her own.

'But we must see Stan first.' Lily was suddenly alert. 'He'll want to know about today and we've got lots to tell him.'

'Let's go now then.' Tom got to his feet. 'We can eat later.'

Lily didn't stop talking from the moment she ran into Stan's front room, hardly pausing for breath as she told him about her room. 'They let me paint the wall,' she told him proudly. 'And then we cooked a huge meal for all of them! There was ever so many there. Alan came with his dad! He's a general,' she told him in awe. 'And he's going to give the doctor lots of money so he can help more men.'

'Really?' Stan was giving the little girl his whole attention, listening intently. 'You've had an exciting day, haven't you?'

The animation left her face as she nodded. 'I don't want to leave you and June and everyone, but it's a nice place. Dora's told me why we have to go and she doesn't tell lies.'

'Of course she doesn't.' Stan smiled. 'And you won't be leaving us. We'll come and see you all the time. Wandsworth isn't the other side of the world. As soon as my leg's better I'm going to get myself a motor car, and we'll all be able to go out for rides.'

'Oh.' Lily's eyes opened wide. 'Could we go to the sea? I've never seen it. Mum said it's beautiful. She used to live by the sea.'

'Where?' Stan asked.

'Sweetie.' Dora immediately knelt in front of her sister. 'Did Mum ever tell you the name of the place?'

The girl screwed up her face in concentration. 'Don't think so. I was only little when she told me.'

'How come she never told us anything?' Tom complained.

'She said it was a long way from London,' Lily announced. 'She spoke funny to me and said that's how they sounded. It made me laugh.'

Stan was leaning forward eagerly. 'I think she must be talking about a regional accent, but which one? Can you talk like it?'

Lily shook her head.

Tom now joined in with a passable Scottish accent. 'Like that?'

'No.' Lily looked at her brother in amazement as he had a go at Welsh, making them all laugh.

'That was terrible.' Stan was highly amused. 'Have you heard anyone speak like it since then, Lily?'

'Hmm? Ray sounded a bit like it, I think.' The little girl was gazing from one to the other, trying hard to be helpful.

'Oh, yes, he did have an accent, but it was hardly notice-able.' Dora turned to her brother. 'You spent some time with the men today, did Ray say where he came from?'

'John told me Ray had been in the navy and was at the battle of Jutland. Since coming out of hospital he's been living in London, but his home was Liverpool, I think John said.'

'Liverpool!' Stan hit the arm of the chair with his hand. 'Damn! Why didn't we think of that? Lily told us your mum and dad met where the big boats are. We assumed it was Southampton or Portsmouth, and that's where the police have been making enquiries on the off chance that she went back there. No wonder we're not getting anywhere. We're prob-ably looking in the wrong place!' He struggled to his feet. 'I'll go and tell Reg. Well done, Lily. That was clever of you to remember. I never spoke to your mother so I didn't know she had a northern accent.'

'She didn't,' Dora told him, perplexed by Stan's reasoning. 'She spoke just like us. Well, better than us actually. Dad told us to listen to the way Mum spoke because she'd had a good education.'

'She gave us lessons,' Lily said sadly. 'She was ever so clever. I wish she hadn't gone away.'

'So do we all, sweetie, but she wouldn't have left us if she hadn't been forced to. She loved us, you know that.'

'Come on, urchin.' Tom took his little sister's hand. 'Let's go home and get something to eat. I'm starving. Do you want to eat with us, Stan?'

'Thanks, but I'm having dinner with Win and Reg tonight.' He was already moving towards the door.

'We'll see you tomorrow then.'

'Is Reg home?' Stan asked as soon as his sister opened the door.

'He's in the front room. And don't drink too much. Dinner will be ready in half an hour.'

He grinned at her. 'Time for a quick one then.'

'You make sure it's just one,' she scolded, then disappeared into the kitchen.

Stan stood in the doorway, and when Reg looked up from reading his paper, he said one word. 'Liverpool!'

'Sorry?'

'You're looking in the wrong place. The big ships Lily was talking about are in Liverpool.'

'You sure?'

Propping his crutches against the wall, Stan fell into a chair, and told his brother-in-law what Lily had said.

'That's interesting, but it doesn't mean the little girl has remembered it right. Win!' he called. 'Could you come here a minute?'

She looked in the door. 'I'm busy, Reg, what do you want?'

'You spoke to Mrs Bentley, didn't you? Did she have an accent of any kind?'

'I only spoke to her a couple of times outside the school, and no, I didn't notice an accent.'

'Thanks,' Reg smiled at his wife. 'That's all I wanted to know.'

When they were alone again, Stan couldn't let the subject drop. He had a strong feeling that the answers were in Liverpool. 'This needs to be followed up. We haven't uncovered any useful information about her in London, but there's a chance we could have more luck in Liverpool. It makes sense, Reg. That's probably where Mr Bentley sailed from when he was a merchant seaman.'

'I don't know, Stan.' Reg was still doubtful. 'All we've got are some vague memories from a little girl. She could be imagining things. Dora and Tom didn't know anything about this, did they?'

'No, but from what I've gathered Mrs Bentley seemed to speak more freely to her youngest child. I don't know why, but I do believe Lily. She's a bright kid.'

'I'm not sure we can widen the search any more. I'm sorry, Stan, but the feeling at the station is that we should abandon this case. Enough time's been spent on it already.'

'I'm not surprised.' Stan couldn't hide his disappointment. 'I'll have to go to Liverpool myself.'

'No you don't!' Reg was adamant. 'You're not fit enough yet. Leave it with me and I'll see if I can persuade the super to send someone to Liverpool. I'm not making any promises though. You know how it goes, Stan.'

He nodded and sighed inwardly. He couldn't ask for more than that from Reg. 'Thanks.'

'I could end up back on the beat if this turns out to be another waste of time,' he said dryly.

'Or you could be looking at promotion if it isn't.'

'You're letting your imagination run away with you, Stan.'

They were both grinning when Winnie called them to the table. They had been so busy talking that they hadn't even had one drink.

The next day, after his visit to the hospital, Stan called in at the station, unable to wait until the evening to find out if they were going to have a look at Liverpool.

'What did the doc say?' Reg asked as soon as he arrived. 'Are you going to get rid of those crutches soon?'

'Another week, he reckons, if all continues to go well. He's pleased, he said I'm healing well.' He sat down. 'Any news?'

His brother-in-law didn't have to ask what he was talking about. He nodded. 'I'm going up to Liverpool tomorrow. The super's given me two days, and if I can't find anything then we're to drop the case. There isn't much more we can do.'

'I understand. I hope you do find something, but two days isn't long enough. I should be more active soon though, so I'll be able to take over again. That woman's somewhere and I'm determined to find her. Her children have a right to know what's happened to their mother. It's the only way they're going to be able to put this behind them and get on with their lives.'

'Maybe, but have you thought that what we find might ruin their lives? There's something very strange in this woman's background, and my instinct's telling me we ought to stop this right now!'

Stan was shaking his head. 'No, I'm never going to give up! You'll find all the information you need in Liverpool. I'm sure of it.'

'I hope you're right.'

Stan smiled, feeling more hopeful after his talk with the doctor this morning. His chances of a good recovery were excellent and he now had a future to look forward to. 'You're being too pessimistic.'

Reg shrugged. 'There's one thing I'm sure about now. We're looking for a body.'

'That's how I feel. And we must find her to end her children's agony. Wish I could come with you tomorrow, but I've got to go to the hospital again. My leg's stiff and they're trying to get it moving again.'

'That's more important than tagging along with me. Do as they say, Stan, and you'll soon be back here working with us again.'

'Yes, I can't believe it. And if it hadn't been for Dora, I would never have visited the Wandsworth house and met the doc again.' He gazed into space for a moment, then sighed. 'I owe her so much, Reg.'

'Why?' His brother-in-law frowned, puzzled. 'It was Doctor Burridge who persuaded you to have the operation.'

'But if it hadn't been for Dora I wouldn't have considered it. When I first arrived back home I didn't care if I died, at least it would have been an end to the constant pain. But then I met a lovely, caring girl and I began to long to be well again. That's why I took a chance on the operation. She means a lot to me, and I don't care what's in her past.'

'Ah, I thought that was the case. She's a fine girl. Have you told her how you feel?'

'No, and I'm not going to. She's got enough to deal with at the moment. And if can't get back in the police, then I'm never going to tell her.'

Reg frowned again. 'But I thought you said the doc was pleased with you?'

'He is, but he can't guarantee anything yet. The next couple of weeks will be crucial, then we'll know how successful the operation has been.'

'Well, whatever the outcome, you'll still be better off than you were. Being in pain all the time would have led you to an early grave.'

'I know, and I'm grateful for the improvement, but I want more. I want my life back!' Stan stood up. 'Good luck in Liverpool.'

The next two days were an anxious time for Stan. Not only was he eager to know if his brother-in-law was having any success, he was enduring long sessions at the hospital. He felt as if he was learning to walk all over again. After relying on crutches and sticks, the thought of walking without such props seemed a daunting task. He gritted his teeth in determination. No one had ever said this was going to be easy!

After one particularly gruelling morning, he arrived home exhausted. All he could do was slump in a chair, close his eyes and rest. It wasn't long before he drifted off to sleep . . .

The sound of the front door opening and closing woke him. He opened his eyes to see Dora standing by his chair.

'Are you all right, Stan? I knocked but you didn't hear me.'

Sitting up straight, he nodded. 'Just a bit weary, that's all. The doc's a hard man when he needs to be.'

'I was going to invite you to eat with us, but I'll bring the dinner to you.'

'Thank you.' He glanced at the clock and gave a wry smile. 'I've been asleep for three hours and I don't think I can move just yet. Tell me how things are going at the house. Doc told me the workmen have moved in already.'

'Yes, the general certainly didn't waste any time. There are men all over the roof and others are tearing the kitchen apart. Our flat will soon be ready and we're hoping to be able to move in sometime next week. You must come and see it as soon as you're able to.'

'That won't be long now.' He spoke with confidence, any hint of doubt banished from his tone.

'That's good. You rest now and I'll come back with your dinner in half an hour.'

'Thanks, Dora.' He caught hold of her hand, brought it to his lips and kissed her gently. 'I don't know what I'd have done without your quiet support through this.'

'That's what friends do for each other.' She smiled and hurried away.

In fact it was Tom who arrived with the meal. 'Dora told me I mustn't stay because you're tired. She said you're to go straight to bed after dinner. We'll collect the plates tomorrow.'

'Thanks, Tom. I feel so useless at the moment. Dora never says anything to me, so how are you doing?'

'All right. You mustn't worry about us. Our big sister's taking good care of us. Night, Stan.'

He watched the boy leave, his heart heavy. They'd come to him for help and they had ended up helping him!

After finishing his meal he dozed in the chair, not seeming to have enough energy to drag himself upstairs. It was midnight when Reg walked in, and Stan was immediately awake, eager to hear the news.

'I saw your light on. I've only just arrived back.' Reg tossed his bag on to a spare chair and removed an envelope from his pocket. 'I've got a marriage certificate.'

'Ah, good.' Stan held out his hand. 'Let's see it then.'

'You're not going to like it.'

When he read it dismay made him shake his head in denial. This couldn't be right. 'Divorce papers?' he asked.

'None, and his wife didn't die until two years ago. Bentley never married Harriet, and that means—'

'I know what it means,' Stan snapped.

Reg sighed, looking as distressed and exhausted as Stan. 'I wish we'd left this alone, because what I've found out is going to blow that little family's world apart. The fact that their parents weren't married is only the beginning.'

'There's worse?'

'I'm afraid so.'

Twenty-Nine

'Can't you sleep?' Tom sat at the table, rubbing his eyes. 'It's past midnight, Dora.'

'Is it? I hadn't noticed, there's so much to think about and plan. We'll be able to move to the flat soon, and I'm wondering where the money's coming from to pay for the furniture to be shifted. The rooms at Wandsworth are quite large so we're going to need everything we have in this house. It could cost quite a bit.'

'Why don't we ask Dobbs if he knows someone who would do it for us cheaply? He's got connections – hasn't he?'

'Of course,' Dora said wearily. 'Why didn't I think of that?'

'Because you're too tired! You've got to stop worrying away the nights,' he told her sternly. 'Things are looking better for us. We've got somewhere decent to live – rent free – and you've got a full-time job with the doc. And look at all the friends we've made. We're doing all right.'

She nodded. 'I know we have a lot to be thankful for.' She gave her brother a tight smile. 'But I still can't help worrying.'

'You must! I'm not a kid, Dora! Put more responsibility on me. I can take it! You're not facing this alone. We're in this together, remember.'

'Oh, Tom.' Dora's eyes misted over. 'What would I do without you?'

'You'd manage well. You're a lot stronger than you realize, Dora. Come on.' He pulled her out of the chair. 'Get some sleep and things will look brighter in the morning.'

She didn't protest; her brother was quite right. Sitting alone at night and brooding was not a sensible thing to do. She must try to be more positive – just like him. Things were working out well for them. It was unlikely that their mother would be found now. Too much time had gone by – nearly two months – so they must be through the worst of this nightmare. They needed to look to the future and leave the past behind them. It was hard though, and she knew there would be more sleepless nights. Perhaps she would be able to rest once they had moved. She hoped so, and earnestly prayed that things would get easier from now on.

As soon as Dora arrived at the house the next day, she went straight to Dobbs and explained about the cost of moving. 'Do you know anyone who'd do it at a reasonable price?' she asked.

He patted her shoulder. 'Don't you worry now, I'll find you someone. You go and have a look at what the boys have done upstairs. They worked till it was dark. You'll be surprised.'

Surprised wasn't the word! The transformation was astounding. Each room was clean and freshly painted – even the windows had been polished. She had foolishly been worrying all night when in fact she should have been counting her blessings. The young men had worked tirelessly to make this place habitable, and their kindness overwhelmed her as she wandered from room to room. When she reached Lily's room, she stood in the doorway, speechless. It was in a delicate shade of pink. But it was the far wall that took her breath away, and the man completely absorbed in what he was doing. She must have gasped out loud, because he turned.

'Good morning, Dora.' He stepped back. 'Do you think your sister will like this?'

On the wall was a meadow with wild flowers and animals of every kind. Hovering above them was an angel, smiling straight at Dora. The figure shimmered in silver and gold, and had the most gentle face imaginable.

'Oh, Ray! I've never seen anything so beautiful!'

He smiled, pleased with her response. 'This is an angel to look over you. I wanted to give you a gift and this is my way of thanking you.'

'I think you've got that the wrong way round. We're the ones who need to thank you.'

'Not so.' Ray shook his head. 'I was afraid to go out, sure everyone would recoil at the sight of my injuries – John practically had to drag me here. And you didn't seem to notice my scars at all, not even your little sister, and that surprised me in a child so young. I'll always be grateful for that because it really lifted my confidence.'

Dora had been transfixed by the painting as Ray spoke, now she tore her gaze away and fastened on Ray. 'I'm sure you've been imagining you look worse than you do. The scars are healed and they're really not that bad.' She tipped her head to one side and smiled. 'That eye patch makes you look quite dashing.'

A deep chuckle rumbled through him. 'Thank you for that, Dora.'

She walked closer to the painting, examining it in detail. 'And you're a very talented man. Don't you ever forget that!'

'I won't ever forget meeting you and your lovely family. The doctors have done all they can for me, but I've been staying in London. I was hesitant about going home and facing my family and friends. But not any more. The painting's finished and I'm going home today.'

'They'll be so pleased to see you.' She reached up and kissed his cheek. 'Will you let us know how you're getting on?'

'I'm going to stay in touch with John, and I'll want to know you're happy in your new home.'

'We will be,' she said softly. 'We've got a guardian angel to look after us now. Thank you, Ray.'

He nodded. 'I hope everything works out well for you.'

'You too.' She watched him walk away, and then sat on a wooden box to gaze at the wall. A wonderful sense of peace swept through her as she looked at each animal, smiling at the comical expressions on some of the little faces. But it was the face of the angel that touched her the most. It was compelling – that was the only way she could describe it. Ray was a talented man and must have an inner gentleness to be able to produce work like this. He deserved to have a full and productive life.

'We've got to tell them, Stan.' Reg paced around the desk where his brother-in-law was sitting, looking as stubborn as he'd ever seen him. 'You've had the night to make a decision. When you walked in the station this morning, I hoped you were going to agree.'

'Well, I'm not! Damn it Reg, do you know what you're asking?' Stan thumped the desk with his fist. 'This will destroy their lives! Their parents did a good job of hiding this, and that's where it should stay – hidden. Bury it. Please, Reg.'

'You know I can't do that. It's all on record now. But suppose we did do as you ask and dropped the whole investigation without saying a word, what would happen if it came to light later and we'd kept it a secret from them?' Reg sat down heavily. 'They'd hate us. Is that what you want?'

'No!' Stan ran a hand over his eyes, trying to think of the right thing to do. The Bentleys had a right to the truth about their parents, but . . . 'Dear God, Reg, I don't want to hurt them.'

'Neither do I, but what choice do we have?'

'None!' Stan lifted his head, his decision made. There was no way they could protect them from this, but they mustn't just barge in and drop such a bombshell in their laps. They had to do it as carefully as possible. 'They'll be moving in the next few days. Can we at least let them do that in peace?'

'A week, that's all. I'll say our enquiries aren't yet completed. But we can't sit on it longer than that. There are other people involved now, and that could cause even more problems than we've got already.'

'You didn't give them Dora's address, did you?'

'Of course not. And they didn't ask, so I don't think they'll cause any trouble. But . . .' Reg shrugged. 'We can't be sure.'

'No, we can't bank on that. Now they've had time to think about it, they might want the necklace back. I hope Dora's still got it.'

'Try and find out, Stan. If they have got rid of it we'll need to get it back.'

'What a bloody mess!' Stan exclaimed.

'We guessed from the beginning there was something unpleasant in their mother's past. Now we know, and it's worse than I expected. The only thing we can do is help them as much as we can. They're going to need all the love and support we can give them.'

'We'll do that.' Stan stood up. 'I must get to the hospital, and then I'll call in at the Wandsworth house on my way back.'

'Try with just one stick,' the doc ordered. He watched carefully as Stan took one step, and then another. 'How does that feel? Any pain?'

'No, it feels good.' He smiled for the first time since hearing

Reg's news. He continued walking, marvelling at how normal it felt now.

The doctor nodded in satisfaction as he watched. 'As you know, that leg's now about an inch shorter than the other one, but we can build up the shoe, and then you shouldn't limp quite so much. Bring another pair with you tomorrow and I'll get that done.'

'Thanks.' Stan sat down, sighing with relief. It really did look as if the leg was going to be all right, and there was no pain at all from his back. 'Can I do away with the crutches?'

'Yes, as long as you use two sticks while you're out. And don't overdo it. You've made remarkable progress and I'm proud of you, my boy. Just be patient for a little while longer.' Dr Burridge glanced at the clock. 'Same time tomorrow.' Then he hurried away to his next appointment.

It was bedlam when Stan arrived at Wandsworth. There were men clambering on the roof, throwing slates into the front garden, and the entrance hall was full of wood and rubble.

'Whoops! Mind how you go, sir!' Dobbs began clearing a passage so Stan could get in. 'Don't know why they have to make such a mess. Can I get you some tea? We've got a stove fixed up in the back room.'

'Not just now, thanks. I'm looking for Dora. The doc said she should be here.'

'She's upstairs. Looking a real treat it is. It'll be lovely having them living here. Nice kids, they are.' Dobbs shook his head. 'No news of their mum I suppose?'

'No, nothing,' Stan lied, and headed for the stairs.

He found Dora in the kitchen scrubbing away at the sink. 'This is all looking very nice,' he said when she glanced up.

'Stan!' She dried her hands, smiling. 'You must have a look at this. Come with me.'

He followed her into another room and stopped in astonishment.

'Isn't it beautiful?' She spoke softly. 'Ray painted it for Lily.'

'Extraordinary,' Stan agreed. 'He must be very talented. Is he here now? I'd like to meet him.'

'He was earlier, but he's gone home now. He lives somewhere near Liverpool, I think. Lily was right about his accent, though it's very slight. Have you followed up on that yet?'

'That's up to the police.' He fixed his gaze on the painting, unable to look her in the eyes as he lied. 'They're not eager to do anything about it.'

'I don't expect they are. A little girl's vague memories aren't much to go on, are they?'

'No. Has Lily seen this yet?' He quickly changed the subject. Dora looked almost happy today, obviously pleased with the way things were working out for them. His insides churned, knowing that soon he was going to shatter their hard-won pleasure.

'Doc's here, Dora!' Dobbs called up the stairs.

'I've got to go, Stan. The men are in the back room, so why don't you go and see them? We can't cook a meal at the moment but there will be sandwiches.'

'I'll do that.' Then he remembered what he'd come for. 'Do you know when you're moving?'

'In about three days. Dobbs arranged it all for me.'

'Ah, he's a useful man to have around.' He smiled casually and joked, 'Don't leave anything behind, especially Lily's necklace. She might like to show it to the angel.'

Dora laughed. 'Don't worry, she won't let me forget it.'

As she hurried away, Stan let out a pent-up breath. Thank God! She still had it.

Thirty

The next couple of days were so busy that Dora hardly had time to think, which in a way was a blessing. Lily had gone into raptures about the painting on her wall; disappointed that Ray was no longer here, she had written a letter to thank him. John had promised to send it for her. Even before they moved, Tom had attacked the garden. If left to himself he would have dug up everything, but fortunately John was there to stop him doing too much damage. They had started digging over a section at the end of the garden for a vegetable plot. Now the flat was finished, the young men had enjoyed doing something useful and were tackling the front garden.

The kitchen downstairs was finished too, and the cook Mrs Chandler, sent by the general, was arriving on Monday. Dora had already met her and liked her on sight. So did Dobbs. She was a large, friendly woman and insisted on being called Lizzie. The workmen were still clambering about on the roof, but they would be finished in a couple of days. The full beauty of the fine house was being revealed after years of neglect. Dr Burridge was delighted to see his old family home coming back to life.

Dora was working at the hospital today and needed to find the doctor to remind him about his next appointment – he'd forgotten again. She was hurrying along a corridor when she saw a tall man walking towards her. She stopped in amazement, waiting until he reached her.

'Stan!' There had been little time lately to talk to him, or see how he was doing. 'You're walking so well! This is wonderful. I'm so happy for you.'

'Hello, Dora.' He bent and kissed her cheek. 'I'm down to using one stick now, and the doc reckons I'll be able to do away with that soon. They've made a small adjustment to one of my shoes and that's balanced me. It feels good to be able to walk properly again.'

'I'm sure it does. Just wait till Tom and Lily see you. As soon as we've moved you must all come round and we'll hold a party to celebrate your recovery.'

'We'd like that. Have you got a definite date for moving yet?'

'Tomorrow. Dobbs has arranged for a van to move our furniture.' She glanced anxiously at the clock on the wall. 'Please excuse me, I've got to find the doctor or he's going to be late – again!'

'You'll find him in room twenty-three. I'll help you with the move, if you like.'

'That would be wonderful. We need all the help we can get. I never realized we had so much stuff. Thank you. See you tomorrow.' Then she hurried away.

The door to the room was open and she could hear the doctor's voice before she reached it. She knocked and peered in.

'Ah, are you looking for me, Dora?'

'Yes, sir, I'm sorry to interrupt, but you have an appointment at Roehampton in half an hour.'

He looked puzzled for a moment, and then nodded. 'So I do. You'll have to excuse me, gentlemen.' He turned and followed Dora back to his office.

She handed him a small case. 'All the papers you need are in here.'

'How did I ever manage without you? I've been told that my timekeeping has improved.'

'It won't today if you don't leave at once, sir. You're still going to be late however fast you drive.'

'Not by much.' He paused by the door. 'I won't need you any more today. I'll be coming to the house tomorrow afternoon, so I'll see you then. I'm sure you have a lot to do. Have you got enough help?'

'Plenty.' Her smile broadened. 'I've just seen Stan, and he was walking so well. Isn't it wonderful!'

'He's done well, and I'm pleased with the result, but his fast recovery is down to his determination.'

'His sister calls it stubbornness,' she laughed. 'Now,' she urged him out of the door. 'Try not to be too late, eh?'

He left, chuckling quietly.

Glad of the extra time to continue packing, Dora went straight home. She soon lost track of time, and was surprised when Tom and Lily came in.

'My goodness, is it that late?' She bundled clothes into an old suitcase, only managing to close it with her brother's help. 'I'd better get tea, you must be starving.'

'Don't bother to cook tonight.' Tom followed her down the stairs and into the kitchen. 'We've got too much to do.'

'We must have something. What would you like?' she asked Lily.

'Boiled eggs and bread and butter.' This was one of her sister's favourites.

'That'll do.' Tom was already in the larder. 'We've got eggs we must eat up before tomorrow.'

With that decided, the simple meal was soon ready. While they were eating, Dora told them about seeing Stan, and the party she had suggested by way of a celebration.

'Yes please!' Lily clapped her hands. 'Can we invite everyone?'

'We ought to,' Tom said. 'They've all worked hard for us and this would be a good way to thank them. We've got three things to celebrate really – moving into our new home, Stan being well again and the work on the house finished. We'd never get everyone in upstairs but I'm sure the doctor will let us use the room downstairs. I'll ask him.'

'I like the idea, Tom, but how can we afford it? We'll need food, and something for the men to drink . . .'

'You leave that with me. I'll have a word with Dobbs and see what we can come up with.' Tom smiled confidently. 'And there's always the pawnbroker.'

'True.' Dora grimaced. 'That man greets us like old friends when we go into his shop.'

Her brother laughed. 'Well, it won't be for much longer. Once we don't have to pay rent, things will be easier for us.'

'And what a relief that will be,' Dora said with feeling.

Lily finished the last of her egg and stood up. 'Can I go and see Stan now? I want to see him walk.'

'Me too. You coming, Dora? We'll clear up when we get back.'

'All right, but we mustn't be long.'

Lily was out of the door with her brother right behind her. Dora looked around at the mess the house was in and shrugged. It would wait for an hour, she decided, and made her way to Stan's.

When she arrived he was walking across the room with her brother and sister watching intently.

'That's wonderful!' Tom was clearly impressed. 'You hardly limp at all.'

'Does it still hurt?' Lily wanted to know.

'No, little one. It's all better now.'

'That's good, isn't it, Dora?' She spun round to her sister. 'Very.'

Just then Winnie and June arrived.

'Stan can walk properly now,' Lily informed them, as if she was telling them something they didn't already know. 'And when we've moved, we're going to give a *big* party. Everyone can come.'

'That's settled then,' Tom whispered in Dora's ear. 'We'll definitely have to pay another visit to the pawnbroker.'

It was nearly two hours before they managed to get away. Dora was puzzled by Stan. He should have been delighted with his progress, but he seemed rather subdued. He was probably tired, she decided, pushing away the thought as she set about getting everything ready for the morning. The movers were coming at nine o'clock.

She was up by six, moving around quietly, not wanting to disturb her brother and sister at this early hour. Tom joined her by seven, so they gave Lily breakfast in bed.

At nine o'clock a van arrived with Dobbs driving. 'Borrowed this off a mate,' he told Dora. 'Thought me and Tom could manage with the loading. He's a big strong lad, but I 'spect we'll need to make more than one trip.'

'We'll help as well.'

Dora spun round to face Stan and Reg, standing there in their old clothes with sleeves rolled up ready to work.

'It's my day off,' Reg told them.

Another car arrived and Alan got out. 'Need any help?'

'We do.' Dobbs looked round at the assembled crowd. 'Now we'll soon get this job done.'

Dora was quite overwhelmed by everyone's generosity, and smiled as Lily danced up to Alan.

'Can I come with you in your car? Stan too, because he mustn't work too hard.'

'Of course you can both come, and there'll still be room

to put some of the more delicate things in as well.' Alan turned his attention to Stan who had walked over to him. 'Well done, my friend. I'm very happy to see you well again.'

He nodded. 'It was my lucky day when I met Doctor Burridge.'

'All right!' Dobbs shouted to gain everyone's attention. 'Let's get on with it.'

They sprang into action. It took three trips before the house was empty. On the last run, Dora went with the van. Her heart was sad as they drove away, and she didn't dare look back or she would have cried. It felt as if the last link with their mother was being broken. It was an awful feeling, and she was glad that her brother and sister were already in Wandsworth. They had been spared seeing the house empty; the house that had been their home, made for them with love and care by their mother. Now both had vanished from their lives. It was a hard step to take, but it would be for the best in the end, she was sure.

There was great excitement at the house and Dora forced away the sadness. She had expected tears from Lily, but the little girl couldn't wait to move into her room with the beautiful painting on the wall. Tom also seemed to have no regrets.

'We've done the right thing,' he told her, knowing her well enough to read the expression on her face. 'We couldn't have stayed in that house, and we've been very lucky to be able to come here. Let's try and put the past behind us, Dora.'

'I know.' She squeezed his arm. 'I'll be all right once we've sorted everything out.' She watched the activity, amazed that so many people wanted to help them. The house was full of willing helpers, insisting on doing something regardless of any disability they had. Smiling at her brother, she said, 'It seems that in this dreadful time for us we've been showered with many blessings.'

'We certainly have.' He hefted a dining chair on to his shoulders, looking very mature for his age. 'Do you realize what isolated lives we lived when Mum was with us?'

'I never thought about it at the time, but I can see it now. I thought Mum didn't make friends with neighbours because she was working too hard. But it wasn't that, was it? We know now she had secrets, and she hid them well, even from us.'

Tom grimaced. 'I'd dearly love to know what she was up to, but perhaps it's best we don't.'

'You might be right. Don't carry that, Lily!' Dora rushed to her little sister who was tottering along clutching a large vase. 'It's too heavy. You'll drop it!'

'Don't just stand there, Dora,' Alan chided playfully. 'We need you upstairs to tell us where to put the furniture.'

'Oops, sorry.' She ran up the stairs, taking the vase with her. The flat was in utter chaos. 'Where do we start?' she gasped.

Alan appeared beside her, shook his head and shouted, 'Sergeant!'

'You called, sir.' Stan walked into the room.

'Get some men to sort out this bloody mess. Dora will tell you where everything goes. There are enough men milling around.'

'Yes, sir!' Stan came smartly to attention and saluted.

Dora's earlier gloom was now a thing of the past, and she laughed. 'The general should have come as well and made it a military operation.'

'We've got our orders.' A deep rumbling chuckle came from Stan. 'The captain's more than capable of taking over the operation. Now, where do you want that table just coming through the door?'

With Alan now directing things from downstairs and Stan upstairs doing the same, the chaos was soon transformed into a smooth operation. In no time at all the flat began to look like home.

As soon as she could get into the kitchen, Dora grabbed her brother and sister. 'Help me make tea and sandwiches. They must all be gasping by now.'

Their lounge was a large room, but it was packed when they took in the refreshments. The tea had just been handed round when the door burst open and the general strode in.

'You timed that well, father,' Alan said dryly.

'Didn't I.' The impressive man actually smiled as he relieved his son of his cup. He winked at Lily, making her giggle.

Dora quickly poured Alan another cup of tea, and Lily held out a plate of sandwiches. 'Would you like a sandwich?' she asked politely.

'Hmm, what are they?'

'Cheese.' She giggled again. For some odd reason, the general always made her act like this. 'They're good. I made them myself.'

'Ah, in that case I'll have one. Cheese is my favourite.'

At that moment Dr Burridge also arrived, making Tom leap up and mutter, 'I'd better make another pot.'

The general shook the doctor's hand. 'We must put our plans into action now the house is ready.' He glanced at Dora. 'Most of the organization in the early days will fall upon your shoulders, my dear. But Mrs Chandler will soon be able to take over everything to do with the food, and with Dobbs, they should be able to run the place quite efficiently. That's a good man you've got there, doctor, and we must pay him a wage.'

Dora watched the surprise on Dobbs' face, and saw his mouth twitch at the corners. *He heard that all right*, she thought with amusement.

'I agree.' The doctor turned to face the men in the room. 'Gentlemen, I have to take Dora away from you now. Can you manage without her for a while?'

'We've got a captain and a sergeant to keep us in order,' John remarked, making the room erupt into laughter.

Knowing she could leave everything in their capable hands, Dora followed the doctor down to his office, listening to the laughter coming from her new home. It could only be a happy place after such a lovely beginning. At the start of this nightmare she had been afraid that her brother and sister would be taken from her and placed in someone else's care. But that hadn't happened, and she suspected that was due to Stan and his family. She hadn't asked – hadn't wanted to know. All that mattered was that they were still together, and she was feeling quite light-headed with hope for the future.

Thirty-One

It was a week before Dora could give any thought to the party. Lily's continual requests finally wore her down, and they had settled on the coming Saturday afternoon, leaving her only two days to make the arrangements. Thank goodness she had Dobbs and Lizzie, who had said over and over that they would be happy to help. Her little sister was so looking forward to it, and she had been very good, attending the new school without protest, although it meant making new friends. Tom had also taken to his school without uttering one complaint, but then she had never expected him to complain. If he didn't like something, he would keep quiet and sort it out in his own way. Dora was well aware that this was a great upheaval for both of them, but they appeared to be settling down well and she was immensely relieved about that. It had worried her that it had been necessary to put them through this move. She had been almost running from one job to another and hadn't thought about visiting the solicitors as planned. But it didn't matter. It would most likely be a waste of time, anyway.

On the day of the party Dora had been at the hospital all morning, and their guests would be arriving at three o'clock. With only two hours to spare she hurried home.

'Ah, there you are.' Dobbs met her at the door. 'Everything's ready. Lizzie's made a fine job of the food. Wonderful cook, that woman is.'

'What?' All was ready? She was sure she hadn't heard that properly.

He smirked. 'That's my word. Come with me.'

She followed him along the passage to the back room, gasping in amazement when she saw the long table against the wall. It was loaded with all kinds of food, and there was a barrel of beer right in the middle. Tom and Lily were standing with Lizzie, proud grins on their faces.

'Where did all this come from?' She had given Lizzie what money she had, but it would never have bought this sumptuous feast!

'Auntie Winnie and June have been here.' Lily dragged her sister over to the table, telling her who had donated certain items of food. 'The beer came from Uncle Reg and Stan. And John's going to play the piano for us.'

'I didn't know he could play.' Dora glanced at her brother for confirmation.

'Says he's out of practice, but he'll knock out a tune for us.'

'Well I never!' was all she could say.

Dobbs urged them towards the door. 'Now I think you should all go upstairs and make yourselves look pretty.'

Tom raised his hands in horror. 'I'll have a job to make myself look pretty!'

'What?'

'Oh, he's gone deaf again, Lily.' Tom shook his head in mock dismay, but his eyes were glinting with laughter. 'Come on urchin, let's see if you still fit into your party frock.'

Dora took one last look around, wondering how this party had got so out of hand. She had intended it to be a small affair, but it had gathered momentum. Heavens above! She didn't even know how many were coming.

'Stop fretting, girl.' Dobbs pushed her towards the door. 'This was the doc's idea. He's asked all the men to come and bring their families with them. He said it was time everyone learned to laugh again. This was his family home, so he's delighted it's come to life again, and helping a few people as well. You make sure you come down here with a smile on your face. Me and Lizzie are here to see everything goes smoothly.'

'I will, and I'm sorry if I seem such a worrier. Thank you both for all you've done. I'm sure the party will be a great success.'

'There's no need to apologize.' Lizzie gave her an understanding smile. 'You're having a hard time, what with your mother missing and the responsibility for those two youngsters of yours weighing heavy on your shoulders. I don't suppose you give a thought to yourself.'

'I am the eldest, and they depend on me,' she pointed out.

'True, but you've got to ease up on yourself and remember

you're surrounded by people who love and admire you. If there's anything you can't handle, you can come to any of us for help. And Stan would walk through hell for you. Now off you go and get ready.'

Dora had much to ponder as she walked upstairs.

'Look! It's too small,' Lily wailed as soon as she appeared. 'It's the only good frock I've got.'

'Let me see.' Dora knelt in front of her sister. 'Hmm, you've grown, but there's plenty of material in the side seams and the hem. I can soon let it out for you, sweetie.'

'Can you?' Her face brightened at once.

'Of course. Take it off and bring me the workbasket.'

An hour later, after much snipping, unpicking, sewing and pressing, the frock slipped easily over Lily's head.

She stood in front of a mirror, turning this way and that as she inspected the finished garment. 'You are clever, Dora!' She threw her arms around her big sister. 'It looks lovely. Can I wear my necklace?'

'I don't see why not. It is a party, isn't it?'

'Goody.' Lily beamed at her brother as he walked into the kitchen, freshly washed and wearing a clean shirt. 'Dora's made my frock fit, and she said I can wear my necklace.'

'So I see. You're going to dazzle everyone in the room.' Tom frowned at Dora. 'You'd better hurry. We mustn't be late.'

'Goodness!' Dora scrambled to her feet. 'Get the necklace for Lily.'

'I'll see to it, you hurry.'

'Thanks.' She dashed to her bedroom with only half an hour to get ready.

'Isn't Reg home yet?' Stan asked when he went to collect Winnie and June.

'No, but I expect he'll come straight to the party when he's off duty. You know how it is, Stan.' His sister gazed at him with affection and said softly, 'I didn't think I'd ever see you like this again, looking fit and moving without pain. You're a handsome devil, in a tough sort of way.'

'Thanks – I think. Is June ready? We'd better get going.'

'Here I am.' June danced into the room wearing a pale lemon frock. 'This is new, Uncle Stan. Do you like it?'

'Very pretty, and so are you.'

She smiled, delighted with the compliment. 'Will there be lots of people at the party?'

'I think so, but you know quite a few of them will be ex-soldiers wounded in the war, don't you?'

She nodded. 'Mummy told me all about that, and I promise not to stare. I never stared at you when you couldn't walk, did I, Uncle Stan?'

'No, you're a good girl.' He took hold of her hand. 'Let's go, shall we?'

The Bentleys were standing just inside the room to greet the guests as they arrived, and it made Stan's temperature rise when he saw the little girl was wearing the necklace. They had no idea of its value, and he hoped no one else in the room could tell that it was real diamonds. There were at least twenty people there and it was good to see the young men with their families. The general had just arrived with his son and the doctor. John was playing the piano as background music, and Dobbs was even wearing a tie, making this a very special occasion indeed!

Dora looked lovely, if a bit flushed as if she had been hurrying, in a frock of pale blue. He wanted to get her to himself, but she was too busy at the moment. He would have to be patient and choose his time.

'Have a drink, Stan.' Tom handed him a glass of beer. 'Is Reg coming?'

'He'll be here if he can, but he's been delayed.'

At that moment the doctor called order. 'Welcome, we're pleased you could all come to this little gathering. We have much to celebrate. Thanks to the generosity of General Harrington, the house is now in a fit state for us to extend our activities.'

There was a round of applause, which the general took with good grace.

'I am personally delighted that Dora and her family are now living in the flat upstairs. We wish them much happiness in their new home. And we are also here to congratulate Stan on making a good recovery. Entirely due to his own courage and determination.' The doctor smiled at Stan. 'Well done, my boy.'

Stan smiled, embarrassed at having attention drawn to him

like this. 'You've got that wrong, sir. My recovery is entirely due to your skill as a surgeon.'

'Raise your glasses to the doc,' John called. 'Without him some of us would still be in wheelchairs.'

There was a heartfelt round of applause for the man who cared enough to give unstintingly of his time and skill. He held up his hands for quiet. 'It's my pleasure to work with so many fine young men. Now, I suggest we tuck into this splendid food.'

Stan was about to go over to Dora when he saw her smile at someone who had just arrived. He turned and saw a young man. He was tall, even taller than Stan's six foot one. His left arm was missing; there was a patch over his left eye and his face was badly scarred.

'Ray!' The yelp of delight came from Lily as she hurled herself at him. 'Thank you for my picture, it's beautiful. Did you get my letter?'

'I did, and John told me about the party, so I just had to come.'

Ah, he must be the artist, Stan thought. He stood back and watched the crowd gather round, welcoming him with genuine pleasure.

'Stan, come and meet Ray.' Dora urged him forward.

After the introduction, Stan stayed with Ray, and he liked him at once. He spoke with a soft, musical voice, and there was a gentleness about him. It wasn't surprising that he was such a talented artist. One tragedy of the war was that men like this had been sent to the trenches, and the lives even of many who came back had been shattered in one way or another. Right from a young child Stan had been tough, and when faced with the horror of war, he had fought with grim determination. But for someone as sensitive as Ray it must have been nothing short of purgatory.

John abandoned the piano and joined them, bringing a tray with three pints of beer.

Dora also arrived with a plate of sandwiches. 'How are you getting on at home, Ray?'

'All right, thanks to all of you. You gave me the confidence to face my family and friends. I've been working hard and finished a couple of paintings. A local gallery is taking an interest in my work. They put them on show and even sold one.'

'That's wonderful! One day when you're famous I'll be able to say we have an original of yours on our wall.'

He laughed at the compliment. 'Would you mind if I took photographs of it? I've brought a camera with me.'

'That's a lovely idea. Tom, Lily,' she called. 'Take Ray upstairs so he can take a picture of the angel.'

Lily bounced with pleasure. 'Can June come too?'

'Of course she can.'

Stan watched them leave, and when John went back to the piano he was finally alone with Dora. 'Tom's been telling me about his garden. Will you show me?'

She nodded. 'He's very proud of it.'

The afternoon was warm with a slight breeze to stir the air, and although all the doors and windows were open, it was pleasant to walk outside. There was a high wall around the entire garden, making it into an oasis of calm in busy Wandsworth.

'He has been working hard.' Stan surveyed the freshly dug-over plot. 'What's he going to grow?'

'Everything. By next year he reckons we won't need to buy another vegetable in the shops.' There was laughter in her eyes as she looked up at him.

'It's good he's found an interest. This is a lovely spot.'

'Yes, it is.' She was serious once again. 'We've been very lucky. I know you didn't want us to move, but it was the right thing to do. That house was too expensive for us, and it held a lot of memories. We're happier away from it.'

'You were quite right to come here. I was being selfish, not wanting to lose you.' He reached out and turned her to face him, then lowered his head and kissed her on the lips. Standing up straight again, he said, 'I want you to know I love you, Dora. And have done from the moment we met.'

When she went to speak he placed fingers on her lips to stop her. 'Don't say anything, let me finish. Now I can move around again I want to be able to take you out, spend some time on our own so you can get to know me better. And I hope, in time, that you'll love me enough to marry me.'

'Oh, Stan, I do already love you, but it wouldn't work between us. I could never leave Tom and Lily. I'll have to stay unmarried until they're grown up.'

'My darling girl, I wouldn't dream of separating you from

them. Where you go, they go, I know that, and I wouldn't have it any other way.' He stopped her again before she could speak. 'I'm not asking for a decision now, just remember I love you – all of you – and no matter what happens I want us to be together. Will you remember that? It's important, my dear.'

'I'll remember.' She smiled shyly. 'And I look forward to getting to know you better.'

Stan breathed an enormous inward sigh of relief as they walked back to the house. He'd told her clearly how he felt. All he could hope was that when the truth came out she would turn to him, and not away.

When they rejoined the party he saw his brother-in-law had arrived. He was still in uniform. 'You obviously didn't have time to change,' he said. 'Had a busy time?'

Reg took a long swig of beer. 'Had one hell of a day.' Pulling Stan aside, he said quietly, 'We've found a woman's body.'

Thirty-Two

Propping herself up in bed, Dora stared at the fingers of moonlight filtering through the half-drawn curtains. She was bewildered. Stan's behaviour had been bizarre. Had that been a proposal of marriage? If so then he hadn't wanted an answer from her – hadn't given her a chance to speak. If he didn't want to know how she felt, then why say anything? She rubbed a hand over her eyes as the questions ran through her mind. And most confusing of all, he had then made a point of telling her that no matter what happened he would be there for them. They had known that from the moment he had agreed to help them. Perhaps she shouldn't have told him she loved him, but he had taken her by surprise. She had never been in love before – never even had a boyfriend – so how was she to know what was the right thing to do? Of course, marriage for them was out of the question. No man could be expected to take on responsibility for the three of them. And she loved him too much to place such a burden on him, no matter how willing he appeared to be. No, she would be wise to forget this ever happened. He had probably acted strangely because he was feeling good about his recovery . . .

Her bedroom door opened and a little face peered in. 'You awake, Dora?'

'Yes, sweetie, can't you sleep either?'

Lily padded to her in bare feet and climbed on the bed, snuggling up to her big sister.

'I'm too excited. It was a lovely party, wasn't it? And Ray came to see us again.'

'That was a nice surprise, and we might see him tomorrow because he's staying at John's tonight.'

'Hmm, hope so.' Lily yawned. 'He took pictures of the wall and said he'd send me one. I can take it to school and show them.'

'Have you made a special friend yet?'

'No, but they're quite nice, and I like my teacher. But I do miss June.'

'I expect you do.' Dora smiled down at her. 'Did June have a good time at the party?'

'Oh yes, they all did – except Uncle Reg. He didn't look very happy.'

'He could have been cross because he was late and hadn't had time to go home and change. I don't suppose he liked coming to the party in his uniform.'

'Hmm, 'spect so . . .'

Dora studied her sister's face. Lily had fallen asleep in mid-sentence. She leant back against the pillows and closed her eyes, Lily's gentle breathing making her relax.

Sleep was the last thing on Stan's mind. He was at the station examining the contents of the handbag found in some bushes close to where the body had been discovered. It had been buried in a shallow grave.

'We're going to have to ask Dora if she recognizes anything here.' Reg began putting the items back in the bag.

Stan's mouth was set in a grim line. 'But she can't be asked to identify the body!'

'No, that's out of the question. You met the woman, so do you think you could do it?'

'I'll try. We've still got the photograph of her, so that might be a help. Any chance of doing it now?'

'There's always someone at the mortuary. Let's go.'

They walked out of the station together. Stan said, 'After we've done this I'd like to see where she was found.'

Reg nodded as they got into a police car.

The mortuary was almost in darkness except for a dim light over the door. There was only one elderly man on duty. He led them along a corridor and into another room, then he turned on all the lights.

'If it is our missing woman Stan might be able to identify her,' Reg explained to the assistant.

The man nodded, gave Stan a thoughtful stare, and then pointed to a covered figure. 'It ain't gonna be easy, sir.'

Conscious that he mustn't make a mistake, Stan took his time as the sheet was pulled back.

'If you're not sure, then say so,' Reg advised.

There was no doubt in his mind, and he nodded. 'That's her.'

'Positive?'

'Yes.'

They thanked the attendant and went outside, glad to get out of that place. Stan lit a cigarette and drew the smoke in, releasing it on a long sigh. Reg did the same and they smoked in silence.

They stubbed out their cigarettes, and Reg swore under his breath. 'They were all so happy at the party, and now we're going to ruin everything for them. Still, at least they'll be able to have a funeral. But we're not going to be their favourite people when we tell them the truth, Stan.'

'It's got to be done, and far better coming from us. Now, let's go and see where she was found.'

Reg took him to a large patch of waste ground, and walked in about twenty steps. 'She was in a shallow grave just here. Some kids were playing and found her.'

'Hmm.' There was a bright moon shining and Stan could see the area quite clearly. They were close to a cluster of low buildings. 'We're back to Roger Grant again, aren't we? If he is responsible then he must be stupid to leave the body so near to the factory.'

'Panic, I expect. This was probably the only place he could think of where he wouldn't be seen. But proving it was him will be difficult.'

Stan's expression was grim. 'I'll leave that to you. My concern now will be for her children.'

'They're going to need you.' Reg shook his head sadly. 'We'll see them tomorrow and ask if they can identify anything in the handbag. Then we'll have the unpleasant task of telling them the whole story. I'll ask Win to come with us. We can leave June at our neighbours'. Now, I think we should get some sleep.'

'You're joking, of course!'

'Where's June?' Lily asked as soon as they arrived.

'With our friends next door.' Winnie looked around. 'Is Dora home yet?'

Tom was already filling the kettle so he could make tea for their visitors. 'She's been at the hospital all day, but she should be home any time now. Good party, wasn't it?'

'Yes, very enjoyable.' Winnie helped set out the cups.

Stan had never considered himself a coward, but he didn't want to do this. As he looked at their smiling faces, he felt sick – afraid that in a short time he was going to lose them. He loved them all.

At that moment the door opened and Dora came in, breaking into a smile of pleasure. 'Oh, what a lovely surprise! Are you going to stay and help us eat some of the food left over from the party?'

Both Reg and Stan were on their feet, unable to relax enough to sit down.

'We need to talk to you first.' Stan glanced at Reg, the slight nod of his head indicating that he wanted his brother-in-law to start.

Removing the handbag from its paper wrapping, Reg tipped the contents on to a table near Dora. 'Will you tell me if you recognize anything here?'

There was a deathly stillness in the room as the youngsters stared at the items. Dora's hand was shaking as she reached out and picked up a powder compact. After turning it over and over in her hands, she held it out for Tom to see. When he nodded, Stan felt his insides clench. He'd known it was their mother when he'd seen the body, but this confirmation still jolted him.

'Dad gave this to Mum before he went to France. She never went anywhere without it.' The colour had drained from Dora's face. 'You've found her?'

'Yes,' Reg told them. 'And I'm sorry to have to tell you that your mother is dead.'

Stan wanted to reach out and comfort them, but the three Bentleys had drawn close together, effectively shutting out the others in the room. He saw Winnie move towards them and then step back. The little tableau was saying, *This is our grief, it's private.*

'How did it happen?' Tom was the first to speak. 'And do you need us to identify her? I'll do it, if you do.'

Reg spoke now as a policeman. 'She was killed, but we don't have details as yet. And Stan carried out the identification for you.'

'And you're positive it was our mother?' Dora sounded as if the words were being forced out.

'Yes, I'm sure.' Stan's mouth was set in a grim line, hating every second of this. And what was to come.

Winnie was busy handing out cups of steaming tea, but no one seemed to want them. Still standing, Reg continued. 'There are things we've found out in the course of our investigation, and if we could save you from this we would, but you must be told. You might want to put Lily to bed.'

Dora's head shot up. 'Whatever you've got to say can be said to all of us.'

'Very well. Stan will explain.'

Clamping down on the feelings he had for them, Stan also took on the role of a policeman speaking to a bereaved family. It was the only way he was going to be able to do this. When he spoke, it was in a firm, impersonal tone. 'Your mother's name was Harriet Duval. Your father, Ted Bentley, was a merchant seaman sailing out of Bristol. Then he changed to a ship from Liverpool, and it was there he met your mother. When he went back to sea she discovered she was expecting his child. Her family are middle class, quite wealthy, and intolerant. They felt their daughter had disgraced the family name, and they turned her out. No one knows how she survived, but she did, and by the time Bentley arrived back from a long voyage, Harriet had a baby daughter.'

It was as if the youngsters in front of him were frozen in ice, neither moving nor speaking. Drawing in a silent breath, he continued, knowing that they were going to find the next piece of news devastating. 'Unfortunately, they weren't able to marry because Bentley had a wife in Bristol. They decided to move to London and live as husband and wife.'

Although no one spoke, Stan could feel the shock waves rebounding from the silent figures. His mouth was dry and he longed to stop this torture, but he knew the complete story had to be told. 'When your father was killed, your mother took the flat in Bloomsbury. But there, according to her neighbour, Mrs James, she gave dinners for men who needed somewhere for discreet business deals. She also acted as hostess when this was required. The book you found is a list of her clients. We're unable to trace any of them to find out the extent of her services because she only listed Christian names. She's protected them well.'

Stan was aware how bad this sounded, but they really didn't have anything else – not one tiny piece of information to prove that what their mother had been doing was completely legal and respectable. He couldn't take his eyes off the horrified faces in front of him, and was relieved to hand over to Reg. 'Reg has more information for you.'

'The Bloomsbury police have now discovered that your mother didn't own the flat, as her neighbour had said, but was renting it. Also, there's a will with the solicitors we visited. He'll see you when you feel up to it, but won't disclose anything until he's got a death certificate, and it'll take a few days before that's issued. However, there'll be no harm in introducing yourself to him. We don't know yet who killed your mother, but we have our suspicions.' Reg paused for a moment. 'I've met the Duval family, and the necklace you have belongs to them. It's very valuable, but they haven't asked for it to be returned as yet. We don't know why your mother never sold it when she was in need of money – we can only assume that it meant a lot to her. Perhaps she kept it as a link with the family who had rejected her . . . Finally, you can go ahead and make the funeral arrangements. Around two weeks' time should be all right.'

'We're very sorry to bring you this distressing news.' Stan gazed at the silent figures, alarmed by their faces, drained of every bit of colour. He stepped forward, wanting to comfort, needing to let them know that it didn't matter what their parents had done. He loved them and nothing would ever change his feelings for them. But they wouldn't even look at him. He had never felt so helpless in his life. 'Dora . . .'

She turned her head away. 'Please go.'

Winnie stooped down in front of them. 'Let us stay till you feel better. And don't worry about the funeral costs. We'll help you with that.'

'That's our responsibility. There's nothing else you can do for us. We want to be left alone now.'

Stan was alarmed by Dora's abrupt attitude. His worst fear was being realized – they were turning away from them. 'We can't leave you like this!'

It was Tom who spoke, his voice vibrating with anger and distaste. 'Dora's asked you all to go. I'm telling you to leave – now!'

Knowing that they were doing more harm than good by staying, they left.

Thirty-Three

Dora felt as if she had been torn apart as horror and shame rested on her like a heavy weight. Lily was sobbing, and she gathered her in her arms. Tom and Lily were going to need protecting from the disgrace. It was unlikely that Lily fully understood what their mother had been doing; she was crying because they had just been told their mother was dead. The little girl had probably been holding on to the hope that she would return to them one day. But Tom knew. That was clear to see as she looked at him. She kissed the top of her sister's head, rocking her in her arms. 'Shush, sweetie, we'll get through this. It's terrible, but we guessed something like this must have happened to her, didn't we?'

Tom could contain himself no longer. 'We're bastards! How are the hell are we going to live with that?'

'Not easily, but we've got to stay calm, Tom.' She was concerned. Her brother was vibrating with fury. 'There's going to be a lot to deal with. We're really on our own now and we can't expect much help or support. Once this becomes known we'll be branded with the disgrace, even though we knew nothing about it.'

'We're not the only illegitimate children in the world,' Tom snorted in disgust. 'And they manage all right.'

'And so will we, but we have to face the fact that things might be difficult for a while. This is bound to make a difference to our lives, and I want us to face that right from the beginning.'

'Stan will help us.' Lily looked up, her face puffy and red with tears. 'He's our friend.'

'Make her understand, Dora. She's got to know what we're facing.'

'Listen, sweetie.' Dora smoothed back Lily's hair. 'We can't count on anyone being our friend now. Our mum and dad didn't get married, and it's possible Mum has been earning money in a way that isn't very nice. It's unlikely we can keep it a secret for long.'

The tears were coming again in streams. 'But they loved us, and we haven't done anything wrong.'

'No, we haven't, but society frowns on unmarried people having children. Those children are called illegitimate.'

'And that's bad?'

Dora nodded. 'But we'll be all right. Now, we must all eat even if we don't feel like it. Then we'll try and get some sleep. In the morning I'll send notes to your schools saying you won't attend until after our mother's funeral. I'm sure they'll understand. Our first job will be to see the undertaker and then let Reg know who it is. Next we'll visit the solicitor and tell him who we are.'

'What about Mum's family?' Tom asked. 'Hadn't we better get their address from Reg and let them know about the funeral?'

'I suppose we must. It would only be polite. But from the sound of them, I doubt if they'll come.'

'What will happen about this flat, Dora? Are we going to be allowed to stay after this? The doctor's a kind man, but will he want three illegitimate children living in his house? The scandal might harm the good work he's doing here.'

'Oh no!' Lily wailed, wide-eyed with distress. 'I can't leave my angel.'

'I'll see Doctor Burridge in the morning and tell him what's happened.'

'I won't leave my picture. Ray did it for me!' Lily was in a terrible state of agitation, waving her arms around, gasping sobs shaking her body. 'I don't care what people say about Mum. We haven't done nothing! Mum and Dad loved us. You know they did. They weren't bad! They were lovely!'

Dora would normally have corrected her sister for using a double negative, but tonight wasn't normal and she ignored it. She had to do something now, or Lily was going to make herself ill. She reached for her purse to see how much money she had. Satisfied, she stood up. 'Take care of Lily, Tom. I'll go now and see the doctor. He's probably still at the hospital.'

She didn't even remember the journey; it was as if she had been detached from the world – as if she was no longer a part of it.

'Dora, what are you doing here?' The doctor saw her as soon as she walked in the door, then he reached out quickly to steady her. 'My dear, what's happened?'

'I have to talk to you, sir. Can you spare me a few minutes?'

'Come to my office.'

Once there she gripped on to the back of a chair to steady herself, Lily's terrified face vivid in her mind. Without hesitation she told him the whole story. She wasn't going to hide anything from him.

'I'm so sorry.' He took her by the arms and made her sit down, then poured a glass of water and placed it in her hands. 'You shouldn't have rushed over here. You're in a state of shock.'

Taking a gulp of water, she gazed at him, pleading in her eyes. 'I'll understand if you don't want me to work for you any more, but can we stay in the flat? Please. We'll pay you rent . . .'

'Of course you can stay! What on earth makes you think I would want you to move?' He studied her intently and then sighed. 'Our arrangement stands, Dora. Why would you think otherwise?'

'Because of the disgrace . . . People will frown when they know our background, and we don't want to cast a shadow on the vital work you're doing.' Her voice was husky with shock.

'What disgrace? What your parents did wasn't your fault, was it?'

'No.' She looked puzzled. 'But—'

He waved his hand to stop her. 'Tell me, Dora, when you met the shattered young men, did you shun them? Have you judged them as lesser people because they have a disability?'

'Of course not! They couldn't help what happened to them.'

'Exactly!'

'Sorry?'

'What your parents did does not reflect upon you. You have nothing to be ashamed of.'

'Others may not see it that way.'

'Then that's their problem, not yours.' He smiled gently. 'You take a few days off to deal with the arrangements, and then come back to work. You know I'm never on time if I haven't got you to keep me in line.'

Relief surged through her and she dragged herself to her feet. 'Thank you, sir. I'm so grateful. I must get back and tell my brother and sister.'

'I expect they're worried, so I'll take you home and have a word with them. Shall I?'

'Oh please! They're very upset.'

On the drive to Wandsworth, Dora suddenly realized what she was doing by dragging this man away from his work, and felt ashamed. She had acted in panic by coming to him, and that was something she couldn't ever remember doing before. But then, she had never been faced with such a frightening situation. She was doing lots of things she had never done before! 'I'm sorry, sir, I shouldn't have come to you so late. I should have left it until the morning, but I panicked.'

'You did the right thing, Dora. I don't want you making yourself ill with worry. You've shown great courage in dealing with the distress of the last few weeks, and you're going to need all your strength to carry you through the difficult times ahead. I can at least take one burden from your shoulders right away.'

When they reached the house, Dora was beginning to suffer a reaction from the shock, and her legs almost gave way as she climbed the stairs. The doctor said nothing, but placed his hand under her arm to steady her.

She was still feeling guilty about dragging him out like this, but when they walked into the flat and she saw the distress on the faces of her brother and sister, the guilt vanished. She had done the right thing.

The doctor went straight to Tom, placing his hand on his shoulder and giving a reassuring smile. Then he stooped down to Lily, who was holding on to her brother, her eyes red from crying.

'Are you going to make us go away because of our mum?' she whispered.

'No, this is your home now, and I hope you'll be living here for a long, long time. Nothing – *nothing*,' he emphasized, 'will ever make me change my mind. Now dry your eyes, my dear.' He stood up and addressed the three of them. 'Dora's told me everything. What your parents did is no reflection on you, and you mustn't take on their guilt. It sounds as if your mother acted out of love for you – her children. You don't need to judge her harshly. Remember she was treated disgracefully by her family. They're the ones who should feel shame – not you.'

A little colour was coming back to Tom's face now. 'That's

kind of you to say those things, sir, but society will stand in judgement against us.'

'Sadly that's true, but I believe you're all strong enough to rise above such prejudice. I want you to know that it makes no difference to me, and it won't to any of your friends. You can rest assured that your home here is secure, and so is Dora's job with me.' He turned his head and smiled at Dora. 'She's the best assistant I've ever had. I have no intention of letting her go.'

'Thank you, sir.' Tom held out his hand, unable to conceal its tremor. 'We were sure everyone was going to turn against us. This kind of thing is considered disgraceful.'

The doctor shook hands, treating Tom like an adult. 'You're to come to me if you need help. I'm a good listener, as any of my patients will tell you. And don't forget that you have many friends who will continue to support you. Now, I've given Dora time off to deal with the funeral and any other business.' He bent down to Lily again. 'You're quite safe, my dear. You must be brave and help your brother and sister as much as you can.'

'I will.' Lily tried a smile but wasn't very successful. 'Will everyone know what our mum and dad did?'

'The only thing people need to know at the moment is that she's died.' He stood up again. 'Say as little as possible for a while, in order to give yourselves a period of mourning to get through the funeral. If they catch the culprit who did this it will all come out in a trial. But that's some way off and he might never be apprehended.'

'I hope he is!' Tom said forcefully. 'Whatever Mum did, she didn't deserve this.'

'No, she didn't.' The doctor looked at his watch. 'I must go, Dora. Will you be all right now?'

She nodded. 'Thank you for coming, sir. It's been a great help. I think we might be able to sleep now.'

But, as the long night dragged on, Dora knew that rest was going to be impossible. They had guessed that their mother had been doing something she didn't want them to know about, but this was beyond belief. Their life had been a sham of respectability; an illusion. And tonight that illusion had crumbled around them. She'd had to send Stan away, not being able to look him in the eyes and see disgust where there had once been love. He was lost to her now. He was a decent man, and no matter what the doctor said, it would be wrong to expect him to want to take on three illegitimate children. The word cut through her like a physical pain, making her groan in despair. Dora felt the shame, and the last thing she wanted from anyone was pity. That would be the final humiliation. There was great sadness for her mother and the awful way she had died and been treated. It must have been terrible to be turned out by her parents. She knew that if she ever met them, it would be hard to be polite.

With a tremendous effort she clamped down on the distressing thoughts, turning her mind to what needed to be done the next day. Settling back she made a mental note of the tasks, praying that she would find the strength and courage for what was to come.

'Stan!'

He spun round at the sound of his sister's voice. 'What are you doing here? You should be fast asleep by now.'

Winnie grimaced. 'So should you. Reg and June are sleeping peacefully, but I can't get the picture of those youngsters out of my mind. What a nightmare! I don't understand why they sent us away like that.'

'I do. They're ashamed, and fearful that society will now reject them, including their friends.'

'Damn society!' Winnie swore. 'And surely they know we wouldn't turn away from them because of something their parents did?'

'No they don't, and it might take a while to convince them that it makes no difference to us. They're very close and they'll cling to each other to survive this disaster – or disgrace, as they see it.'

'They shouldn't have to suffer like this. What can we do, Stan? Can't this be kept a secret?'

'I wish it could, for their sakes, but it's bound to come out eventually.'

'You're right, of course.' Winnie sat down heavily and bowed her head. 'Poor little devils. You'll watch over them, won't you, even if they try to turn you away.'

'I'll be beside them every step of the way.'

Thirty-Four

'Right! What've we got to do today, Dora?' Tom had a determined gleam in his eyes but was quite calm.

'We'll get more done if we work separately. The first job will be to make arrangements for the funeral. I'll go to the one in the High Street – Chandlers. Then I'll visit the solicitors and introduce myself to them as Reg suggested. He'll have to talk to us now we know Mum's name was Duval.' Tom nodded agreement, and she was grateful for his strength of character. He might be a bit volatile at times, but he always pitched in when anything needed doing. 'I'd like you and Lily to go to the police station. Tell them who the undertakers are, and get the Duvals' address from Reg.'

Tom nodded again. 'We'll meet you back here for lunch. How are we going to pay for the funeral?'

'I don't know yet.' Dora rubbed her tired eyes. 'I'm hoping there might be an insurance policy at the solicitors. If not we'll have to raise the money somehow. We must do this properly. She was our mother and we know she loved us. We owe it to her to see she has a dignified funeral.'

Silent tears were trickling down Lily's face. All this talk about funerals was upsetting her. She whispered, 'What do you want me to do, Dora?'

'As I've said, I want you to go with Tom. You can write down everything Reg tells you. Can you do that for us?'

She swiped away the tears and nodded. 'I've got a little notebook. I'll take that with me.'

Glad that was settled, Dora stood up and began clearing the table. She hadn't been able to eat. It felt as if there was a large empty hole inside her and food wouldn't have stayed there. She still hadn't come to terms with what they had been told, but there was far too much to do today and she had to get on with it.

'Leave that,' Tom told her. 'We'll clear up. You've got a lot to do, so you'd better be on your way. Have you got enough money for your fare?'

'Yes.' She picked up her purse. 'Thanks, Tom. I'll see you both later.'

'Head up, Dora,' he said sternly as she reached the door. 'We are *not* going to carry the shame for something our parents did. It's not our fault we're illegitimate. It's not as if we had any say in the matter.'

She straightened up and forced a smile. Her brother was a sound thinker, and that was just what they needed to remember in order to get through this. And get through it they would! She was absolutely determined. 'You're quite right, Tom.'

Dobbs was just arriving when she came down the stairs. He stopped and stared. 'My God, girl, you look done in. What's up?'

There was no point evading the question. It was going to be known soon enough, but for the moment she would only mention one thing. 'They've found our mother. She's been killed.'

'Oh, that's terrible news.' He was genuinely upset. 'I'm so sorry, girl. Is there anything I can do for you?'

'No, but thanks. We've got it all under control.'

Once outside Dora felt like bursting into hysterical laughter. All under control? It didn't take long for the lies to start coming, she thought bitterly as she made for the High Street.

By the time she reached the undertaker's she didn't feel quite steady enough to go in, so she kept walking. She wasn't going in there until she could conduct the business without breaking down. It was about fifteen minutes before she felt in control enough to turn back.

Much to her relief the undertaker was dignified and businesslike. If anyone tried to sympathize with her at the moment, she would not have been able to cope. The arrangements were concluded quickly and she stuffed the papers in her bag, not looking at them. Time enough to study the details tonight when Tom was with her. She had chosen a good-quality coffin without giving the cost a thought. They were going to have to sell quite a few things to pay for it, but she didn't care. How she would have loved to have Stan with her today. She had never felt so alone in her life, but this was probably how it would be from now on. At least she had Lily and Tom, and without them life would now be unbearable.

Stopping halfway along the High Street, she gazed around, lost for a moment when her mind went blank. Where was she going? A bus! She had to catch a bus to the solicitors'. That's right, she had to go to Bloomsbury next.

Pretending to look in a shop window, she called herself all the names she could think of. This was no time to be falling apart. She had things to do, and a brother and sister to look after. The news had been horrific, but they knew now what their parents had been hiding all these years. They had loved each other, that had been plain to see when they had been together. Looking back now, she could see that their mother had changed after their father had been killed, but they'd put it down to grief over losing the man she loved. Why she had done the things she had was a mystery and would probably remain so. Perhaps that was for the best.

Feeling steadier again, she caught the bus. What was done was done, and whatever the consequences, they had to work their way through this nightmare. It felt as if she had a notice around her neck telling the world that she was illegitimate, which was ridiculous. Tom had declared that they didn't need to carry guilt around with them. She must remember that, but it was hard. The cloak of respectability they had worn had been torn from them.

From the bus window she could see people going about their daily business and she wondered what secrets some were hiding. There was nothing to single anyone out, and that was how it was with her. The shame was inside, out of sight, and it was up to her to see that it didn't ruin their lives.

She rested her forehead on the window and calmness filled her. This would not ruin her life! If she allowed that to happen it would drag down her brother and sister as well, and she wouldn't do that to them. The next couple of weeks were going to be distressing, but she would be strong.

The bus stopped and she got off. The weakness of mind and body had left her, so she stepped out confidently. It was only a short walk to the solicitors'.

'Can I help you?' a young man asked when she walked in.

'I'd like to see the person who is dealing with Mrs Duval's affairs. I'm her daughter.'

The man disappeared into another office, returning almost at once. 'Mr Graham will see you, Miss Duval.'

He held open the door and she walked in, not bothering to correct him about the name.

A rather elderly man stood to greet her. 'Please sit down, and tell me what I can do for you.'

'My mother is dead, sir, and I believe you hold papers of hers. I would like to know what they contain.'

'I'll need to see a death certificate, and proof of your identity, before I can do that.'

'My mother was murdered, so there will be a short delay before the death certificate is issued.' Dora was pleased with the way her voice sounded, firm with no hint of weakness.

'I'm sorry to hear that . . .'

Dora continued. 'I was brought up under the name of Bentley, not Duval.'

'I see.' He narrowed his eyes and stared at her intently. 'You have something to identify you as Bentley?'

Opening her bag she took out an official letter given to her by Dr Burridge stating the terms of her employment. It was something he had insisted she have, and now it could prove useful. After handing it over she sat back while he read it. 'If you are in any doubt, then the police will confirm that what I have told you is true.'

He folded the letter carefully and gave it back to her. 'You understand that I cannot show you the will until I see the death certificate?' When she nodded, he continued, 'But I will tell you that Mrs Duval has mentioned three names. Can you tell me what they might be?'

'Dora, Thomas and Lily Bentley.'

He nodded, his expression softening. 'Have you made arrangements for the funeral?'

'Yes, this morning. It will be in ten days' time.'

'Ask the funeral directors to send the bill to me and it will be paid out of your mother's estate.'

'Estate! What estate?'

He stood up and opened the door, bringing the meeting to a close. 'I will tell you next time you come, Miss Bentley.'

Dora walked out of the solicitors' in a daze. If there was money, then it could be from doubtful earnings – she refused to admit to the word that was forcing its way into her thought.

No one really knew what her mother had been doing, and she wasn't going to label her in such a disgraceful way. Let people think what they liked, to her children she had been a loving, caring mother, and that was how they would remember her. It was a relief to know that the funeral expenses would be paid. If there was anything left over, they would keep it for Lily.

When she arrived home, Stan was there with her brother and sister. Lily was still subdued and grieving for their mother, but thankfully she was too young and innocent to understand all they had been told. They hadn't enlightened her, but she wasn't daft and obviously knew something was very wrong.

She went immediately to Dora, holding tightly to her hand. 'We saw Uncle Reg and he showed us around the station. The policemen gave us tea and biscuits.'

'That was kind of them, sweetie.'

She nodded. 'Tom tried on some handcuffs and he couldn't get out of them, but they had a key. They put them on me, but my hands were too small and I just pulled them out again.' Lily was chattering nervously. 'Stan wasn't there, but he's come to see us now. He's bought a car. Did you see it outside? Did you see about burying Mum . . . ? Was it all right? Did you have enough money?'

Dora knelt in front of her sister. 'Everything's been taken care of, my love. The solicitor said that Mum has left enough money to pay for the funeral.' She kissed Lily's cheek and forced a smile. 'You're not to upset yourself. How about making me a cup of tea? I'm gasping.'

'It's ready. I'll get you one.'

As soon as Lily hurried off, Dora stood up. Stan had been watching, not speaking, and Dora wished he wasn't there as a witness to their grief and struggle. 'Have you come to find out when the funeral will be?'

'No, I came to see if there's anything I can do for you.'

'There's nothing. We can deal with this ourselves.'

His face darkened with frustration. 'Damn it! Don't turn away from me.'

'Just a minute!' Tom stepped up to Stan. 'We know you want to help, but Dora's right, there's nothing anyone can do for us at the moment. And I won't have you raising your voice at my sister like that. Don't you think she's got enough to cope with?'

Stan lifted his hands. 'I apologize.'

'You must give us time,' Dora explained. 'What we've found out has knocked us off balance. We're feeling lost. The best thing you can do is leave us alone while we try to sort out our lives.'

'All right.' He couldn't hide the regret he felt at their withdrawal from him. 'But you're not getting rid of me – ever! So while you're sorting yourselves out, remember that. Also remember what I said to you at the party, Dora. I'll step back for now, but only for a few days. The sooner you sort yourselves out the better it will be for all of us.' Then he turned on his heel and walked out.

'We've upset him,' Lily whispered. 'We shouldn't do that, Dora.'

'I know.' She sighed deeply. 'We'll apologize when we're feeling better.'

Thirty-Five

The station was almost deserted when Stan arrived the next day. After being told by Dora to leave, he had stormed home, feeling as if he had deserted them. It was not in his nature to stand back and watch people suffer. He had dragged Alan back to the trenches even though he might have been dead. He didn't consider himself especially brave; it was just the way he was, and his instinct was to stay and protect the three youngsters while they were suffering so badly. But he had to respect their wishes. He didn't want to do it but he understood their reasons, because he had struggled with similar emotions when he had returned home injured. Just like them he had needed time to come to terms with the change it was going to make to his life; the last thing he had needed were well-meaning people around him. Although he could see what the Bentleys were going through, he didn't think it was right for them to be alone at this time. He had seen shame in Dora's eyes, fury in Tom's, and heart-rending grief in Lily's. He would stay away for a couple of days, and that was all.

'Hello, Stan.' The super looked him over, and after a moment gave a nod of approval. 'I see you're walking well now. How strong is the leg?'

'Good.' He did a turn around the room to show him. 'Getting stronger every day.'

The super looked him straight in the eyes. 'When are you coming back to join us?'

'Tomorrow? I've already put in my request to be reinstated. I can start work as soon as a decision is made.'

'You'll let the police doctor have a look at you?'

'Of course.'

'I'll see it's hurried along.'

Stan was elated. 'Thanks. I'd love to get back to the job.'

'I know that, and we need good policemen.' His gaze swept around the empty room. 'As you can see, we're short handed.'

'Where are they all?'

'Reg has taken a team to bring in Roger Grant for questioning and do a quick search of his home. We need to find out if he had a close connection with the Duval woman. There's nothing concrete to tie him to her at the moment. Do you think he killed her, Stan?'

'Yes, I do, but I think we'll need a confession, and that's unlikely. If he's got any sense he'll keep his mouth shut.'

The super nodded in agreement. 'I hate to see a murderer go free.'

'If he did do it I'd want to see him swing.' Stan's mouth set in a firm line. 'There are three youngsters left to cope on their own.'

'Everything will be done to find and convict her killer.' The super slapped Stan on the shoulder. 'Look forward to having you back with us.'

He had only been gone a couple of minutes when Reg strode in.

'Have you got him?'

'Yes, he's in one of the cells.' Reg smiled grimly. 'Thought we'd leave him there for a while in the hope it might loosen his tongue. We didn't find a damned thing to suggest he knew her.'

Stan's fury surfaced. 'I wish I could interview him!'

''Fraid not, Stan, you know we can't let you near him.'

'Not for much longer. I think my chances of getting back on the force are good.' He told his brother-in-law about his talk with the super.

'That's wonderful!' Reg was obviously delighted. 'It'll be like old times. I don't think I'll wait any longer. I'll go and talk to Grant now.'

'Good, I'll wait.'

'It might take some time, Stan.'

'I'll wait!'

Left alone Stan glanced around the empty room. Not long ago he had believed that working as a policeman again had been an impossible dream, but it looked as if that dream was about to come true. He couldn't wait. His life was really taking a turn for the better, but that wasn't the case for the three bewildered Bentleys.

It was two hours before Reg returned. Stan knew immediately from his expression that he'd had no luck with Grant.

'He's not saying a bloody word!' Reg exploded. 'I'm damned sure he knows something, but we've had to let him go.'

'I know it's frustrating, but keep at him, Reg. I'll see you later.'

His brother-in-law nodded and then grinned. 'If he still isn't talking the next time we bring him in, I'll let you have a go at him. That should shake him up a bit.'

'I'll keep you to that.' Stan waved and left the station, heading for Wandsworth. He hadn't promised not to call on John and the other men at the house. Lizzie was a good cook so he would have lunch there.

Dobbs met him as soon as he got out of the car. 'You've heard the sad news? Of course you have. We're terribly worried about those lovely kids. They're suffering bad, and they don't deserve that. What happened to their mum?'

Stan walked inside with him. 'I don't know the details yet. The police are still trying to piece it together.'

'I hopes they find the bastard that did it!'

'Me too, Dobbs. Who's here?'

'Most of the regulars, but they're all rather quiet today. You go along and cheer 'em up. Dinner will be ready in half an hour.'

'Look forward to that.' Stan walked down the corridor and stood in the doorway watching the scene. The room was full, as many of the disabled now brought their families with them for a meal, and it was becoming a popular meeting place. John was idly tinkering on the piano in a distracted way; some were playing darts or cards. There was little talk. At one table, Pete was amusing Lily with card tricks.

She looked up, and her wan little face tore at his heart. He smiled and held out his hand. 'Hello, sweetheart.'

After a slight hesitation she came over to him, taking his hand and gazing at him uncertainly. 'Are you still my friend?' she whispered.

He swept her up in his arms. 'I'll always be your friend. Nothing will ever change that.'

She rested her head on his shoulder, saying nothing.

John stopped messing with the piano and joined them, deep sorrow in his eyes. 'Any news?' he asked softly.

Stan shook his head and turned his attention back to Lily,

lifting her chin so he could look at her face. 'Are Dora and Tom here?'

'Dora's out, she's got things to do, but Tom's in the garden.'

'Are they all right?'

'Think so.'

Stan knew that was all he was going to get out of the little girl, so he said, 'Do you think Tom would mind if I have a look at his garden?'

'Be all right, I 'spect.'

John grimaced at Stan. 'You might get hit over the head with a shovel. He's not just angry, he's boiling mad. I left him digging over the ground like a maniac. You want re-inforcements with you?'

'Might be a good idea.' Stan put Lily down, still holding her hand. 'You coming with us to see your brother?'

'Better. He's not happy.'

The sweat was streaming off Tom as he slammed the spade into the ground time and time again. He was so lost in what he was doing that he hadn't heard their approach.

'Has that piece of ground offended you?' John asked dryly.

'What?' Tom spun round.

John pointed to the beautifully dug-over soil. 'That's prepared enough, don't you think?'

'Oh.' Tom pitched the spade into the ground, watched it quivering upright for a moment and then wiped his hands on his trousers. 'I'm just working off my frustration. Hello, Stan, any news?'

'They've got someone in for questioning, but there's no proof he's the one. I'd like to have a go at him myself, but as I'm not a policeman they won't let me near him.'

Tom nodded, pulled the spade out of the ground and tossed it to Stan, who caught it in one hand. 'You want to have a go. It's a great way to let off steam without hurting anyone.'

They grinned at each other, knowing they both had short tempers at times. He tossed the spade back to Tom and watched him lean it carefully against a tree. The tension between them had completely disappeared, and Stan felt as if he had won a victory. Two of the Bentleys were now treating him like a friend again. That left only one to win over – the most important one.

Lily tugged his hand. When he bent down to her, she whispered knowingly, 'He's all right now. John's been talking to him and helping him.' She gave the other man a tremulous smile. 'Haven't you, John?'

'I certainly have, little one.' He looked pointedly at Tom. 'We're all here for you.'

'We know that, and thanks, but you'll have to forgive us, we're so bloody furious.' He grimaced. 'At least I am. Dora's devastated and so is Lily. I could tear the bugger who did this to pieces.'

'Don't swear, Tom,' Lily reprimanded. 'Dora will be cross if she hears you.'

'She won't know unless you tell her.' A gleam of devilment came into his eyes and he dived for his sister, swinging her high in the air. 'I'm bigger and stronger than the two of you put together.'

'You're all dirty!' She pummelled him with her fists until she was safely on the ground again, then said smugly, 'I'll soon be too big for you to do that. I'm growing out of my clothes faster than Dora can alter them. So there!'

Stan and John gave each other a slight smile of relief as they listened to the bickering. It was such a normal thing for brother and sister to do.

Lily pushed between the two men for safety, her little face serious again. 'Dora went and got the doctor last night 'cause I was crying so much. He was ever so nice. He said we don't have to leave here, and he still wants Dora to work for him. I cried ever so much because I didn't want to leave my angel.'

Tom stepped in immediately to stop his little sister saying anything else. 'Come on, urchin, I'm gasping for a cup of tea.'

'All right. Lizzie will give you one.' She started to follow her brother, then turned back to Stan. 'Are you staying? Dora might be home soon.'

'Yes, I'm having lunch here.'

'Oh good.' Then she tore off to catch her brother.

John was frowning. 'Why would Lily think the doc would turn them out? Is there more to this, Stan?'

'It isn't my place to say, but they're going to need all the help and support we can give them.'

'There's no question about that. We're all very fond of that family.' John's frown deepened. 'Bad, is it?'

'Couldn't be worse.'

* * *

Stan hung around until four o'clock that day, but if Dora had
arrived home she had gone straight upstairs without speaking
to anyone. He hesitated at the bottom of the stairs but forced
himself to walk away. If she had wanted to see him then she
would have come downstairs. Lily would have told her he
was here. Patience was not a virtue he possessed in any great
measure. But if he wasn't very careful he could lose any
chance he had with her, and he wasn't going to risk that. He
walked away, knowing he wouldn't be able to keep on doing
this. He loved Dora and the children, and couldn't imagine
his life without them. They weren't going to get rid of him
very easily!

Reg came to see him just after six o'clock, looking tired
and dispirited. He slumped into a chair. 'You know, Stan, I'm
absolutely sure Grant has something to do with this mystery.
He's far too nervous, but . . .' He shrugged helplessly.

Handing his brother-in-law a large whisky, Stan said, 'I feel
the same, but his Christian name doesn't even appear in her
book.'

'Perhaps he wasn't a customer.' Reg tossed back his drink,
shuddered, then handed the glass back to Stan for a refill.
'He's quite well connected, so perhaps his role was to find
clients for her?'

'That's more than likely. But unless he talks there isn't
much you can do. Let him stew for a couple of days and then
bring him in again.'

'Already thought of that.'

Two days later Stan was at the station waiting for the police
to bring Grant back in. They had asked the neighbour, Mrs
James, to come and see if she could identify him. He wasn't
allowed anywhere near Grant, of course, so he found a quiet
corner out of the way, determined to stay there until the interview was over.

It was nearly three hours before Reg appeared, and Stan
was immediately on his feet. 'Well?'

'The neighbour said she thought he was the man who came
when Mrs Duval moved into the flat, but she hadn't seen him
since. When faced with this, Grant at last admitted he'd known
her. But he insisted that all he did was lend her money to set
herself up in business. She repaid him six months later, with

interest, and that was the last he saw of her. His alibi is that he was having dinner with his father on the night she disappeared. One of the constables went to check and the father said it was true. His son was with him till around midnight.'

'Ah, but where did he go after midnight?' Stan asked. 'Does he have a witness for the rest of the night?'

'No, he was home to bed, alone, he insists, and we can't prove otherwise. We've had to let him go.'

'Bad luck, Reg.' Stan was torn between two points of view. He hated to see a murderer escape justice, and yet, if there was no trial then the truth about the Bentleys' mother might never come to light. They could be saved from a public humiliation, and he wished that with his whole heart.

Thirty-Six

B ut that was not to be. Two days later Tom rushed home with a newspaper in his hand. 'Look at this!' He opened it to the second page for Dora to see. 'How the hell did they get hold of all that? And how dare they call her that when there's no proof!'

Dora read the headline with mounting horror. PROSTITUTE MURDERED. It was all there. The connection between Bentley and Duval was clearly stated, and even their own names had been printed. Now she was just as furious as her brother. 'They must have got this from someone who knows us. And there aren't many people who know our mother used the name Duval.'

'Well, that narrows it down! It's only the police, Stan, and the doctor of course.'

Dora was very frightened, and her fear was showing itself in anger. For the first time in her life she was consumed with fury. 'The doctor wouldn't have spoken to reporters. I trust him completely.'

Her brother's fists were clenched as if he wanted to hit someone. 'That leaves someone from the station, or Reg or Stan. I'd never have believed either of them would have done this to us!'

Dora surged to her feet. 'Get Lily, Tom. She's downstairs. We're going to find out who's responsible for this. Right now!'

Stan wasn't at home so they went straight to the station. Tom stormed up to the front desk and slapped the newspaper down. 'We want to see Reg Tanner.'

'And why do you want him, young man?'

'Just tell him the Bentleys are here!'

Before the constable had time to leave his desk, Reg and Stan appeared, drawn by the raised voices.

'Have you seen this?' Tom waved the paper at them.

'Yes we have,' admitted Reg. 'And we're very sorry—'

'Sorry?' Tom was absolutely furious. 'Do you know what this will do to us? Do you?'

Knowing that they weren't going to get any answers by shouting, Dora laid her hand on her brother's arm to quieten him. 'Let them explain.'

The boy clamped his mouth shut and glowered at the men in front of him.

'As I was saying,' Reg continued, 'we're trying to find out how the reporter got hold of this information.'

Tom couldn't hold his tongue any longer. 'Someone close to us talked, and there aren't many who know all these details.'

'Now just a damned minute!' Stan spoke for the first time, rounding angrily on them. 'Are you accusing us of selling this story to the press?'

'Well, someone did! And we want to know who it was.'

When Stan spoke his voice was like ice. 'We'd never do anything to hurt you. And you're wrong about us being the only ones to know the details. Everyone at the station here and at Bloomsbury knows. It's a matter of record.'

Dora felt awful. She had been in such a blind rage that she hadn't even considered that.

Tom was looking uncomfortable now. 'We never thought of that.'

'That's obvious,' Stan almost growled in disappointment at their accusations. He could understand their fear, for this could have distressing consequences for them, but it hurt that they should even consider him responsible. 'Try thinking before you go accusing people of betraying you. And calm down, Tom. You're frightening Lily.'

The little girl had been very quiet, and Dora had forgotten that her sister was with them. She bent down, knowing just how upsetting Lily found arguments. She was such a gentle child. 'I'm sorry, sweetie.'

Her bottom lip trembled. 'I don't like it when Tom shouts. And he shouldn't say things like that to Stan and Uncle Reg. They love us.'

'I know, and we're sorry, aren't we, Tom?' When she looked up, Stan was nowhere to be seen. 'I'm sorry, Reg. We were very wrong to storm in here like this. Please, will you forgive us?'

The door opened with a crash, and Stan marched in holding

a small man firmly by the collar. 'Look what I found lurking outside, trying to listen to our conversation. Johnson, he said his name is.'

'Get him off me! He ain't a copper.'

Reg tossed Stan a pair of handcuffs, and before the reporter, Mr Johnson, knew what was happening he was securely chained to a heavy chair.

'What you doing?' He was eyeing Stan with a great deal of distrust.

'I'm making a citizen's arrest. You got a cell free, Reg?'

'You can't do this. I haven't done nothing!'

Reg picked up the newspaper and waved it under the reporter's nose. 'How about cruelty to children for a start?'

'What you mean . . . ?' His gaze rested on the youngsters. 'Ah.'

'We'd like to know where you got your information from.' Dora spoke politely, her anger having drained away as she witnessed the scene in front of her. If she hadn't been so upset, it would be hilarious.

'I can't reveal my source.'

'Was it someone from here?' Reg demanded.

The reporter gave a snort of disgust. 'None of you lot will give me the time of day.'

'True. Friendly with someone at Bloomsbury, are you?'

'I got friends,' he answered defiantly. 'But I don't care what you do to me. I ain't telling.'

'There's an invitation if ever I heard one. He doesn't care what we do to him, Stan.'

'Tempting. You'd better let me have him. I don't want you getting into trouble for beating up a suspect.'

'Suspect?' The reporter tugged at the handcuffs. 'I ain't no suspect. I ain't done nothing. I'm only doing my job! You got no right to hold me here.'

Stan shook his head and tutted. 'How did you ever become a reporter? Your English is atrocious.'

'Makes you wonder how people like this get jobs.' Reg made a show of searching for the key, and when he found it he tossed it from hand to hand. The reporter watched every move with fascination. 'I might consider removing the handcuffs and letting you go with a caution if you apologize for the harm you've done.'

'Why should I?'

'Because you've just ruined our lives, Mr Johnson.' Dora spoke quietly. 'And made us accuse honourable men of being underhand. And we're ashamed of that.'

Taking hold of Lily's hand and urging her brother forward, they walked out of the station without looking back.

The next morning, armed with all the necessary papers, they went to see the solicitor. He told them that after the funeral expenses had been paid, there remained the sum of two hundred and ten pounds to be shared between the three of them. It seemed that their mother hadn't used a bank, but had kept the money in a safe at the solicitors'. It was a large sum, but it meant nothing to them because of the way their mother may have come by it. On the other hand their mother had obviously intended they should have it, because it was in an envelope with their names written on it.

'I suppose we could buy a house with it,' Dora said without enthusiasm.

'No, Dora!' Lily was immediately agitated. 'I don't want to move. I like it where we are.'

'Me too.' She smiled at her sister and then glanced at Tom. 'How do you feel?'

'I like it where we are,' Tom said, dismissing the idea. 'Let's put it in a bank. It'll be security for Lily in the future. I don't want any of it, Dora.'

'Neither do I, and I agree that we keep it for Lily.' Dora gave her brother an understanding glance, knowing he was feeling as she did. They would never be able to spend the money on themselves.

Over the next few days they went out only to get necessary shopping, not wanting to meet reporters asking questions about their mother. It would be common knowledge by now, and they didn't feel up to facing the pity they would see in people's eyes.

Stan didn't come round, and Dora wasn't surprised. They had behaved disgracefully towards him and Reg, and they must have hurt them. She doubted if the men would ever be able to forgive such distrust. They would probably never see them again.

She sighed sadly, feeling very alone, but guessed that was

how it would be from now on. All they could hope was that the scandal would soon die down, and then they might be able to make some kind of a life for themselves.

Stan was spending more and more time at the station. His home didn't seem so inviting now Dora and the children had moved away.

The door opened with a crash and Reg erupted into the room, his face like thunder. 'The bloody man's gone! His father said he's cleared out the safe at the factory and disappeared. He's got enough money to go miles from here, even abroad if he wants to. Damn it! This proves he's guilty. We should have held him on some charge or other. Now we've lost him!'

Stan watched his brother-in-law rage, understanding how he felt, but knew that there was no way they could have held Grant. 'There was no proof, Reg, you had to let him go. But you obviously made a good job of making him nervous,' he said dryly.

'Too good!' Reg gave a wry smile, calming down. 'All we can do now is keep looking. We might get lucky one day and find him.'

'You never know.' Stan knew as well as Reg that Grant was probably a long way from here by now, and the chances of catching him were slim. Not a satisfactory end to the disappearance of Mrs Bentley.

Thirty-Seven

The day of the funeral had arrived so quickly. It was a clear, sunny morning, but Dora was dreading it. It would be a poor turnout with only the three of them to say farewell to the mother they had loved but, on reflection, never really known. The coffin was going straight to the local church, St Mark's, just around the corner. The service was at eleven o'clock and it would only take them fifteen minutes to walk there.

'We'd better go.' She straightened her hat, put on her gloves and made sure that her brother and sister were immaculate. They might be the only mourners, but that was no reason to turn up looking untidy. It was important to Dora that the funeral was a dignified affair. Their mother deserved that.

Silently they walked to the church, carrying a single rose each to place on the coffin. Even Tom hadn't complained about walking through the streets with a flower in his hand.

'Oh look!' Lily tugged at Dora's hand. 'There are lots of people there.'

'I expect there's another funeral or something.' Then Dora's steps faltered as she recognized the people waiting outside the church. Winnie was there with June, John, Ray, the doctor, Dobbs, Lizzie, and many of the regulars from the house. There were also two policemen in uniform. One was Reg, and the other Stan.

Dora's throat constricted as she gazed at them. The kindness of each one of them overwhelmed her. And Stan was back in the force. She was so proud of him, for he had fought hard to get fit enough to be able to put on his uniform again. She had seen little of him over the last week or so, and she felt guilty about that. It was entirely her fault. She knew he had been around the Wandsworth house, but she hadn't wanted to see anyone.

'Stan looks good in his uniform,' Tom remarked. 'What a difference in him from the man we first met.'

'Yes, he's made a remarkable recovery. I must congratulate him.'

'Yes, you must, Dora.' There was a reprimand in Tom's voice, and she knew she deserved it. 'Everyone we know's turned up. They don't give a damn about our past, and neither should we! Mum's going to get a real good send-off.'

'And they've all brought flowers.' Lily was bouncing up and down, impatient to get over and see everyone. 'Lots of lovely flowers.'

Dora started to move forward, and then stopped again. 'Oh dear, we should have laid on food at the house, but I thought we'd be the only ones attending. None of them knew Mum.'

'They know us, though,' Lily pointed out innocently. 'They've come to be with us.'

'Of course they have.' All the shame and confusion Dora had been feeling melted away at that moment. Her sister was absolutely right. 'We can scramble something together. We'll ask them all back, Tom.'

'We must. Lizzie will help us. Come on, Dora, let's go and thank them all for coming.'

It was only when they reached the church that Dora noticed Stan and Reg were standing either side of a couple she didn't know.

Reg stepped forward, turning to face the man and woman. 'These are your daughter's children.' He turned back again. 'Dora, Tom, Lily, this is Mr and Mrs Duval.'

She was astounded that they had had the nerve to come, but this was not the time or place to tell them what she thought of them. She remained silent.

Tom however was not so reticent. Clearly offended, he said abruptly, 'You aren't welcome here.' Then he took hold of his sisters' hands and led them into the church.

It was a moving service, and with so many friends attending and singing the hymns, an emotional affair. Not one of them had known their mother, but they had come to support the three of them. She was in awe at the love being shown to them. It was almost too much for her, and she struggled to maintain her control. Lily was being very brave and she must do the same. Their mother would have expected it of them.

They dropped their roses on to the coffin, and while the vicar led them in a final prayer, Dora glanced at their mother's parents. They were stony-faced, and clearly surprised by the number of people attending the funeral. It was quite a sight. There were two policemen standing to attention as the coffin was lowered, several young men on crutches or using walking sticks, and many others paying their respects to the daughter they had turned out all those years ago. She hoped their consciences were troubling them. The expressions in their eyes told her they were, and Mrs Duval could hardly take her eyes off Lily. Dora almost felt sorry for them. One heartless act years ago had deprived them of three fine grandchildren.

When it was all over, they went round thanking each person for coming, and inviting them all back to the house.

As she moved towards the unwanted guests, Tom caught her arm. 'You're not inviting them back, are you?'

'Yes, I am. It would be rude not to, and we've been brought up better than that. Do you realize they're our grandparents?'

'Hell, I never thought of that. But I don't want anything to do with them.'

'Neither do I, and once this is over we'll never see them again.' She walked over to them. 'There will be refreshments back at the house if you would like to join us.'

'Thank you, we'd like that.' It was Mrs Duval who answered. Mr Duval couldn't take his eyes off Tom.

Finally he fixed his gaze on Dora. 'Will he talk to me, do you think?'

'I doubt it, sir, but I'll ask him.' She went over to her brother. 'Mr Duval would like to talk to you, Tom.'

He merely shook his head and went to stand with John and Ray.

Stan was close by and Dora went over to him. 'Congratulations, Stan, I'm so pleased you're back in the force. I know it's what you longed for.'

He inclined his head. '*One* of the things I long for, Dora,' he said quietly.

She let the remark go. 'Would you be kind enough to bring Mr and Mrs Duval back to the house?'

'Of course.'

She watched as he made his way over to them and ushered them towards his car. Turning, she bumped into Tom. 'Oops!'

'Sorry, Dora. I've just been talking to Dobbs and Lizzie. We don't have to worry about refreshments. They've got it all laid on for us.'

'That's very kind of them.' Dora blew out a breath of relief. 'We haven't got anything to worry about then, have we?'

'Not a thing.' Tom patted his sister's hand. 'Everything's going to be all right from now on.'

'Yes, it is.' She smiled for the first time that day. 'We'd better get back.'

Lily was subdued as they walked back to the house, and Dora hoped she wasn't going to upset her more by the decision she had made. 'Sweetie, you know that man and woman are Mum's parents?'

The little girl nodded. 'They didn't look very nice.'

'I expect they felt uncomfortable being with people they didn't know.'

'Hmm.'

Dora continued. 'You know the necklace we said you could have when you're older? Well, it belongs to them, and I think we should give it back. I'm sorry, sweetie, but we shouldn't keep it. It's very valuable.'

Lily thought about this for a moment, then said firmly, 'I don't want it if it's theirs.'

'Good girl.' Dora stopped and gave her a hug. 'You can give it to them if you like.'

Lily nodded. If she was sad about giving up the necklace, she didn't say so. Dora was very proud of her.

Stan was waiting just inside the front door for them.

'What have you done with them?' Tom asked dryly.

'Inflicted them on the doctor.'

'Oh, poor man.' Dora pulled a face. 'We've got to pop upstairs first. Lily's going to give them back the necklace.'

'Good, that's what I thought you'd do.' He stooped down to Lily. 'That's very generous of you and deserves a reward.' Removing a small black box from his pocket, he took out a rose pendant on a gold chain, with a small diamond in the centre of the flower. He placed it around the little girl's neck. 'There, not as sparkly as the other one, but it looks nice on you.'

Lily rushed over to the hall mirror. 'Is this for me?'

'Yes, do you like it?'

'Oh yes!' She turned to her brother and sister. 'This is much prettier, isn't it?'

'Much nicer, sweetie. Thank Stan properly.'

'Thank you.' She hurled herself at him, pulling him down so she could kiss his cheek. 'I'll wear it always.' Then she grabbed hold of her brother. 'Come on, let's get the other one and give it back.'

As they thundered up the stairs, Dora gazed at Stan, filled with gratitude. 'That was very kind of you. I don't know how to thank you.'

'Just don't shut me out of your life, my darling.'

'I'm sorry for the way I've acted, Stan. I was so hurt and confused, and sure that everyone would turn against us once they knew the truth about Mum – even you – and that was insulting. Today has shown me how wrong I was. We're surrounded by true friends.'

'You know I want to be more than your friend.' He took another box out of his pocket. 'I'm afraid I can't get down on one knee yet, but it would make my happiness complete if you'd marry me.' He flicked open the box to reveal a solitaire diamond ring.

'Oh, Stan!' Dora's eyes filled with tears. 'I do love you so much, and I thought I'd lost you. Of course I'll marry you. But you do realize that the three of us come as a package, don't you?'

'Of course, and I wouldn't have it any other way.' He smiled affectionately. 'I'll have a ready-made family. How lucky can a man get?' Then he placed the ring on her finger and took her into his arms.

The sound of clapping broke their embrace as Tom and Lily threw themselves at Dora and Stan, nearly knocking them off their feet.

'I guess we're all happy about this,' Stan laughed. 'I think it's time we told our friends, don't you?'

Lily held tightly to Stan's hand, with the velvet box clasped firmly in her other hand. 'You come with us,' she whispered as they walked into the other room.

Stan nodded, serious once again. 'I'm going to be a witness that the jewel's been returned to them.'

The four of them walked up to Mr and Mrs Duval, and Stan stood Lily in front of him, resting his hands on her shoulders.

She held out the box. 'This is yours. You can have it back.'

Mr Duval took it, but his wife touched his arm and shook her head. 'Let them keep it.'

'We don't want it.' Lily held up the pendant she wore proudly around her neck. 'I've got a much nicer one now. Stan gave it to me, and he gave Dora a diamond as well. He's going to be my dad, because he loves us!'

There was a stunned silence in the room for a moment, and then it erupted as everyone swarmed round to congratulate them. The next few minutes were chaos as drinks were poured to toast the happy couple – or the happy foursome, as Tom and Lily were also included in the toasts.

A sad day had turned into one of joy, and Dora was sure their mother would have been happy for them. Looking round she noticed that her mother's parents had gone, and she was pleased they'd had the chance to meet them and return what was rightfully theirs. Who knew what the future held? They might even be able to forgive them one day.

A beam of sunlight caught the ring on her finger, making it burst into a rainbow of many colours. Only a short time ago it seemed as if their lives had turned to dust, but their future had been diamond bright all the time.